BLOODSONG

BLOODSONG

JILL NEIMARK

RANDOM HOUSE NEW YORK

Library of Congress Cataloging-in-Publication Data
Neimark, Jill.
Bloodsong / Jill Neimark.—1st ed.
p.   cm.
ISBN 0-679-42005-3
1. Young women—New York (N.Y.)—Fiction.   2. Manhattan (New York,
N.Y.)—Fiction.   I. Title.
PS3564.E355B57 1993   813'.54—dc20   93-261

Manufactured in the United States of America
9 8 7 6 5 4 3 2
First Edition

In memory of Hortense Neimark

As if through a straw, you drink my soul.
I know—It's bitter and intoxicating.
—*Anna Akhmatova*

ACKNOWLEDGMENTS

Thanks to Jim Landis, who from the time I was twelve years old and he read my first scribbled poems, was my truest writing compass; Howard Dickerson and Alina Bloomgarden; Mercura Fine Arts; Ricardo E. Alegria of The Institute for Culture in Puerto Rico; Miriam Trokan and the Rowland Company; and Jan D'Esopo and Hector Gandia, who offered me a porthole into the wonders of Old San Juan. But most of all thanks to David Rosenthal, who in a few astonishing conversations changed the fate and shape of this book.

BLOODSONG

ONE

I'm in love with a murderer. In his own quiet way he's extraordinary—honey in his hair, his mouth, his voice—a stillness in his eyes—and he moves with a panther's luxury. He's kind to me. I think his heart is breaking. He comes here every night but he hasn't said he loves me yet.

He can do things with my body that other men sense and hate, he pulls me down in the dark with a lost boy's smile, and his eyes are the phosphorescent blue of grottos or wolves. Then he sleeps, and in sleep he shudders, the way a child shudders and twitches while dreaming. When he wakes he's seldom rested.

I've known him for seven weeks, and only yesterday he admitted he killed a man. When he told me last night he finally came into focus, and I could see the dark stain at the center of him and the beauty fanning out from that center.

He says he killed for love. It should chill me, and it does, but I can't give up my happiness. He was—he is—my happiness. He never has to do much, just appear at my door, rocking on the balls of his feet, silent, diffident, and all of him reaches me, like the mystery of wind: the way his high-top sneakers are slightly scuffed, crafted of white leather with thick long laces that he has wound round and round his ankles; how his socks are whiter still, bleached to brightness by the Chinese laundry on Eighth Avenue, two blocks from the room where he lives; even his comfortably baggy denim overalls and the rectangular "Osh Kosh B'Gosh" label sewn on the front bib. I reach out to cover the label with both hands because suddenly it pierces my senses like a small sun, so ordinary and so uniquely him, and I call him my blue-collar baby—though he isn't really, he's a wanderer with a bitter privacy in him.

"Let's have a talk," I say.

"Let's not, Lynn," he replies, mocking an old cliché, "let's just say we did," as he holds me in my crooked hallway with the towering, narrow walls typical of pre-war apartments on the Upper West Side. I admire this hallway, because it seems like a room itself, a room so thin and long that it's useless, and yet here it stands in every apartment on the A line. The first time Kim visited he nicknamed this hall "the gallery" because I'd hung a series of prints by Balthus—flour-soft girls with their radiant, almost evil sexual heat —and he paused dutifully in front of each one, as polite and studious as if he were a guest being introduced to members of my family. It was a touching formality, because earlier that night he'd been in a car accident, and in spite of the pint of cognac I'd slipped him when we left the emergency room, he was walking with pain.

Whenever he comes to see me he stops first in my kitchen, opens the freezer, and in the bluish light untwists a can of Budweiser from a six-pack lying on its side. The can is fuzzed with ice that melts under his fingers. He taps it so it won't foam, pops the top open and drinks with the abandon of someone who can never appease his thirst because his thirst is of a different nature. Occasionally he'll spend the entire night making love to me, moving deep into my body with that same thirst—"I'm a perfectionist. Don't you realize that yet?"—so that I, who need exactly this kind of never-ending sex in order to feel whole, order him to stop. He stops. I can't stand it when he stops.

And so I tell myself there are many kinds of murder. Long before I met Kim I witnessed a murder, on a Labor Day weekend, and what stays with me after all these years is how easily I passed by. I was walking along Seventh Street in the East Village, wearing a snug, black lycra dress, with a peony-red silk scarf belted around my waist, going nowhere and feeling lonely, when twelve or fifteen boys spilled out of McSorley's, the battered Irish alehouse with scrolled iron windows, scarred tables and sawdust drifting like snow across the floor. They came swerving into the street, whooping and howling, stabbing at trash bags heaped at the corner, prying out bottles and hurling them gaily into storefronts and cement stoops so that a glorious, carnival song of bursting glass filled the street—until one boy sunk a knife into another boy's chest and for a moment the two stood staring at each other, alert and stunned. The other boys scattered and disappeared.

He looked about sixteen, this stabbed boy, with his pocked face and sweat-soaked blonde hair and bony shoulders, and already he was dying. A crowd gathered around him. They seemed no different than the kind of crowd that throngs around a street performer, straining, half-awed by this boy's hipbones twisting, his eyelids fluttering.

A few blocks later I stopped for a hot dog. It was good, the soft cool bun, the crunchy skin in my mouth. I wanted to eat for hours. On my way home to the Upper West Side I stopped at fruit stands for pears and apples, chunks of chocolate, cheese—blue, brie, smoked—and I stood in the street and opened the plastic bag and began to eat with my fingers, eating as I moved, migrating home, brushing against strangers, waiting with the crowd for the light to change. I knew that for the next week I'd call up friends and say, "I saw a boy killed on East Seventh Street." I'd tell each friend a different part: how the kids erupted into the street, how they tore open trash bags as if they were disemboweling carcasses, how like a circus it all seemed, how a few small stigmata of blood dried on the boy's shirt and that was the only visible sign, death's neat little entry point, how I ate melting cheese in the afternoon sun. I would tell this, too: at the first fruit stand, the one on the corner, I bought a bottle of seltzer, shook it up and let it spurt like champagne over my fingers. I've always loved life when I could stand aside from it.

I stood thirty yards away from a murder, my world was safe, and I floated away like a new balloon.

I've lived in New York for eight years. After a while it becomes an addiction. It's morning and a policeman nudges a man with his nightstick; the man is swathed in blankets. Around the corner, a woman in a mink coat and running shoes buys bagels at the deli and stuffs them in her briefcase. You drink coffee in gold-rimmed cups at the Plaza, from cracked mugs at your lover's. You watch a woman smear herself with chocolate syrup and raw eggs in a loft on the Lower East Side, and afterwards you applaud, and file out with the other guests. You read about it in the newspaper. You eat fried okra in a restaurant in Harlem. You attend a reading by a man dying of AIDS. He's frail and alone, like a rumpled graduate student who just spent all night in the library stacks. He reads of the time he took his lover's shaving brush and shaved off his chest hair, so that he would be an eternal teenager. Later that week, at Alice Tully Hall, you are careful not to rustle your program while listening to the Kronos Quartet. Dressed all in black, they play contemporary music. You like it. You're relieved you like it.

At a streetlight a man swaggers toward you, tapping his head with a red plastic mallet. He circles you, this Rumplestiltskin of the city, rattling lightly all over his skull. Suddenly he stops, grins, and blows on the mallet. "It's a whistle, too, see?" he entreats, and opens a brown bag. "A dollar each. Buy one for your kids."

And you bury yourself in somebody new whenever you want. You stop by an apartment sale in a friend's building. The owner is slouched at an oak table in the kitchen, stroking his silver beard. His wife has left him. "I don't want to do it," he says flatly. "Sell all this, I mean." He glances at a row of copper-bottomed pots hanging like harvest moons from a beam over the window. "Will you stay?" he says, and you turn to see him watching you. "Stay for coffee," he amends. For an instant you sink, sinking like someone dropping off to sleep, and all is yours: the luminous pots, the husband, the home.

And the city has a way of spitting up, out of its hothouse millions, the one person you shouldn't see. A few months before I met Kim, I stopped at the corner of 77th and Columbus to watch a puppeteer make a donkey dance on the curb, hooves and knees and open mouth clacking. The man's calloused fingers were magic—an almost imperceptible shift and the donkey's tail whipped through the air, another shift and all four feet shot out, a flick of the thumb and he collapsed. I looked up then, gazing absently across the street, and saw Stephen, the man I was wandering home to. He was smiling eagerly at a woman in a pink leotard and flared skirt.

She put her hand on his shoulder to steady herself, removing her pumps and massaging each foot with slow, purposeful circles. Then she stood on the concrete in her bare feet, comfortable and abstracted, while he knelt and searched through her wrinkled tote bag until he found flats. He slipped them onto her feet and for a long moment went on kneeling, one hand clasped around her ankle. I had never known he wanted to kneel before a woman.

I met Kim through a personal ad I placed after I broke up with Stephen. I never mentioned I'd seen him with another woman—I guess I was too proud—and so I told him I hadn't gotten over an abortion I'd had a year earlier.

For most of my life I'd thought I was sterile. I hadn't had periods since my brother disappeared when I was fifteen. I used to imagine my uterus was bloodless, as white as knuckles when you're clenching your fists, but I must have ovulated sometime in January because that spring I had fevers, kept falling asleep in the afternoon, ate boxes of bitter chocolates. One night while Stephen was playing chess, I ran out to the corner drugstore, bought a home pregnancy test, came back and poured my urine into a plastic petri dish. I stood there watching the pale circle darken, mutating into the most unbelievably inky blue.

"Look at this. They say if it's pale blue you're not pregnant. Would you agree it's pale?"

He gazed at it in surprise. "No, it's dark," he said. Then he began to laugh.

"What's so funny?"

"You're so funny," he said. "Saying it's pale when it's dark enough to fill my fountain pen."

"You sound proud," I murmured.

The next morning over breakfast he said, "Isn't there a time limit on these things? Three months or something for an abortion?"

I stared at him.

"You'll check into it, won't you?" he asked, and then amended, "I'll go with you, of course."

"Stephen, what was last night all about?"

"Last night?"

"Yeah. What was the stud act in bed last night?"

"But . . . you're already pregnant. It's the best contraception around."

"So you were just having fun?"

"Weren't you?"

I had to have the abortion twice. First I was strapped to the padded examining table while the clinic doctor inserted a metal cylinder into my cervix. It hurt. When the pain subsided he withdrew the cylinder and inserted a thicker one, removed it and wedged in a thicker one. I was being stretched. Then a sound came not unlike the gurgling of a dentist's air pic sucking up saliva: it was the inner shell of my womb whisking down a plastic tube.

A week later they called to tell me I was still pregnant. The fluid contained no placental tissue, no life. I had the second abortion in a hospital where they put me to sleep and discovered another chamber in my uterus. When forming, it had begun to divide in two, but stopped midway and took the shape of a small, lopsided heart. Embedded in the wall of that second chamber was the child.

Ever since the abortion I get my periods. I love them. I like to watch my blood, which looks like clots of red silk, dripping into the toilet bowl. Sometimes I half crouch, not sitting, not standing, and move so that it splashes on the ceramic. It's the color of cranberries, and when I clean myself with bunches of Kleenex it looks like sloppy fingerpainting on the tissues.

I got the idea of advertising from a friend of mine who had run a personal. She had long brown hair, but before the ad ran she cut and bleached it and described herself as a blond gamine with two kids (she actually had three, but the third was a newborn and that didn't count, she said). Another friend, a gay actor, used to lie in bed after a fight with his lover and make late-night phone calls to party lines. He'd call Texas Talk and Bad for You and 540-TOOL, find a husky voice he liked, and tell the man he was straight, but might be persuaded.

But I didn't know what to write. That I was born in Connecticut? That I'd worked in the stables after school for two years, and spent my summers at the homes of friends, because my parents liked to be left alone? That at fifteen I'd nicknamed myself the Keeper of Secrets and at twenty-two I started writing. That the person I loved first, my brother Cob, vanished fourteen years ago, vanished the way troubled teenagers sometimes do, except he never returned, and that I still got an occasional card from him, always postmarked in a different city.

That those cards made me sad because they said so little. The last one had a picture of a man floating on a raft in the Pacific. "Hello, beaner. I'm writing from another place I'm about to leave. Some people I know in Montana bought a boat and I offered to drive it to the coast for $500. Don't worry I'm okay. I'm not eating red meat, and studying the stars."

How could I say, in a few lines in the back pages of a magazine, who I wanted to love?

But, actually, I could say anything. It was only an ad.

"You know, when you fought Muhammad Ali he left the ring in a dazed condition, wasn't the same man by his own admission . . . so goes the song. I'm a 29-year-old writer. Short blond hair, long neck, dark eyes. You're a mystery, a messenger, an invitation, a wanderer, my half-brother, and when I meet you I'll feel like I've seen you before."

About a hundred men responded, by letter, or by phone to my voice box number. Their messages were like a hundred different handprints, casual, desperate, confiding, ordinary, strange. A few were married or deeply entangled with a woman, but most of them had slipped from one lover to the next. If they believed they were good-looking, they sent photos. One man was sprawled in a hammock bear-hugging somebody else's child; another was running on a winter beach, his collar turned up smartly to protect him from wind; a third stood on the steps of the pyramid at Giza. This one was sunburnt; a necklace of blisters popped out on his bare neck, but he looked starry-eyed and high, the photo probably snapped by a girlfriend in happier times.

Kim didn't leave a message on my voice mail, he sent a short letter about three weeks after the ad appeared. I no longer have the envelope; I have his cigarette stubs, the napkins he's written numbers on, I have his voice on my answering machine, again and again and again, but I no longer have that first envelope. It was white and nondescript, and I remember opening it to find a picture torn neatly down both sides so that only the face was left—riotous, unruly hair, a sweetly curving mouth, a sprinkling of freckles across prominent cheekbones, and a faintly smiling irony in the wide, clear eyes.

Our first phone conversation was awkward; we seemed to have nothing in common. Kim told me he'd just come up to New York from San Juan, where he'd lived for many years. He was thirty-three years old, a welder at a plant in Brooklyn, and had grown up near St. Paul, Minnesota. His father was a pilot who'd made a small fortune through canny investments, but Kim never took his dad's money. He was self-educated, and most of his jobs had required challenging, physical labor.

There was a simplicity to metal, he said; once you knew what a torch could do, you'd learned something honest and enduring—your fingers knew it, and your eyes, and it became a part of you that was unchanging when all else kept changing.

We met the next night in the Algonquin Hotel—his neighborhood, my choice. I like the warmly panelled lobby where you can drink cognac in big, stuffed chairs. It was nearly eight o'clock and busy. Still, I saw him: a man shifted slowly on a loveseat at the far end of the room and I knew it was Kim.

He looked older than the picture. Something had blighted his face, bringing the cheekbones and forehead out too far, punching dark circles under the eyes, straining the mouth. Often since I've wondered . . . was his face really the ruin I saw? Or was it some quirk of my own sight? Was it the face, or was it me?

I almost turned around and left. Instead, I opened and closed my purse, checked my watch, and walked into the ladies' room, where I flung my head down and shook it methodically so that my hair fluffed into a small cloud. Finally I went out to meet him.

"You made me wait so long I was ready to leave," he said, though not unkindly.

"Are you sorry now?"

"I don't know yet," he said, and held me with his gaze. "But I was getting hungry, so I reserved a table in back. Want some dinner?"

I let him walk ahead of me. Even now, I like to watch him move. Heads don't turn, but he exudes a simple confidence, and you can see the whole man in his walk: the graceful, half-joking aloofness, the balance, ease, and the solitude—nobody ever fits his pace, he manages to separate himself in a crowd.

By the time we'd sat in a quiet corner in back I decided I liked him, but then I grew shy. I rolled my linen napkin into a cylinder, then folded it into a triangle, and then a boat. He seemed amused, and willing to let me go on folding.

"So," I said finally, "what were you doing down in Puerto Rico?"

"Escaping to paradise," he answered quickly.

"For six years?"

"You get used to having a beach for your backyard."

"Then why did you come up here?"

"I just did, that's all. Tell me about your writing."

I decided to tell him part of the truth—about science reporting, but not the heady rapture of science itself, not how the mysterium tremendum flows through every corpuscle and nerve, through stardust and radio waves, ice floes and wheatfields. I kept my dizzy love of science from Kim, because I've found that it's only scientists who understand.

"I just went down to a place called Monell Chemical Senses Center. It's an institute in Philadelphia devoted entirely to research on smell. They have a whole laboratory full of marmosets, these tiny dark nervous monkeys that shriek like bats. Marmosets have a very unusual mating pattern." Our eyes were locked. He was perfectly still. I told him there was one dominant female in a pack, the only one who reproduced. She kept all the other females sterile by rubbing the trees with her scent glands. Some mysterious secretion in those glands was a contraceptive. The monkeys would inhale her scent while they were climbing and be rendered sterile.

He laughed. "I think I know a female like that."

"Do you? Anyway, now I have to sit down and write the piece. I have a hard time writing. I'm a slow writer."

"How long did it take you to write your ad?"

I thought. "It was off the top of my head. But that's just having fun in the personals column. It didn't seem to matter. Have you ever answered an ad before?"

He shook his head. "I never thought I would."

"Why do you need to now?"

"When I read it I thought it was about me." He was smiling.

"So did a hundred other guys. You've got to have a better reason than that."

He leaned forward into the light as he put out his cigarette. His hands were powerfully muscled, lightly chapped. A thin etching of grime—from the day's work?—shadowed his fingernails. I loved his hands—strong and battered like his face.

"So," I repeated, "there's got to be more to it than that. There must be a reason you even sat down to read the personals in the first place. I bet you don't usually do that, do you?" From that first night I asked a thousand questions. I didn't walk into this blind, I went with my divining rod to the ground. "Did you just break up with someone?"

"Did you?" he retorted.

"Yeah," I admitted, and he nodded too, and at that moment the waiter came.

He's too intelligent to be a welder, I wrote the day after I met him. He lives in a big Times Square hotel, a cut above the SRO's, he says, but still, it's a decaying relic, home to gays, hustlers, gypsies, psychics, night messengers. He paid for dinner and drinks with cash he kept extracting from a thick billfold. When he went to the bathroom I looked inside it—why else would he have left it on the table? I flipped through dozens of cards in sheath after plastic sheath, addresses from all over the country.

He never asked my last name. When I asked if he'd ever been in love, he said, Yes, but I loved the wrong person, and he said it as simply as someone would say, Yes, but I took the wrong turn and that's why I'm late. I wanted to ask the most stupid, obvious question: Why did you choose the wrong person? But instead I asked him how he liked New York, and he said, I've been in New York before and I can tell you, New York and I are not in love with each other. I like the desert and the ocean.

"I like buildings," I told him once we left the restaurant. "I like things made by man."

"What's your favorite building?"

"The Flatiron on Twenty-third Street. You walk down Fifth Avenue and it looks thin as a wafer, pasted on the sky. It's actually shaped like a triangle. But I like lots of other buildings. I like Grace Church. I like the meat-packing factories on the West Side, too."

He started to touch my pearls, the neck of my cashmere sweater, moved closer and by that time we were both a little drunk and talking about letting feelings flow, about not freezing moments, and we went walking back and forth on the side streets, in a drizzling mist of rain. The rain reminded him of San Juan, where his world was water, where for two years (he said) he'd been manning a forty-foot catamaran at the port of Fajardo on the island's northeast tip. Each day he'd taken tourists sailing to the tiny islands speckling the coast, waited while they went diving, delivered them to soft, white beaches, fed them beer and heroes and sped them home on the evening wind. But the catamaran was not the boat he owned and loved: that was a British lark he'd bought from a guy in St. Kitt's, a boat rarely seen in those waters. He loved it because it was a delicate thing, stable only when skimming at high speeds.

At two A.M. we stood on Central Park West near the Museum of Natural History. The pavement and the park and a cloud-flecked sky stretched in sleepy silence all around us, and he said,

"I want you," so quietly there was no need to respond.

"You'll have to wait," I told him anyway.

"I'm waiting," he said, and we started to walk again, and were silent for a long time, until he told me that the night before he couldn't sleep, so he walked up the West Side, right past the corner where we were standing. He said it was one of those times he'd walked all night. "The other night I was trying to walk out on my own life."

I asked him to describe his life, and he told me about his friend Cheeks, who has a late-night interview show; told me how he takes the L train out to Brooklyn, where he works, so early in the morning that it's always nearly empty. Out of habit he slides into the corner of the last car, shaking out the *New York Times* like a curtain, hugging his coffees between his legs. He always buys two coffees and that's his breakfast. This is how he reads the *Times*: a cursory glance to national news and sports and then he spends the rest of the ride poring over the classifieds section marked "Business Opportunities," and life after life passes before him: he'll fly heli-

copters down the Ivory Coast, buy a farm in Guatemala and plant a
thousand rows of cocoa trees, get married . . .

"It's because I know I'm not going to do any of it."

"It's like when I'm walking down the street and see somebody
interesting, and I pretend to be them," I said. "Everything in me
just stops, and I soak them up like a sponge."

He laughed. "Who do you want to be?"

"There isn't anybody I wouldn't want to be, for at least a minute."

We stopped in the park behind the museum, and he took my
arm and said, "If I had to guess one thing about you, it would be
that you're going home to write about me."

"Why do you say that?" I protested, but I was pleased. I almost
wanted the night to end, so I could go home and live it again in
front of my computer. "I will write about you," I whispered.
"What else are you going to tell me?"

"You'd rather figure it out yourself, wouldn't you?"

And then he pulled me inside his arms and sucked my lower lip
in his teeth, twined my hair, roughly and yet with precise economy,
as if he were coiling rope, so he could pull my head back and bare
my neck, and when he put his mouth to my throat I felt what I've
been waiting to feel forever. I could have screamed. I stumbled and
he held me from behind this time, kissing me like an animal licking
another animal's wounds, but then I saw a cab way up the avenue,
a little yellow toy twenty blocks away, and as the string of candied
lights on Central Park West turned from red to green I leaned out
of his embrace and waved it down.

"I'll call you tomorrow," I said, because I couldn't bear giving
him my number, since I'd have to wait for him to use it. "I'll call
about six. Will you be home?"

"I get off work at four," he said, and I settled back into the cab
and observed my body with a kind of cunning. By that time I
didn't feel a thing. Not heat or hunger or even the dark pulse of
addiction. I went home and slept and woke and went back to sleep
and dreamed that he came to me, lay down beside me and bit
through my skull, shoulders, spine, searching for the heart of me
that I could not give him because I had never given it to anyone,
and he went on biting through the sheet, the mattress and bed-

spring and floorboards, and even though I was bit and sundered I got down on my knees in amazement to watch him, and he turned in the dark, his eyes fixed on me, curious and steady, and the next thing I knew we were back on the bed, watching long seams rise on my body where the bites had been. He moved his fingers along the seams and his light touch pleased me. "My god," I said when he stopped, "I've missed you."

TWO

I love him. When I'm not with him it hurts, so I go
find things to hold me. And many things hold me.
I drink the way he drinks, holding my head back
like a circus performer swallowing fire. I play Rickie
Lee Jones—her mournful, pizzicato croon. I talk to
a beggar on Broadway because Kim flipped coins
into her frayed paper cup until there were no coins
left, intent on the game. She fell silent, caught and
becalmed by something in his eyes.

When my favorite things fail me I go to his factory. I take the L train and then the G and I'm
there, walking past a grid of narrow townhouses
slicked with aluminum siding and fenced in by cement yards.

It's the end of the day and Kim shuts off his
torch, removes goggles, visor, leather gloves, and
the heavy canvas jacket that protects him from slag,
the metal flecks that fly out from the torch like rain
from bicycle wheels. He spits his last bit of welder's
chaw into a plastic cup and pulls on a blue baseball
cap with "Dodgers" scripted in bright yellow
across the brim, fitting it on backward.

He doesn't see me in the doorway, and the

whole man is mine, weaving through the five-thousand-foot concrete plant, past immense columns of rolled brass, slabs of steel and sheets of tin. Everything is coated in metal dust. The hiss of blowtorches drowns out his voice as he calls the name of José Ramirez, a bushy-haired Latino. Kim puts an arm around José, who's half his size—short, powerful and fat. "My man," José mutters with pleasure. His maroon t-shirt is drenched with sweat, his springy beard coated with metal bits, his thick black hair pulled into a ponytail. Kim tells me they've been like brothers since the gray dawn, weeks ago, when he showed up at the plant and offered José (who was loitering before punching in) a taste from his twelve-ounce paper tumbler of coffee.

He lets me put on the welding helmet; the window's so black I see only a slow-moving spark. If I lift it, he says, brightness will singe my eye and make the surface peel like sunburned skin. I hold the torch. He steadies my hand and draws the flame down. The sheet of brass separates, like water being parted.

Because I'm the only woman in this factory, I become beautiful. The men make jokes, they ask how much I cost, and offer to teach me the fine art of metal fabrication. For a moment I love them all, one long receiving line of dusty males.

Kim stands a few feet from me. I come close—everyone's watching and I don't care—and turn his cap around so the visor's facing the front and say,

"Now I'm under the awning."

At last I'm under the awning. He understands the kooky meaning of it: Just you and me alone in the world. Nobody can hear a thing we're saying.

Then Kim and José and I walk out to the street,

to the trees that grow into fences by the river, the
kind you see under subway gratings and in the rub-
ble of abandoned lots, their scissored leaves a sort
of greenless green. Kim bobs his head to the right,
the left, and tells us that he's fitting the skyline into
the diamond spaces of the fence.

So Kim tilts his head, absorbed in his task, and I
try to envision his face when he shot a man. I try to
see him without this signature of sadness. He's
wearing a t-shirt with *Expect a Miracle* printed
across the front. He told me he bought it his first
night here; he'd gone out to get a soda, and there
on the corner was an old Filipino in a trance, listening with closed eyes to headphones, seated behind
a table blazing with yellow t-shirts. Each was folded
to show the words *Expect a Miracle*. Kim tapped
the vendor on the shoulder, and the man opened
his eyes. "Twelve dollars. Buy two. Bring you extra
miracle," the man said, closing his eyes again. And
Kim stood there, looking at those cotton shingles
of yellow and blue, like a hundred bumper stickers
promising impossible heaven.

What did he do then? The night was hazy and
cool, so he walked to the river, past the flashing
marquees of the theaters and the crowds milling
outside, past white limousines on side streets,
cracked stoops, cigarette shops, until he reached
the highway and could see the lights of Jersey fleck-
ing her hills. His mind was on murder. Murder had
used up all his luck, that miraculous current of luck
that had been his inheritance.

Just ahead was the aircraft carrier *Intrepid*, per-
manently docked at 46th Street, its bleak cannons
proud against the night's glow. Kim walked in the
shadow of its hull and settled himself on the cement, resting against a fence. The murmur of the
river bore him back to Old San Juan, a city bound
by water like New York. He folded his new t-shirt

four times and fitted it against the back of his head for a pillow. He didn't mind the irony, the touch of pathos, in trying to join miracles to murder. With his head cradled against twelve dollars of hope, he closed his eyes and began to fall.

THREE

I call him at six P.M. the day after we meet. He doesn't say a word, not even hello, just picks up the phone and waits. At least he could have hung up on me.

I don't know why but something in me is breaking and I can't let it. Is this what they call love at first sight? I don't think so. It's my body that's caught fire. It's my body that wants rescuing. Okay. I'll go down. I'll go down and kick his door in.

Nobody stops me in the lobby of the hotel, which has the dreary faded feel of an old municipal building. I pass a woman in a flimsy housedress, a man wearing black leather wristbands with spurs, and a dusty corner office near an old ice machine. The hotel long ago fell into disrepair; built in European style, with small rooms and shared baths, it's the kind of place nobody wants anymore. Kim said the owner bought it in '62, and in the first five days two people killed themselves.

I take the elevator to the seventh floor and at the end of a dim hallway is Kim's door, painted black and cracked so deeply and in so many places that it looks scarred with light. I rap and hear nothing, but when I press my face to the cracks I can see it all—a towel thrown into a little sink, an oil painting of Indian chiefs, a narrow window and twin bed with rusted metal casters. Huddled in the center of it all is Kim, knees bent, fists at his mouth.

The phone receiver is on the pillow where he must have dropped it when I called. I knock at the door and his eyes open. "Go to hell," he mouths, and rolls over. As if he doesn't know or care who knocked.

I could watch him like this for hours. He's lying on his back, perfectly still, as if he'd fallen from an immense height. Lying there in a kind of stunned trance. For a long time he and I don't move, as if we're invisibly hinged, held in suspension on either side of his door. And then a shadow falls on his face, except it's a shadow from inside, appearing suddenly at the surface like a birthmark—a shadow of brooding purpose and half-shaped resolve. What's he planning?

"Lose something?" A teenager with a tight bow of a mouth has come out of the hall bathroom and interrupts.

I walk a few steps away from Kim's door, reluctant. "He's home but he's not answering. Do you know him?"

"I seen him around. A couple times in the last two weeks."

"He's only been here two weeks?"

He shrugs. "I knew the gypsy who used to live in his room. She read my cards once in a while, but then her sister popped up from Jamaica with a kilo of hash and they split. And that was two weeks ago."

As he turns the key in his door I see that his entire left arm has been burned, healing into slick, surreal knots of skin. He catches me looking.

"My old man threw a pot of boiling water at me. So I bashed his teeth in with a frying pan."

". . . I'm sorry."

He disappears into his room, and I have that familiar sense of giddy lightness when misfortune has not touched me, instead has touched a stranger. It whispers to me. This place. Looking down the jailhouse row of cracked doors, listening to the low buzz of fluorescent light, I suddenly hear Kim's voice, low and tired:

"Guess what. She found me."

With my back against the wall, I slide down on my haunches. But it turns out he's not speaking of me.

"She was in the lobby of La Concha. Apparently she'd been walking up and down Condado Beach all day, stopping at phone booths. She sounded drunk. So she called fifteen times. I don't understand you, Cheeks, did you have to pick up the phone and give her my number? . . . Do I have to move again? . . . No, I don't think she'll come up, not to stay anyway. She hung up on me. Yeah, I know, that's just Katie. Listen, I'll talk to you tomorrow. Give Ginny a hug."

The bed creaks, there are footsteps, water runs from the tap and suddenly the door opens and he's so close I can touch him, dressed in blue jeans and a t-shirt, running his fingers through damp hair, utterly out of place in this gloomy hallway.

"I thought you were asleep—"

He breathes out slowly. "No you didn't. How long have you been here?" Softly he fingers the cracked wood, and then crouches, swinging the door toward his face, and looks through the fissures. "I meant to tape these holes up. Haven't had any time, though." He turns and his mouth smiles though his eyes do not. "So. Hello."

"Why didn't you say anything when I called?"

He seems surprised. "When?"

"Half an hour ago."

"I'm sorry. I thought you were someone else." His tone is tolerant but with a steeliness in it; I shouldn't press further.

"Who?"

"Someone I didn't want to hear from. You didn't give me your number, so I couldn't reach you. But I would have located you somehow. I wasn't about to let you go. Why don't you come in?"

"Why don't we go out for a drink?"

"Come in first," he counters. His fingertips brush my collarbone through my shirt.

"I want to go out."

"I'd rather not."

"Why not?"

"Not in the mood. And I'd like you to myself."

"You must be joking. Half an hour ago I was on the phone listening to the sound of traffic outside your window, waiting for you to say hello or hang up. You left the phone off the hook. You couldn't have cared less if you saw me."

He shakes his head in astonishment. "I thought about you a lot today. If you really believe I don't give a shit, why did you come down?"

"I honestly don't know."

"Why aren't you dating some writer or artist, anyway?"

"I usually do."

"So what's got you interested in a factory worker?"

"Is that how you think of yourself?"

"Good question."

"I'm interested, that's all. Tonight, I'm interested. I haven't called the other guys who answered my ad and told them to forget it because I've just met the man of my dreams."

"Look, I'm actually flattered that you want to see me." His tone is slightly exasperated, but tender. "I even came home to wait for your call."

"So why did you leave the phone off the hook?"

"I told you. Somebody got to me first. I was afraid she'd call back," he says bluntly. "And don't ask who she is. Come in?"

He intends to bend my will tonight and I like it, so I step forward and he propels me inside, kicks the door shut and in one fluid, unthinking motion pulls his t-shirt over his head and drops it on the floor. His chest is a shock: sleek and chiselled, starker than I've seen, the puckered, tight nipples at the center a deep red the color of mud. I want them in my mouth.

He lets me watch him, calmly as a slave for sale. Here in this crumbling, unreal hotel room, a humid cocoon that could be in the slums of Tokyo or Texas or Guam, anything is possible. He starts to unbuckle his belt.

"No thanks," I protest. "Spare me the strip show."

"You looked like you were enjoying it."

"Uh-uh." I look past him at the stained wall. On the bed is a nubby brown blanket, brittle from industrial detergent; next to it a pine nightstand with one unsteady drawer, a rotary phone and a small lamp sporting a cracked red accordion paper shade. A large window has loosened from its frame, leaking noise—metal gates being shoved close, trucks hurtling down pitted side streets, the wheeze of busses. I say to him, "You just want to fuck me? That's it?"

"I just want you to stay."

I shake my head, confused.

"Maybe I want to pull you in before you get a chance to think. I didn't want you to see how I live. I don't even have a bathroom. I have to take a leak down the hall. Will you sit down?" He pulls a chair over to the bed, removing a buttery, scarred leather jacket from the seat—then he leans back, cocks his head a little, and tosses the jacket across the room, so it lands squarely on the bureau. He smiles.

"Who's the woman you didn't want to hear from?" I mean to sound indulgent, but my voice trails out. I say her name to myself: Katie. Names have their own, mysterious vibration, and Katie's name seems both tough and soft at the same time.

Tapping a cigarette out of a crumpled pack, he says speculatively, "You're a smart woman. You don't need to play detective."

"But you interest me. Are you going to answer?"

"Right now, I'm inclined to answer."

"Okay."

"So. Let's get this over with. What exactly is it you want to know?"

"For starters, why *are* you staying in this scummy hotel?"

His laugh comes just a beat too late, and I know I've stung him and I feel a hot prick of pleasure. Already his pain means something to me. His answer comes slowly. He tells me that his best friends, Cheeks and Ginny, live four blocks away, and he could have rented from them, since they own their building, but he doesn't want them breathing down his back. He's got a few other friends he'd do anything for, anything, but he's a loner. "I'm telling you this because I don't want you to be hurt later."

"That's a pretty speech. But why are you here?"

He lights his cigarette, inhales, holds the smoke in. "This hotel? It's a place with no strings. Besides, I stayed here my first week in New York, when I was seventeen."

"Are you selling drugs?"

"Drugs," he echoes, with a whiff of bitterness. "That's the last thing I'd sell. I don't take them. I don't sell them."

"I've never tried any drugs," I lie, a small lie, because the one time I tried cocaine I hated it. Just a pinch under my tongue while the man who'd offered it to me sniffed long greedy draughts up each nostril. He was middle-aged and had the spectral face of an alcoholic, but what I remember most about him was his hands, shapely and feminine, capped with manicured nails. He repulsed me but when those nails gently scraped the back of my neck I floated into his arms.

"I think I know why you like this place."

His eyes rest on me.

"It numbs you."

"You think that's what I want?" He leans forward, alert and curious.

"It's like when you have a pain in one place and you hurt yourself somewhere else. Then you don't feel the first pain anymore. That's what this place is to you."

"I don't feel numb at all."

"No," I admit. "You don't seem numb. But I'm right, though, aren't I?"

"Close enough."

"Once when I had a fight with a boyfriend I went to a hotel like this. I lay in the dark," I tell him. The bedspread was orange cotton. The plaster ceiling had begun to flake and swell, like dried sea foam. In the bathroom down the hall I laid my makeup on the scratched aluminum counter and was curling my eyelashes when an old woman in a torn robe came in. Her hand darted out and stayed there, half-open, until I placed the eyelash curler on her palm. She turned it over and over, then dropped it in her pocket and left. "I stayed for three days, Kim. I was completely anonymous. And I was only twenty blocks from home."

"Yeah, it's like falling off the end of the earth."

"Just for three days."

He smiles. "Puerto Rico wasn't any different. Except it was four years. Shut your eyes. The noise here reminds me of Old San Juan. It's like rush hour in the old city."

"You miss it?"

"I started missing it before I left. I'm still going strong."

"So you'll return, then."

"Never."

"Never?"

"It's out of my hands. And," he adds, "it's none of your business."

"Would you have stayed there forever?"

"What do you mean would I have?"

"If it wasn't out of your hands?"

He's silent, but like last night he's intrigued by my questions.

"I miss the water," he says finally.

"There's water here."

"Yeah, but I'm not working on it." He shrugs. "I'm crazy about boats, but if you really know how to handle one it kind of disappears. Then it's just you and the water."

"Welding inside a factory in Brooklyn must be torture."

He smiles. "I like it. I told you already I like it."

So—I make mental notes—he's one of those men who finds grace in physical work. Maybe one of those men so unknown to himself, so shaped by contradictions, that he hopes a boat or a torch can resolve him.

"Can I sit next to you?"

He gestures to the bed. "Don't change your mind."

Our arms brush as I stretch myself on the sagging mattress, adjusting my body so I won't feel the springs, breathing in cigarette smoke that Kim keeps breathing out. He doesn't kiss me or hold me but manacles my wrist.

"Such small wrists." The voice betrays his eagerness. "How can you write all day with such small wrists?"

I twist my hand sharply in his.

"Oh," he mocks me, smiling. "I see. Sinews of steel." Then he pauses. "My god."

"My god, what?" My voice sounds lazy in my ears.

"I just realized your entire body must be like that."

"Sort of. Sometimes I think of myself as a greyhound," I admit. I'm drowsy with the pleasure that comes from lying next to him. It's like lying on the ocean floor, already dead and drowned. With his thumb he caresses the clefts in my palm, the heartline, the lifeline; he rubs the blue-ribboned veins at my wrist as if he could erase them; crumples my cotton sleeve between his fingers, turns my head until a tendon rises in my neck and he strokes that, too. A moment later he discovers a pink mole above my collarbone—I've had it since I was ten—and smiles at this oddly comical note.

He's staking out his territory, not just tracing hips and breasts but kneading each calloused elbow and the torn cuticles on my fingers, touching the bristly ridge of shaved hair in my armpits and streaks of tallow-dark wax I haven't cleaned out of my ears. I'm afraid he'll find all the things in me that are rank and pungent. But he doesn't seem to mind. He rests his head on my stomach, and after a short silence tells me he can hear the sounds inside.

"Move your head, then," I order.

"Are you kidding? I love it. Lift your leg up. Tighten the muscle. I want to feel you."

His fingers tease my calf and I hold my breath not to quicken this pleasure. As long as I keep my leg perfectly taut his touch is bearable. He's stroking my leg as if hypnotized. I jerk away. He looks up, half dazed and satiated and—

"What are you doing?" I blurt out.

"I'm forgetting."

"Forgetting what?"

Shaking his head, Kim says, "You're kind of virginal. It's intriguing. Especially after that ad you wrote."

"What are you trying to forget? Answer me, anyway, will you?"

"No."

"Why not?"

"Because I don't know how to answer a question like that. What about *your* secrets? You don't even know what they are."

"Ask me."

"What about that guy you split up with?"

I stare at him. A shudder of anger passes through me.

"What was that for?" he remarks.

I'm silent.

"Tell me."

"He had an affair. I left him. It was completely stupid and predictable."

"Same thing happened to me," he says evenly.

"Really? Why did she do it?"

"People get restless."

"Not when they're in love."

"Who said she was in love."

"Didn't she love you?"

"I don't know." He thinks for a moment. "Probably not."

"Did you love her?"

"I was crazy about her. But I never liked her. She's selfish."

"Is this the woman who's pestering you now?"

"If it were, would I tell you?"

"I guess not."

"So. Back to your story."

"My story doesn't have any blood and guts in it. It's kind of boring."

"Tell me."

I tell him I've lived with men and gotten hopelessly attached to them, but I don't think I've ever been in love. "It just hasn't happened. Sometimes I think I've lived out this parody of love."

"Maybe that's about to change."

"Christ, you're arrogant."

"I just think you're ready for a change."

"Right at the time you come along."

"I have nothing to do with it. I'll just be a witness." He leans against me. "If I'm lucky. I mean that."

"What's the difference to you?"

"I want what you never gave anyone else," he says simply.

"Human nature, right?"

Those men . . . sweat-drenched men, their bodies going soft after lovemaking, lying next to me talking randomly about this and that, talking with self-satisfied triumph because they'd come and I'd come. I tell Kim about them. "None of them had a clue. They thought if I had orgasms they'd moved me. Who cares about orgasms? I can make myself come. So I needed men. That's not love, is it? What's it like being in love?"

"It's been a while," he says patiently.

"I'm glad."

"Why, you don't like competition? Can you hold your own?"

"Yeah, but you seem so intent on getting me into bed. It's like you have no time. People feel that way when they're desperate over somebody else."

I must have hit close to the mark, because he shrugs and says, "This woman got to me once, that's all."

"She's the one who called?" I ask again.

He looks straight at me. "Do you know when to stop?"

"My turn, then. Ask me a question."

"Can't think of any right now."

"Try just one."

"Okay. Did you ever read the Dick Tracy comic books?"

"Nope. Next question."

"There's a reporter in the comics named Sparkle Plenty."

"That's not a question."

"Did I promise you another question?"

"No. But every performance deserves an encore. I want an encore question."

"How about this. Do you want me to describe her to you?"

"Who, Sparkle Plenty? Okay."

"She's just like you."

I laugh. "I'd better go read the comic."

We're silent. Finally he asks, "What is it that's stopped you from falling in love?"

I finger a belt loop on my jeans. "I didn't expect a real question."

"What do you want to do with it now that you have it?"

"I'll tell you a story."

And so I speak, harsh and breathless and apologetic, but brave somehow too, stumbling into a story easier to tell than my own, my brother Cob's story. I've been telling his story ever since he left, and the more I tell it, the more beautiful it gets.

Cob was five years old when I was born. A shy boy, the kind of boy teachers peg as special, as one who will make his mark on life and time. Adults loved him and other children avoided him. He had no friends, and was fastidious as a lonely bachelor, filling his time with small, orderly tasks: each night he laid the next day's clothes over the back of a chair, though no one had ever suggested he do so; he folded his napkin into his shirt collar like a bib before he ate, labelled his school notebooks with a crabbed hand, hung a

calendar over his bed and every night drew three steady lines across
the day before.

The truth was he lived in a glass envelope. It wasn't readily
apparent, since my parents spent the requisite hours taking him for
walks and teaching him words. They bought him toy trucks and
Slinkies and an Etch-a-Sketch, all of which lay hardly touched in
his pine trunk. Occasionally they took him to the zoo or museums.
They executed all their parental duties, but in some final, important way, they didn't really notice him; he was incidental, and he
lived like a straggler continually falling away from the tail end of a
parade.

He said that when I came, everything changed: into the quiet of
his heart burst this colicky infant who howled through the night.
He was drawn irresistably to me, and I fastened my heart on him,
too. Soon I couldn't sleep unless he was nearby, so my mother tore
down the wall between our bedrooms and we lived together for
the rest of our childhoods. We worked together at the stables,
though Cob didn't like to ride as much as he liked to watch me
ride. And I sensed some hunger in Cob urging me to violate
things. Only with Cob was I vital and lawless; with him I simmered
and begged and wept and laughed, but with the rest of the world I
was an inscrutable girl.

I stop speaking for a moment and Kim's eyes flicker darkly as if
he's about to say something. I almost feel as if he doesn't believe
my story. But how could he not? It's my best story, my most
believable story. Besides, it's true.

Nobody but me noticed that Cob had odd, dark lapses; hours or
whole days when he didn't want to talk or move. Instead he drew
back into some inner cave of self. And it was at those times that I
made trouble, left the back door open at night so the cat escaped
and was killed by a racoon, forgot the bath was running and
flooded the bathroom so many times that finally the floor caved in,
took my parents' car at two A.M., went speeding on the rain-slicked
streets, and smashed into a tree. Always I managed to snap Cob
back to me and the world. I was rescuing him from something

unnamed, and he usually repayed me by lying to my parents and taking the blame for my little catastrophes.

One afternoon I was pretending the plush green carpet of our room was a stormy sea, and my mission was to make it across to the chair where Cob was puzzling over an algebraic equation. I leapt from the doorway to a footstool, from there to a small bookcase, then scrambled onto a hightop walnut dresser with potbellied drawers. With a victorious battle cry I jumped onto Cob's bed, but miscalculated and crashed into the headboard. I remember my parents rushing in and how Cob wrapped my head tightly in a towel and held me in the backseat of the car on the way to the emergency room, murmuring my name again and again as if he alone would save me—but what I remember best is the sudden thrilled terror in his face when he first saw what had happened. . . .

I look at Kim. "He lived through me. It really hit home, that night, that he experienced life through me."

"Are you sure you want to go on?"

"Bored? You don't like my story?" I frown. "I can stop anytime. But you won't get another chance."

"That's not what I'm saying."

"What are you saying?"

"You'll hate me for this later."

I stare at him.

"You're like me in that way," he continues. "You play it close to the vest. Talking like this isn't your style."

"Oh, but it is. I like to tell stories." I lean forward. "It's escape, that's all. Sometimes, when I interview a scientist I spend a couple of days with him. We don't just talk science. We start with small, quirky stories, the ones that don't seem to count, and then we tell the intimate ones, and then it's like a love affair."

I hesitate. But he's nodding.

"Then, when it really gets serious, I stop. I always stop but by that time the other person doesn't notice. He's telling me the things about himself he'd never want in print. I interviewed a biologist last week, and by the end of the day he was describing how a colleague had stolen his girlfriend, and how he dreamed that he went up on the hill to this guy's house and shot him."

"You tell a stranger your story because you're never going to see him again," Kim says. He looks tired. Smoky blue moons under his eyes. "But I want to see you again. And I don't have anything to give in exchange for your story."

"It doesn't matter. Do you want to hear the rest?"

"I'm listening." He nods and lights another cigarette. Suddenly he reaches across me, the harpstring of muscles in his shoulder and neck straining as he switches off the lamp.

"I like my stories in the dark," he says. A fluorescent dimness floods the room—the city night, which is always starless and full of light.

For a moment I can't think how to continue. I want Kim to know about the change, of course. It happened when Cob went away to Cornell, seventeen and free, a young drifter with an air of mystery. A certain type of lonely and earnest girl inevitably loved and pursued him, and he submitted. Later there were several short affairs, but he cut them off. He told me that with one girl whom he particularly liked he was impotent. I remember how he described it. *Soft as an old carrot.* So he got out of bed and read her the definition of impotent from the dictionary and she started to cry. He said he was trying to be funny.

When he came home at Christmas the gentle irony in him had soured—he seemed ashamed. He had the kind of sheepish, pained smile you see on middle-aged men walking into porn shops. Yet I believed nothing between us had changed: he was still my brother, loyal and constant. Long ago he had replaced my parents—and my parents, actually, found it agreeable that he should replace them.

Kim briefly places his hand over my mouth. "Wait. Stop. You think your parents wanted it that way?"

"They had each other."

"They had each other," he repeats, disbelieving.

If that's sounds strange, I tell Kim, you have to know my parents. My father was a lawyer, a man as massive as my mother was delicate, with a dour bulldog's face and a naval academy crewcut. When he was twenty his right hand was severed in a boating accident, and he had a prosthetic metal pincer in its place. He was embarrassed by the hook except when alone with my mother, because she teased him about it with a kind of loving gaiety, and called it his war wound. My father silently adored my mother, and she was the only warmth he permitted in his styptic, unripe heart: I think of him as he often was, standing in her vicinity, waiting and watching, his bad arm crossed awkwardly at his waist, the other arm at his side, a bear of a man with the heat of idolatry in his eyes.

Sometimes at night I'd hear them talking when I came up the stairs, carrying a glass of milk and some graham crackers to my room. I'd pause on the landing, holding the old china plate with its scalloped rim and blue design of forget-me-nots. I could see them from the dark womb of the hallway, my mother pouring tea from a small white pot and bringing the cup to my father, and the happiness in his face. Then she'd settle back on the bed, relaxed, sleepy, and glutted. Somehow they completed each other, and so Cob and I formed our own impenetrable duo.

At the end of Cob's junior year I went to visit him. He lived in a rambling house on a narrow, crooked side street with seven other students. I banged at the door but nobody came, so I walked up three musty flights of stairs to a large attic room with sloping ceilings and motes of light. His bed was as neat and narrow as an army cot, his books alphabetized on cinderblock shelves. A parson's table illuminated by an overhead bulb served as a desk. He was standing in the middle of the room waiting for me.

"I was going to come down," he said slowly.

I went straight to him and put my arms around him. A few days later we took off for New York, on our way home for the summer. Cob put his hand out the car window to feel the wind rushing through his fingers, and said to me,

"This is enough, isn't it? You can fail at everything but there's still this."

We stopped in New York late that night and rented a fleabag room in Hell's Kitchen. Tilting his head at the desk clerk, Cob entered us as man and wife ("Otherwise what will he think?") and we went around the corner to a crowded bar, where he said with an eager, fatalistic smile,

"Why don't you go stand over there against the wall?"

"By myself?"

He nodded. "I bet a lot of men will come up to you. You're getting pretty now, you know."

He slipped onto a barstool, winding his legs around the stool's metal legs and pretending to watch the television while he actually watched men come on to me. He had a look of vivid unhappiness.

That night as we were walking back to the hotel we met a dog. She was small, black and shaggy, with a delicate face and one torn ear. She was shivering at us from a doorway. . . . (My eyes have adjusted to the shadows in the room, and I can see Kim clearly now. His face is full and relaxed. He senses my story coming to a close.) "Cob got down on his knees and lifted her face in his hands. The dog instantly became quiet. I think it was love at first sight."

"For him or the dog?"

"For both of them, really. . . ."

When Cob stood up, the dog stood too, her nose quivering expectantly. She trotted at his heels and when we turned into the hotel lobby the clerk was sleeping the sleep of death, his head so far forward that a pouch of fat bulged between his chin and collar, so the dog followed us in. Cob heaved the mattress onto the floor, leaving me the boxsprings, and lay down with the dog while I lay alone. I said to him, from the depths of pleasant exhaustion, "It's just like the old days."

He didn't answer. When I woke the next morning he and the dog were gone. He'd left no message with the desk. I stayed in the room until noon, then wandered the city, careening between anxiety and anger. When I returned at three he was sitting on the bed with the dog.

"Where were you?" I snapped.

With a malicious gaiety: "I was with Sally."

For a moment I was uncomprehending. "You met somebody and went off with her and left me here?"

"No, no, the dog," he said, laughing. He tickled her between the ears. "Sally and I were at the vet's. I've decided to adopt her. I'm going to take her back with us tonight."

He asked me a funny question then:

"Do you think she'll want too much of me?"

"A dog?"

"She needs me. She isn't like a regular dog. See?" He called to the dog and she came. "When I was with her today I kept thinking, this little thing is more real than I am. She seems so gallant and tragic at the same time. She's like a little person, a little human being, isn't she? Aren't you?" And she was—her lovelorn head lifted to him, tail shivering. Cob turned to me. "I need her. I'm like the kid with his nose pressed to the window pane. I feel left out, even left out of my own life. You were the only thing that kept me grounded. And when you go . . ."

"Go where? When I graduate I'm going to Cornell just like you."

"I can't depend on you. I mean I shouldn't."

"What are you doing, breaking up with me?" I joked. But I didn't believe it.

The next night we found a better hotel. One with double beds and a soda machine on every floor. Then we went home to Connecticut. A week later Cob got in his car with Sally and didn't come back. After forty-eight hours my parents asked me to help file a missing persons report. I drove down to the police station alone. I'd been the last to see Cob walking down our driveway, a twenty-year-old boy wearing a black Cornell sweatshirt and a plaid cotton jacket. I remember noticing how nimble and resilient his step was and wondering if the dog had really usurped me. For the rest of the summer my parents kept questioning me. "Was something bothering him? Where did he go? Was he planning it? Was it over a woman? He was seeing someone? Was he in an accident? Why didn't he take any money? Why can't the police find any trace of him? What do you think, Lynn? Did something happen in New York? Talk to us."

It had always been a household of two against two. And so they began to blame me. My silence seemed conspiratorial, and my mother became convinced I held the answer to Cob's disappearance.

"Are you going to tell me you didn't?" Kim asks now.

"I was the most mystified. Really."

He's silent.

"He left everything. He just disappeared."

"I left everything myself, at about the same age, but I called home when I got to New York."

"He wrote me eventually."

"What did he say?"

Late in August, on a humid night eleven weeks after Cob had vanished, my parents came to my room. They were determined to make me talk. I remember fanning myself slowly with a paperback book I'd been reading. My parents liked air-conditioners but I didn't, and my windows were shoved open to bring in the night's dead heat. My father stood, bewildered, his good arm wrapped protectively around my mother. She told me she believed Cob had killed himself.

"If that's what you think, don't come to *me* with it. You and Daddy just keep it to yourselves."

They stood there holding each other. And I could see in them, even then, the deep repose of mutual love.

Eventually I heard from him:

"Beaner, forgive me is all I can say. I'll say more later. Now I'm up to the yin-yang with talk and strangers. On a train to Wyoming. It's surprising how we're all alike at least on trains. It doesn't take much in the way of body or mind to be a traveller. It's mostly soul. I'll write again."

I left the postcard taped to the refrigerator, and it stayed there for years. Sometimes I'd surprise my mother standing in the kitchen, reading the card as if she might, this time, divine some secret meaning or message from it.

In some strange way his absence dazzles me. I still can't believe he did it. He may die on the road someday, and I wonder if I'll feel it physically, or if it will come to me in a dream. I've gotten so accustomed to missing him that I might never know, I might be without a brother right now and not know.

'And that's how it is. I know what you're about to ask. You're wondering why I placed that personal ad. For the same reason I came down here tonight. I'm twenty-nine and I feel absent from my own life. You understand. You're quiet now because you understand. I won't live like this anymore. I don't remember—what's it like to be the most important person to someone? To say, *I'll never get over you. I'll never recover.*

*   *   *

My voice dies out in the darkness and a moment later Kim leans toward me and touches my lips with his, in the most excruciating never-ending kiss. My body stings with the sweetness of it. My heart burns to ashes in his mouth.

FOUR

My life is a series of beautiful accidents. Kim would never have come my way if one night in March, six months before I met him, three men in a ghetto in Puerto Rico had not watched, silently, moodily, while a fourth rubbed cocaine into his skin. The fourth, Raphael Nadal, sat in a folding chair near the door of a tin hut that opened onto a road by the sea, in the slum called La Perla, rubbing the white powder into the flesh between his thumb and forefinger.

His head was all silver curls, cut tight around a swarthy face. Black linen slacks hugged massive thighs. His stubbed fingers rubbed almost dreamily. Inside the room, on a floor of crooked planks, was a foam mattress and a television. Just outside stood Katie, uncertain whether she should look at the sea, or back at her lover.

Finally Nadal was done with his skin test, and he stood, an elegantly dressed hulk framed against a pink aluminum doorway. He looked like some hurtling thing, a javelin or fist, stopped in mid-flight.

"Darling," Nadal said to Katie.

She shoved her hands into her jeans and waited.

"*Carita,* you look, as always, like the little girl who just came downstairs on Christmas morning. Come, sit," he said, and pointed to the folding chair.

He moved toward the men with a strange, creamy lethargy. Katie had seen this mood before: but here it was strange, frightening. She hesitated, then followed, until something in the tone of his voice stopped her. He said, in Spanish,

"Who's the cook?"

One of the men, obese and middle-aged, nodded warily. His skin was a luminiscent grey—the typical hue of a master chef after a lifetime inhaling cocaine's vapors. He looked like a stranded whale, but like most cooks, he was proud of the color. It was a living resumé.

"*De siguro,*" said Nadal. And then he held out his hand: there was a white dusting on the skin where there should have been none. Human skin soaks up cocaine, leaving any impurities behind. The kilos had been cut.

I know it's an innocent, even childish, view, but I like it: if not for that innocuous dusting of white, Katie would have stayed with Nadal, Kim would have stayed in his house by the water, and I'd be alone.

FIVE

"Are you still alive?" Kim asks lightly as he pulls back from our kiss.

"Nearly dead."

He nods slowly, judging my state, then puts his mouth to my breast through my shirt. I let the cotton get wet, until it sticks to my nipple and scorches my senses, then I push him away.

"What's wrong?"

"I can't."

"Can't what?"

"I'm not ready. It's only our second night."

"You think you're going to know me so much better tomorrow or next week?" he says. But he pulls me close. "Don't move. I won't tempt you again. Just put your head on my chest. Go ahead, hide from me."

And I do, lying against him as if he's warm stone. I drift back into sleep, and back into consciousness. It must be hours later; he's crouching by the bed watching me with careful calm, as if he were the interloper in the room and I the rightful owner. I hear his sober voice.

"It's your eyes."

My eyes, he says, are golden brown, but much darker when remembered. "And your hair," he says enigmatically, smoothing my hair back.

"You like it?"

He nods, then stands, shrugs on his leather jacket, and says he's heading out for a pack of cigarettes. I know he can't sleep because he wants me. It's touching and sad, his leaving—as if he's given me his room because it's all he has. The door clicks gently and I lie still, listening to my breath, before I remove my clothes and curl up on my side, the sheet bunched around my knees. He doesn't return, but in some way I'm not surprised. I imagine him reading a newspaper in an all-night diner down the street.

It's morning and I'm lying in Kim's bed pretending he owns me. I'm naked, I've kicked the sheet off and my hands are locked behind my head as I watch a bee that must have entered the room last night. It's circling the ceiling fixture, and I can see by its crazy, looping flight, the way it keeps bunting against the frosted glass and falling back stunned, that it's dying—one of those ill-fated Indian summer bees that hatch in October and are rendered senseless when nights turn cold.

And then, almost as if called to me, the bee dips down to the bed. It's a beautiful, buttery thing, its hind portion hanging loose like a fruit pod, ripe and heavy and swinging. It lands on my hand and I flick it away and it comes back, so I let it stay. I believe it is staring at me, its helmeted head motionless, and I don't know how many minutes pass before I decide that it has died.

I tap it with my fingernail and it feels as light as a flake of ice. I tap it again and suddenly it stirs, flies straight at me and pierces my cheek with its stinger, then plummets like an exhausted champion back onto the bed. In spite of the burn that flows like fluid across my skin, I don't move, I only watch as the bee's whole body begins to expand, its wings moving up and out with a slow, soft, terrible power.

A minute later it's dead and I lift it by one wing and gingerly toss it out the window.

I lie down again, fingering the fire-bathed welt where it stung me. If I were superstitious I'd say the bee was a warning—an omen of disaster. Maybe it was. But I feel at home here.

This is the kind of room that asks nothing of you—a bed, a lamp, a sink, a scratchy AM radio and a stiff cotton curtain with plastic rings that pulls shut against the light. There's a feeling of release in the squalor, because it's so irreducible. I find the same consolation in the *baratillos,* the discount stores in Spanish Harlem. I wander by bins of vinyl sandals stamped with their bald round sale stickers, and I'm comforted. Green, blue, banana, black, shiny as slick paint, some with thick heels and buckles and I buy them all, tossing them in a corner of my front closet at home. There they lie in a heap of brilliance, never worn and yet with a madcap life to them, as if they'd been kicked off in mid-dance. I like them. I like to look at them.

I never had that feeling around a person before, until Kim. He's smooth as a bird's egg and will only crack when he's ready, and then from the inside.

Idly, lazily, I imagine masturbating, but don't touch myself. For years I used to lie on my back with my hand between my legs, and I favored my forefinger. I just unbuttoned my pants and slipped my hand inside. Masturbation was my little seizure, a kind of *petit mal,* when a shutter closed on the world.

Then one afternoon I ducked into a darkened theater to watch *Last Tango in Paris,* and halfway through Maria Schneider spread herself facedown on the floor, no longer a woman but a pear-shaped animal, a rump and back and legs. She shoved one hand under her belly and when she came it was desperate. That night I turned on my stomach, mouth in the pillow, and the bed moved beneath me. That's been my way ever since.

But not now. I want to save myself. He has no idea how I crave him, that at this moment while he's welding metal in his factory I'm lying in his rickety single bed with an unutterable ache between my legs, that I might lie here all day waiting for him to come back, remembering pieces and flashes of him—his sad mouth, his white sleeve, his silence.

I stretch and notice the phone is off the hook; I put it back on. He shouldn't have trusted me alone here. When it comes to other people's privacy I'm uncontrollable, so of course I'm going to search his room.

The pine bureau is innocuous—two pairs of well-worn blue jeans, soft as powder, and a collection of t-shirts bearing nautical insignia. The small, rusted wastebasket contains four empty bottles of Foster Lager Ale (if it's from a six-pack, I wonder idly, who drank the other two?) and a confetti of torn wrappers from Snickers bars.

In the peeling, musty closet, where a dozen starched cotton shirts and three fine suits hang (one wool, two silk), I discover a leather tote bag. It's an intoxicating piece of luggage, melting and rich, and it smells as wonderfully pungent as the oiled saddles and harnesses of my childhood.

Nothing inside. Just to be thorough I check the pockets, and the pockets within pockets, for this is the tote-bag equivalent of a castle, complete with trapdoors and secret chambers. And now comes the warm leap of shame, of pleasure: I find three photos in a zippered pouch. Pictures of Katie, labelled on the back in red ink: her name, the date and the year.

She's about seven in the first one, a little girl with hair cut like a boy's, basking in the sun on a summer day, her fists clenched, her feet (which look like hooves, small, thick and arched) pressed tightly together. She's staring into the camera with a fierce rapture, as if by her look alone she might hypnotize her viewer.

The next one is shot on a sailboat. She's sixteen or seventeen, wearing a sleeveless skintight dress and sandals. Her mouth is open as if she were panting, her hair has been whipped into a tangle by the wind, and she has the same look of biting rapture.

In the last picture she's slumped at a kitchen table, unwashed hair swept back from a puffy, sleep-swollen face. She seems exhausted but the fierceness is still in her eyes.

They're ordinary pictures but I want them, with a jealous, dazed wanting, so I leave Kim's door slightly ajar and go out into Times Square in search of a copy shop. When I return fifteen minutes later, booty in hand, I stop at the front desk.

"Any messages for room 745?"

The clerk, a skinny young Arab with curling black hair and bloodshot eyes, gives me a level gaze. "You don't live in room 745."

"I'm his sister."

"Yeah? He has a sister in Puerto Rico, too."

"I know. Two sisters," I say, and my throat tightens. But I force a smile. "Okay, okay, I'm his new girlfriend, and she's his old girlfriend. She called last night, didn't she?"

The clerk nods suspiciously. "I talked to her this morning. She called the front desk, told me he had took his phone off the hook, and she was worried about him. She said how he has mental troubles."

"He does?"

"She says he disappears for weeks at a time. Just takes off and flies somewhere in the world he's never been." The clerk leans close and says confidentially, "She's got family money, so they don't have to work. We had a nice talk. She's a nice girl."

"Did she ask you to keep an eye on him?" I joke.

The clerk smiles.

"So—any messages?"

He walks over to the wall of boxes. "Just one," he says formally. "From her."

"Did she leave a number?"

He puts the message back in the box. "He knows the number," the clerk says disapprovingly.

Up in Kim's room I lie on his bed examining the photos of Katie, and all at once I think I can see her soul. It's there in each picture, as irrevocable as a scream, and though I can't quite find words for it, I can sense it: feline, insolent, pleasure-seeking. She reminds me of a girl in a motorcycle gang I interviewed. The girl was the gang's honorary member, not just a hanger-on, and she walked like she was doing a slow dance. She told me she'd eaten her own menstrual blood and could hold a burning cigarette to her palm longer than any man. She displayed both palms—smooth and pink. "It's all mental," she said while her gang brothers stood in a circle around us as if we were prize catch, soon to be roasted and eaten. "I gotta psyche myself up . . . so that I don't feel it . . . and I don't burn one little bit. It's like I go under. It's like I go, uh, somewhere else." Then she pulled her hair back and showed me a puckered scar near her ear. "My guru . . . little Johnny, the leader of the pack . . ." and she smiled at a small boy who looked as mean and streamlined as a missile, "tested me once. By surprise . . . See, it don't work unless I'm already under." She told me she called her scar Johnny's Kiss.

I put Katie's pictures back, and shove the tote bag into the closet. I don't close the door, just stand there holding the sleeves of Kim's cotton shirts to my face. Even though they're fresh from the laundry, creased neatly where they were folded and slipped inside brown wrappers, they smell of him. I want that smell the way someone wants a tattoo of their lover's name, hidden on the inner arm.

The phone rings, and very quietly I pick it up and say hello.

There's a short silence, and the caller hangs up. A minute later it rings again, and I do what Kim did last night—pick up the receiver and place it on the pillow.

Suddenly I notice that the cord doesn't fit into the wall jack; instead it's taped to the underside of the table and fed discreetly into the night table. I open the shallow, rickety drawer, which sticks as I pull it, and discover a flashlight, pen and a pad of paper which, when held to the light, shows the faint impression of the letter Kim wrote in response to my ad. And a small, gray answering machine containing two silver microcassettes smudged with use. I lift the machine, press the outgoing message button and get only silence, but when I rewind and play the incoming tape whole conversations unfold. Kim must have rigged the machine to pick up and record whenever he answered. Why is he bugging his own phone?

I push the playback button and listen hunched over, my heart skidding rapidly.

"Hey, didya get home okay?" comes a gravelly Hispanic voice. "What time is it?"

"I woke you? Midnight I guess. Wife's asleep. I'm dying."

"Of what?"

"Thirst. I'm burning up like with a *puta*'s fever. Shouldn't have drank so much. Boss junior gave me a big job tomorrow. I'm gonna tell him I need your help."

Kim is silent until finally his friend asks whether he's gone back to sleep. "No, I was thinking about this old Puerto Rican guy named Manuco, who taught me sailing tricks. You remind me of him, José."

"How come?"

"Gruff old bastard, but loyal."

"I'm fucking stuck to you," José brags. "You only met me a few weeks ago, but you'll find out."

And then he talks, full of guileless braggadocio. He tells Kim he grew up in a little slice of barrio on 110th Street, the firstborn, the oldest of five boys and meant to be Papa's pride, except God gave him kinky hair.

Pelo malo—his relatives whispered when they thought he wasn't listening. Where did he get his hair?

Four brothers followed in six years, and each was creamy-cheeked, "light brights" with their fine coating of *pelo bueno*. "It was like, how come all the others are such a nice color, and not me? So I told my mother she don't love me because I got black blood. I said my papa is a *cabrón*, a cuckold, she gave Papa horns, you know, she slept with another guy and that guy is my real father and he's black. She cried so hard her eyes swolled shut. The next day she strapped me to a chair with a leather belt, and before I knew it my head was smeared with paste from this green jar. But my hair didn't straighten out like she wanted, it fell off in clumps. I woke up with this fucking bald spot a mile wide."

He was twelve, he says, when he discovered the street. On the street were boys who'd been made by hate, and they had their own odd pride in the result; they didn't ever want to be unmade.

"When I was a kid," Kim says suddenly, "I used to like watching bar brawls. I liked to watch a man going down and another man standing over him looking high as a kite. You know that look?"

"Sure I know that look. It's *corazón*, that's all. It's goddamn heart. You never fight unless it's for heart."

I love the conversation, but it seems a luxury—I can't wait for what might come next. I want to sample everything at once. So I fast-forward.

The next voice, a man's, is cheerful and middle-aged. "The keys are still in the same place. I kept them for you even though Ginny and I lost hope you'd ever come back from that godforsaken island. Or should I say godforsaken commonwealth. See you what time?"

"Around seven?"

"Gotcha."

Fast forward. Playback. Silence. And then a sharp whistling

breath. "What's this disappearing act? Where've you been? I was gonna die trying to get hold of you. You won't believe what's happened. Kim? Kim? Are you there?"

When the voice breaks I almost jump; I'd been feeling it flow over me without making sense of the words. Hoarse and pleading, all the sentences run breathlessly together.

Katie.

"I'm here," Kim says. "Are you calling from the condo?"

"God, I'm not that stupid. I've been walking up and down Condado all day stopping at one phone booth after another."

"Where are you now?"

"In the lobby of La Concha. I've got to get out of here, Kim. I've got to come back to the States."

"I'll send you a ticket."

"You will?" Her voice becomes almost inaudible. "You will really, honey?"

"Not to New York. To Boston."

"Boston?" Her voice catches, trembles, and suddenly becomes mocking. "You're going to send me a ticket home to Mama? I'll cash it in. Screw you, Kim."

"You don't want the ticket?"

"Why are you up there, anyway? You always said you hated New York." There's a lovely bitterness in her voice; it's so vulnerable, somehow. "Are you coming back to me? You came back once—"

"Did I?" he retorts.

The line goes dead. Almost instantly I hear my own voice:

"Hello, Kim? It's Lynn."

An odd, muffled silence. Did he let the receiver fall on the pillow?

"Is anybody there? Kim?"

The tape goes on turning in silence. I rewind and replace the recorder.

Still, obeying some urgent inner command, some reflex that's a mix of reporter's bloodhound curiosity, and physical desire, I open the night-table drawer, write my phone number across the empty pad, and toss it on his bed before I leave.

My clothes carry the faint odor of his cigarettes, and wearing them feels like he's touching me everywhere. Outside it's lunch hour and I take the IRT from Times Square to Lincoln Center, moving with a million strangers through the turnstiles, click, click, click, the crowd splitting and flowing like a flock of birds through separate stairways, only to merge again in the street above.

I'm going to visit Sherry—my partner in crimes of the heart—and tell her about the fever in my body, this omnivorous cunt-ache, as she'd call it. This man is what she calls magnificent trouble.

Sherry was my third roommate in New York, and I circled her warily at the beginning, perplexed and intimidated by the rich disorder of her life. She made me shy. Clothes flung on the bed and hanging from the shower rod; paintbrushes and pens and stacks of paper piled along every wall; lipsticks rolling across the bathroom floor and half-used rolls of toilet paper on the top of the tank. This was Sherry: balancing the phone between ear and shoulder, speaking in a low melody to her latest love, pouring cracked pepper into homemade soup, wriggling out of her quilted coat—and she always did it all at once, flushed and impetuous.

And yet she respected my distance. She didn't ask why I brooded, lay alone on a Sunday reading a book. Slowly I melted into her life. We began to eat dinners together. I borrowed her clothes. She introduced me to her old boyfriends. But it was actually a note from my brother that made us friends. It was my birthday, and my parents told me Cob had called home for the first time in three years. They'd given him my new address. I stood in the middle of Sherry's living room and wept. She put her arms around me and I told her the story of Cob. I remember her saying,

"He probably wonders if you read his notes at all."

"I read them."

"Do you keep them?" she asked curiously.

"I don't want to."

"I guess that means yes."

So I went to my bedroom and got out my plastic shoebox of cards and notes from Cob, and she looked through them. She was fascinated; I had never seen her so quiet. Sherry was the first person I told.

Now she's seated at her drawing table, wearing sweatpants and a man's sleeveless undershirt, her thick brown hair swept up and knotted sloppily on her head, three pearls in each earlobe.

"You're forty-five minutes late, Lynn," she says, in a distracted tone.

She starts to put away her tools—brushes, cartridges, bottles of ink. Sherry's drawings of animals are so opalescent people buy and frame the originals. She makes a new series each season, which she sells as prints and cards.

When I'm within a foot of her she looks up and gently touches my cheek.

"What in the world is that?"

"A bee sting."

"It looks like someone punched you." She loosens her hair, a tangle of velvet, and starts to brush it. "Do you want some ice?"

"No, I'm fine. Sherry, listen, something has happened."

"A man," she murmurs, delicately laying a sheet of wax paper over her drawing. She pulls on a white, zippered sweatshirt, rolling up the sleeves.

"I met him two days ago."

"And?"

"I haven't slept with him yet. I want to. I can't think or feel anything else. I haven't been this way since—"

She looks at me with sharp curiosity. "Since when?"

"Since . . . since never, actually."

"So what's stopping you, honey?"

"He came out of nowhere and he lives in a fleabag motel in Times Square."

She's quiet for a moment. "What does this man do?"

"He's a welder."

"Mmm. Nice muscles? Well, whoever this stranger is, I want to hear everything."

We sit in the back of the Saloon Grill and order big salads and glasses of Cabernet. I tell Sherry my story, from the moment I opened his letter to last night's slow, thudding kiss.

"Jesus, the man sounds hot." She nods to herself. "I could pick him out of a roomful of strangers on your description alone."

"I don't want to get lost in him."

"Is that so bad? Besides," she continues, "you've already decided. And it's about time. What did you do when you were a teenager? You never necked in the grass at four A.M."

What's she trying to get me to admit? I live in a glass envelope, but so does Sherry. She keeps men in constant orbit around her, and if a man crashes she replaces him immediately. I've never been blind and howling with love, but neither has Sherry.

"Let me meet him," she offers.

"Not yet."

Dessert is served, a golden, candied pear tart for Sherry, and chocolate mousse for me.

"Did I tell you about the stranger in the deli?" she says, taking up the thread of our conversation. "This will make you laugh and cry. I was buying a dozen sweet rolls the other morning and a big grizzly bear with blond hair and a red beard comes up to me and tells me he's been watching me for years. Turns out he lives on the seventeenth floor of the building across the way, and watching me do t'ai chi in my leggings in front of my window has been a pastime." She blushes. "Not an obsession or guilty peeping-tom kind of thing, but a pastime like going trout-fishing. Well, he gives me a beautiful fairy tale and makes it sound as if we might be each others' destiny, and the long and short of it is that after a few dates I'm in his apartment and he's massaging me for an hour. Up, down, head to toe, and I'm as warm and helpless as a baby when he pauses and whispers, 'Should we?' And you know what I thought?"

"Yeah. 'You blew it, baby.' "

Sherry nods and says softly, "He should have taken me, no questions asked."

"Isn't that the same reason you're not marrying Kyros?"

Sherry gives me a warning look. I go blithely on: "Kyros has a Zen kind of strength. You might admire that but it's a turnoff."

"Everything would be fine if he didn't keep asking me to marry him. Except now he's talking about going to Europe."

"By himself?"

She sighs. "It's his way of forcing me to decide and still being a gentleman about it. Listen, what are you doing later? Do you have an hour?"

"I should get back home. I've got a piece to write about light and diabetes."

"What's the deal? Now diabetics have to walk around with parasols or something?"

I laugh. "This guy invented a device that sends a beam of infrared light through the skin, and detects exactly how much sugar is in the blood by the way the blood vessels absorb light. I interviewed him."

"Was he good-looking?"

"A phone interview."

"A wasted opportunity. Listen, don't go home yet. You should be out when Kim calls. Stay with me. A woman in my building, Dana, is having a party to promote her new line of sunglasses. We can get them wholesale. Her company is called Bizarre del Mundo, which is a takeoff on Bazaar del Mundo."

"Sounds suffocating and tedious."

"And waiting for a phone call isn't?"

"I don't need sunglasses."

"Lynnie, let me tell you," Sherry's voice drops, "when you see these glasses you'll crave them. They're better than that pair of white lace-up boots you bought last winter. These glasses will make you happy."

"Yeah, but for how long?"

Most people choose a witness to their lives, but I can't. Nobody reverberates down to the bone. So I live alone. My work is my refuge; I visit but don't live in other people's worlds. Under the guise of good reporting I ask any question I want, and so I have the freedom of the lover or the child. And usually I ask about love. Vanessa tells me she met Bob on a skiing weekend, asked if she could have the seat next to him, and he said, "Not only can you sit here, you can have my babies." Rosemary says she likes tall American men, but when a small Arab with a sad, little face took her dancing she knew she'd met her mate. James says Nora jerked him off one day on a park bench, and from then on he cleaved to her. He says, "I'm the kind of man who walks along, not noticing where he's going, and his foot strikes something. He bends over and it's exactly what he wants." Henry never loved anyone. He said the most important thing about him was his loneliness. Mary says when she has lunch with a man she used to call her ugly prince charming, she feels nothing. He doesn't even seem ugly anymore.

The people I choose to love are like myself. Sherry is an island.

But Dana, the maker of sunglasses, is another species entirely. As soon as Dana greets us I recognize her: someone who comes to life only when she is being seen, touched or talked to by others. This afternoon her apartment is packed and she's practically trembling with elation. We follow her down narrow aisles formed by racks of sunglasses, and they do leave me awed. They're simple dark-lensed glasses rimmed by fantastical shapes in gold tin—salamanders, camels, cupids, curling leaves, city spires. Like everyone else at the party, I feel a metaphysical thirst, and almost instantly I buy a red plastic pair topped by two fat iguanas.

"How did you make this stuff? It's like . . . Star Trek meets Goya."

She laughs. "Glasses are camouflage, like hats with veils. They're sexy . . . hey, is that a birthmark?" she adds, studying my cheek, then claps her hand over her mouth. "I'm sorry, are you sensitive about it? It's beautiful, really, that's why I asked. I don't know why people torment themselves over birthmarks. I knew a man who had a cherry birthmark on his scalp, and it started to grow down over his forehead, so he had the whole thing removed, had his skin stretched and all. After that he wanted his head scratched all the time. He found it very erotic."

"Actually, it's a bee sting."

"A bee sting," she echoes doubtfully, and gazes at me with a tinge of respect: if I'm joking, the joke is offbeat enough to give her pause.

She brings us to a smorgasbord in the kitchen, and without thinking scoops warm Camembert onto her finger. "Eat, eat. Here," and she holds her finger near my lips. I hesitate until she smiles broadly and sucks at the cheese herself. "My mother used to sculpt my food, she'd push her fingers into the carrots and peas and say, 'Here's the Eiffel Tower,' and it got so that I wouldn't eat my food without my mother putting her fingers in it first."

"Sherry," I murmur, turning away from my hostess, "I'm going home."

Dana hears me. There's a sudden pause and a tightening. "What's the trouble?" she inquires sweetly.

"No trouble—"

"Man trouble," Sherry interjects.

"What kind of man trouble?"

"A fresh cut. She hasn't even gone to bed with him. In fact, I only heard about him over lunch."

Dana lowers her voice. "He isn't married?" she asks hopefully.

I shake my head.

"He might be anyway," she says.

"Lynn's last boyfriend . . . forgive me, Lynn," Sherry touches my arm, "was a hopeless case. A hair-trigger quickie."

"Sherry!"

"Once down, he stayed down," Sherry continues relentlessly, "so you can imagine the poor girl needs her faith restored."

"Are you supposed to see him tonight?"

I shake my head. "You know how it is," I explain. "Waiting for a phone call from a man who's wrong for you."

In a burst of sisterly affection, Dana slides her arm around my shoulder and says the one thing I want to hear—the whispered promise that women exchange in hallways and cafés, powder rooms and bedrooms, the lullaby that calms our late-night crying jags, the words to hold us steady:

"He'll call." Dana, however, adds a variation on the theme: "Just forget about him. He'll pick it up by mental telepathy, and as soon as he's afraid you don't care, he'll be calling every day."

I know the precise spot in the darkness of my living room when I can see my answering machine. I know the moment when I can see the red light blinking.

I see the red light blinking.

And so my choice is made. Actually, I prefer it this way.

Earlier today I joked with Sherry about how she needs three men in her life—old faithful, the demon lover, and the question mark. It's the question mark, the distant shore of a new man, that she desires most. He's her sense of freedom. Sherry has a habit of liking new men. The fact that she and Kyros are closer every day—by now they must be in the same skin—doesn't dampen her ambition for beautiful or accomplished men. Sometimes I think she finds them so her friends will say, *Now* Sherry has finally done it, Sherry has really done it. It's always happening, this dance with men, even when she's alone studying her anatomy books and setting the table with lace cloth for a private dinner, but I—

I play back the message and it isn't him.

SIX

A reporter is witness, rapist, translator—in that order. Cruel, and, when it's done right, a calling.
Someone has to write the rag and bone-shop of the
heart.

The night after Kim tells me of murder, I sit for
hours in the public library at a scarred oak table
that looks like it could serve a feudal mess hall,
poring over *El Mundo,* reading front page notices
of Nadal's death. A homicide team of three has
been assigned to the case. There's no mention of
the fact that Nadal was a human hub for cocaine
flowing from Colombia to America. He's eulogized
as a canny businessman who donated heavily to city
preservation and the arts. His nephew, the article
notes, will take over the family's business dealings.

Again I read the simple opening sentence: *El ca-
dáver de Raphael Nadal fue hallado el domingo por
la tarde en su casa, presentando un balazo en el
corazón.* His dead body was found Sunday afternoon at home, shot through the heart.

But that's not what I want to know.

I want to go to Kim's room and lie in his bed
and listen to it all again, since each telling is always

different. I want to watch that face, that has all the
renunciatory ripeness of a monk's.

Last night he told me about that balmy wintry
evening years ago, when Katie was lonely and hungry and wanting him.

They weren't living together yet. He'd gotten
home around midnight, played back his messages,
and her husky, inconsolable voice filled the house.
"Oh Kim, you wouldn't believe what I saw in the
shop window of the plaza of Rio Piedras. *Pelucas.*
Wigs. Anyway you'd die from the colors, Kim. Purple, pink, gold. For the *locas,* the crazy ladies. I
always wondered where those ladies shopped!
Black faces so *indio,* so *grifo.* And those crazy wigs.
Oh God I love those ladies because they look like
bad Christmas ornaments and they make me
laugh." He turned the volume up but halfway
through the message he was out the door. At his
car he stopped. He was hopelessly intoxicated with
life. Nothing but sea-silence all around him, and
Katie's voice floating out the window and into the
stars. "The *locas* in their *pelucas!* I'm waiting for
you, I'll wait forever!"

SEVEN

It's not Kim on my answering machine, it's Stephen, and I almost call him back. When Stephen found out I was leaving him he went to a movie and came back whistling, tossing his windbreaker on the table and touching my shoulders with bemused tenderness. "Hey, I still like you," he protested. "Aren't I allowed to like you?" In the living room he flipped on a video game, pointed a plastic gun at the television and began to shoot at leaping ducks. All night he sat on his blue-checked couch, a hunter at home, as his ducks went down. He wasn't shooting at me, he was just relieved to be on his own again.

At one A.M., the phone rings (I'm awake, reading about a woman who owns the only robot store in the country. I'm going to interview her tomorrow). I lift the receiver and without warning feel Kim's voice—

"I just came home and found your number on my pillow. I'd like to see you," he says.

"When?"

"Now."

"Are you kidding? Don't you ever rest?"

"Not when I have something more interesting in mind."

"Kim, I was trying to sleep."

"But you couldn't, could you," he replies. "Are you in bed right now?"

"What do *you* think?"

"Do you want me up there?" he asks suddenly.

"You don't even know where I live."

"Are you going to tell me?"

"Yes, but . . ."

"But what?"

"This is too sudden. And it's too late."

"How about going out to hear some music, then? Hop in a cab and we'll go hear Bobby Short at the Carlyle."

"I'm sure you don't give a shit about Bobby Short. Besides, if you're going to spend that kind of money on me I want to choose my drug."

"Choose."

"Not so fast. How do you know about Bobby Short anyway?"

"I've lived in New York City before, remember?" Then he says he used to date an actress who hung out at jazz clubs and cabarets. At the time he was working at a bronze foundry in Long Island City, where many of the workers were sculptors. "They were Russian immigrants, most of them. I was the token blue-collar boy. But they loved working with metal, and I taught them a few shortcuts."

"So I'm your first writer."

"My first writer," he agrees. "So, are you putting on your black dress and joining me?"

"How about tomorrow night?"

"All right. I'll call you tomorrow around six P.M." A silence. "Shall I hang up?"

"You mean now?"

"Yeah, now."

"Maybe in a minute."

"Then I'll cut to the chase. Are you wearing anything?"

I laugh. ". . . A man's shirt. This shirt belongs to an old boyfriend. I don't like nightgowns."

"Will you do me a favor?"

"I might."

"The back of your hand—"

"The back of my hand?"

"Move it along your cheek." He pauses. "Did you?"

"Yeah."

"Now move it down your neck. When you get to the place where the shirt opens, just stop. Just keep your hand there."

"How would you know if I moved it?"

"I'd know."

"I moved it."

"I don't think so."

"You're right, I didn't. But now I'm moving it."

"Not now, either." He sounds amused. "Keep it there, and think of me." And he wishes me a good night's sleep.

The line goes dead. I pull the sheet to my chin, wadding it in my fist, holding it close the way a lover holds a lover. My hand is no longer at my shirt, but a phantom hand remains, impressed like a print in wet sand. Soon I sleep, rocking peacefully between the call that came and the call that's yet to come.

The next day at noon: Feeling fine.

At three: Strolling through the park—school kids chasing and slugging each other with their backpacks, a mother smoothing her newborn's warm head, hoots of joy from an all-girl softball team. I walk and walk, cocooned in my waiting. Sometimes waiting is as sensuous as a love-bite.

At four: Naked in my bathroom in front of a full-length mirror that warps me so I look even longer than I am. I try on a silk camisole and push the strap partway down my arm. It flows like a bracelet, cut into my skin. I don't move. I'm in love with my body.

At five: Feeling tireless, madly sanguine. Giggling, singing "Leader of the Pack" by the Shangri-La's. His call is an hour away.

At six: No call.

Six-fifteen: No call.

Six-thirty: Pacing the apartment, lying down, reading other answers to my ad. I take my phone off the hook and imagine him calling—the busy signal is my petulant "No!" to his lateness. It feels good but not for long. I replace the receiver. I remember the first time I thought I was in love, and how I lay in the dark waiting for a call. And when it came, I went on lying there, letting the machine pick up, and I listened to his voice, as close to me as his breath. I was an eavesdropper on my own life. When he was finished talking, I went to the phone and called Sherry and played her the message. "He likes me, doesn't he?" "Yes, a lot, now call him back."

Seven-thirty: I can't stand dangling on the agony of a phone call —I'm going out.

Eight-thirty: Back home. The red light, little red guillotine, isn't blinking. Sherry once taught me a half-desperate trick: she phones her machine from the street and leaves a message. Just dialing a number gives you a sense of purpose, makes you feel you have someone to love or link with. Oh yes, it's a mordant, half-assed joke but it's better than thinking nobody's thinking of you.

Nine o'clock: I call Stephen and hang up on his answering machine. I call Sherry and hang up on her answering machine. I call Stephen's machine and leave a message telling him not to call me anymore.

Nine-thirty: A sudden, morose tiredness. I don't even know this man, and I don't want to bother. It's not Kim who's hurting me, anyway—it's the way I keep waiting for something that never happens. This is the sort of mood that makes me write letters to my brother. I have no address for him, so I tell the truth, and I save the letters in a pink flowered plastic box at the bottom of my closet. I tell him loneliness is my element, a kind of scalding mother's milk that nourishes me. I tell him I still love him.

Ten-thirty: "Hello, Lynn? You there?" Kim's voice is warm and liquid—he sounds drunk. "I broke our plans . . . what time is it anyway? I have no idea what hour of the night it is. My friend José is here, they just picked glass out of his head for thirty minutes. I'm next. The doctor gave me codeine and I can't think straight . . . what time is it? I wanted to call you."

"Is this your idea of a joke?"

He's silent, and I don't say another thing.

"You there?" he asks finally, a vibrating note of unhappiness in his voice.

"Uh-huh."

"You want me to call you tomorrow, then?"

"What for?"

He's silent again. Finally: "Hey, José, what hospital are we at?

Take the phone and tell her. José, you owe me, sweetheart. You just sent me through a windshield."

I hear his friend's voice: ". . . Look behind you. You're in trouble, my man."

Kim cups his hand over the mouthpiece, muffling his words. ". . . Yeah, I know I'm supposed to be horizontal. But I've got my friend on the phone and she doesn't believe I'm in a hospital. She thinks I'm drunk and making up a story. . . . Lynn, you there? Here's the nurse."

The nurse, who has an Australian lilt in her voice, cheerfully confirms Kim's tale. Kim and his friend, she says, were in an accident while exiting the Williamsburg Bridge early this evening. It isn't clear whether they swerved into a truck or the truck clipped them, but the side of José's jeep was torn off, he lost his steering, and crashed into a brick building. Kim's "forehead is a bit mauled," she concludes, and adds in a teasing tone, "I'd give him fifty-fifty if he doesn't disobey orders and keep wandering around."

"What hospital are you at?"

"Beekman."

Kim: "Tell her I'll call again, after they've stitched me up. The codeine's kicking in."

"Nurse, tell him not to call. I'm coming down."

I slip on white jeans and a sleeveless black leotard bordered with seed pearls, line my eyes with black so they look like wet tar, and snatch a pint of Courvoisier from the kitchen cabinet. I'm not sure Kim should be drinking if he's already half-sweet on codeine, but if he doesn't drink I will.

Halfway down the stairs I stop. Why am I going to this man? Thinking of the other night's kiss, its wet and unholy heat, I only want to see him again. But heat never took root in me like this. Not ever. I remember the way he looked when I stood at his door —my face pressed against the cracked wood, a spy at a strange and landlocked porthole in Times Square—and found a man struck still with grief, rallying for some kind of heroic act which, it turned out, was simply to get up and greet me as if he'd been resting and hadn't heard the knock.

Something happened when I observed him then. He gave an

impression of strength pitted against incalculable loss. And I wanted to be part of him, because this welder in a vagrant's hotel was like me.

There are times late at night, sailing in a cab through deserted streets, when the buildings of the city melt like hills and her bridges lie like inverted harps on her waters. Tonight is such a night.

I like travelling the length of the city. All the stately upper avenues—Park, Fifth, West End—cross and converge, spewing out a starburst of tiny broken blocks; disorderly streets with names like Gansevoort, King, Gay, Lispenard, Prince, White and Gold.

Beekman Hospital is on Gold, just beyond the shadow of the Brooklyn Bridge. In the lobby a male nurse is waving his arms at a patient. The nurse's hospital-green sleeves keep flapping around his elbows, so that he looks like a giant praying mantis. "You can't walk around like this! Either go home or sit down!"

"Just a scratch, bimbos! It was just a scratch!" the patient bellows at no one in particular and stands swaying like a deckhand on a listing ship, his head swathed in bandages, face inflamed, twitching at a blood-matted beard. He scowls at me. "Watcha staring at, sweetheart?"

Helplessly, I shake my head and all at once his mood shifts. He smiles with a strange, touching vulnerability. "Eh, forget it. I'm out of my mind tonight."

The nurse sighs.

"I'll make nice," the man concedes, rubbing his beard with the butt of his hand, flinging off dried flakes of blood in disgust, as if he still cannot quite believe what has happened to him. "I'll sit down but not until you check on my buddy. I'm getting stir crazy."

I walk up to him. "Can I ask you something? Are you Kim Beckett's friend?"

He's nonplussed but then he realizes who I am and his eyes fasten on mine with a rudeness that's more than sexual; it's the stare of a man appraising his friend's girl.

"You're not what I expected," José says finally, in a voice gravelly with reproach.

"Why? What did he say about me?"

He shrugs. "He didn't." I follow him toward a bank of curved orange chairs, each molded into the next, like one long wave of the same, archetypal chair. He slumps heavily into a seat and stares at his black shoes—he has the thick feet of a leviathan.

"I didn't plan on meeting my buddy's girl all banged up in a hospital," he says resentfully. "I was clean today. *Clean.* My shirt had so much spray starch it creased in five places. Now," he pulls at his collar, "nobody would look at me. I'm bogus!"

"I promise not to remember you this way."

He lifts his head to peer at me. His eyes are nothing like the rest of him—they're soft as a pup's.

"You seem nice." He stands. "That nurse gone? Good. I'm gonna get a beer at the Blarney Stone. You wanna come with me?"

"Thanks, but I want to find Kim."

José points to double doors. "He's back there where it says patients only. You're not supposed to go in there, Lynn. Lynn," he repeats. "That's your name, right?"

"Yes."

"What's your whole name?"

"Lynn Hershey." I hadn't even told Kim yet.

"José Ramirez," he responds and we stand there awkwardly, as if we'd been introduced at a party and had taken an instant dislike to each other. His brow furrows. "See ya in a bit." He attempts to swagger off to the door, butts it with both hands and is gone.

On a stretcher in back Kim lies sleeping in a world of white—crisp sheets, sterile counters that glint with surgical instruments, and everywhere the barren sheen of fluorescent lighting. By contrast he appears ghoulish and muddy, like some root yanked up from the earth, dirt still cleaving to its tendrils. I touch his jeans, his belt, his hand which closes reflexively around my finger. His forehead is a shallow, bloody gulch, the skin mopped with iodine so that a rustlike stain, made of eaten-away edges, covers him from the neck up. Threads of skin curl out of the blood.

I look closer. His wound is like those photographs of a human pore, magnified a million times so you see clefts of skin as puffy as paper soaked in warm water. You're mesmerized. You don't want to turn the page.

I look until I'm no longer afraid—fear pops like a cork, and in its wake comes a tenderness I had not expected. I want to touch him, just as he is.

"Are you a patient?" A doctor with a crewcut and wire-rimmed glasses is striding toward me.

I shake my head. The doctor says, courteous and hard, "Only patients are allowed back here."

"I know." I don't move. "This man is my friend. Are you going to stitch him up soon?"

His breath smells of sour coffee. "Do you know what a job this is gonna be?" he says. "He has pieces of dirt and metal and glass as small as sand in his head. It's a miracle none of it went into the eyes, and it's going to be a bitch cleaning him up. I just put him out. He won't wake up for a few hours. Now, if you want to wait . . ." He gestures toward the double doors as he wheels Kim away.

"Why did you do it?" I ask.

It's two A.M. and Kim is fumbling in front of a cigarette machine in the Blarney Stone, a block from the hospital. He just got released. He's clumsily pushing one quarter after another into the slot and tilting his head like a piano tuner, listening to each coin clatter in the change box. Finally he pulls a knob and retrieves a pack of Salems. He holds it up. "Shit. This isn't what I wanted." He repeats the entire procedure, pulls another knob and a pack of Marlboro Lights tumbles into the metal trough.

Three black men watch wearily and without interest as I light a match and Kim cups his hands around the flame. He sucks on the cigarette and loses his balance, stumbling toward the machine and then into my arms. "I'm dizzy," he says in a half-swoon. "It's kind of a pleasant sensation. Don't worry, I'm okay. You know, I don't know how to say this, but I'm amazed you came down." He searches my eyes.

"I came, that's all."

I love holding him this way, in the miserly dim light of this bar, turbaned with bandages like a ruined sheik.

"So why did you do it?" I repeat.

Kim shakes the pack of cigarettes until a few more fall into his

hand, and offers them to José, who is coming from a toilet in back.
"Do what?"

"Nearly get yourself killed."

"Is that what you think?"

"What does Lynn think?" José asks.

"She thinks that I wanted to die tonight."

"I was joking, Kim."

"Sparkle Plenty," he says.

"Suit yourself," I say.

"Did I want to die, José? Did I lean over and twist the wheel out
of your hand?"

José grunts. "You were talking and I got distracted." He turns
to me. "He was talking and I didn't wanna miss a word. Next
thing I know a truck clips me."

"What were you talking about?" I ask José.

He stares at me. "Business," he says, and throws Kim a questioning look. "Kim, you got a light?"

"Take mine. It tastes funny." Kim heads for the door.

"We *coulda* died, y'know," José says. "It's shook him up. . . .
I've only known him a few weeks, but he's my skin."

Outside he's leaning against a mailbox, waiting for us. I dig for
the bottle of Courvoisier in my purse. "Oh, this is really going to
help," Kim says, "this is going to lay me flat on my butt." He
unscrews the top (deftly, for one besotted with pain and drugs),
takes a swig, passes the bottle to José and then seizes my face in his
hands.

"I'm sorry," he murmurs.

"What for?"

"For standing you up, what do you think?" He kisses me, grog-
gily at first, but then his kisses grow harsh and wonderful.

"Lynn's gonna get us home," José announces. "By the way,
where's home tonight? This mornin' I told my wife I was staying in
town."

"My room," Kim responds.

"You've only got a single bed," I interject.

"That's okay; José can sleep on the floor."

"That doesn't sound very comfortable."

"A floor is no problem. Me and the floor are buddies."

"Come up to my place instead."

"You don't mean that," Kim says flatly.

"I do."

He stops directly under the streetlight: "You want me up there?"

"You're in trouble and it's late."

"No, no, no," he says. "I don't give a shit about the circumstances. I don't want to intrude on you. You want to wait?"

I like him this way, more than I'd care to admit. He's as proud and vulnerable as a kid who's fallen off his bicycle, skinned his knees, and is standing there, eyes smarting.

"Kim, if you don't come up I'll never speak to you again."

"You gonna make her beg, Kim?"

"Nobody makes me beg," I say.

Kim's still cautious: "What about José?"

"There's a couch in my living room." I turn to José. "Is that okay?"

José nods. "Just like when I was little. The whole time I'm growin' up I got four brothers and three beds. So who gets the couch?"

When Kim slings his arm through mine for balance, José does the same on my other side. We're laughing like renegades cut from the same bolt of cloth—except I'm renegade only for tonight. For tonight I'm living like the giddy girl I never was, sandwiched between two men who can't stop making jokes, as if it has finally begun to dawn on them that they really did almost die (*Sir, we are not part of a religious cult,* Kim explains to the cabbie). José's hands are folded in his lap, polite before his friend's lady; Kim's leg is thrust over mine, and I feel buoyant, as if I've fallen into the ocean and discovered how to float.

"They're going to love it when we walk in with these bandages tomorrow."

"I'm not scared about the boss, I'm scared about my wife."

"Maybe you'd better head on home?"

"She says we're not spending enough time together," José says, half-aloud. "I'm hardly home all week and not a word of protest, and when I call her tonight she lays into me. She didn't phrase it too good but her heart was in the right place. So I asked the doc to call her. He gave her all the bad news, including we've got to buy a new jeep."

"Call her again when you get to Lynn's," Kim advises.

"No way! If I tell her I'm staying at a woman's . . . See, she's got some crazy idea that ladies are after me." He grabs a fold of his stomach and laughs. "Hey, I look like a fat sailor, that's what. But she don't see me like that."

He tells us that when he was nineteen he rescued his wife-to-be from her stepfather. "She grew up a couple blocks south from me in the Bronx. Skinny little streak of piss, just like her ma. Her ma was a war-bride. We were an item for about a year before she tells me her old man is making her blow him every night. I told the prick I'd bash the fuck out of him if he ever touched her again, and then I married her." He leans his head against the backseat of the cab.

Kim smiles. "You're not usually this soft on her."

"I got things in perspective tonight. You don't need women hitting on you as long as your wife thinks they are. It's almost as good."

"Better, actually."

"Yeah, you say that 'cuz you got your pick."

"But I never did pick. I'm loyal."

"For how long?" I interject.

But he doesn't know I'm thinking of Katie.

"You'll find out, won't you?" he says a little testily.

"Hey guys," I say softly, "we're here."

I live in a crumbling cathedral, a beaux-arts building festooned with curling stone and stained glass. Soot-drenched gargoyles perch above every window. José stands in the long tongue of the courtyard, shaking his head as if he could shake it free of pain, while Kim gives the driver a ten-dollar tip. The elevator is broken, and so we take the stairs, passing doors painted with fluorescent pinks and greens, chipped tiles, candy wrappers and dirtballs and rinds of crushed fruit. "My bladder's bursting again," complains José, and I point him to the bathroom. Kim stops in my hallway, examining the wall posters. "All the same artist," I tell him.

"All thirteen-year-old girls," he comments. "Do you want to be thirteen?"

He stalks my place, slow and predatory as a prospective owner, squinting at the yellowed ceilings, the paint-splattered windows and oak floor that buckles across the middle.

I don't think he likes my home. Clean, spare spaces suit him. The fireplace doesn't work; he places his hands on the mantel as if it were a living thing to be tamed or warmed by his touch, and taps a spot where paint has chipped.

"What poor bastard painted over mahogany? José, where are you? C'mere. Look at this turn-of-the-century stuff. Scrape away the paint, rub the right oils into it, and this wood would look like it's melting. We've got to fix up this place for her, José."

"You own this dump, Hershey?" José inquires, winking at me.

"Nope. The building went co-op but I didn't buy. I'm just a renter."

"What did you call her?" Kim interjects.

"I used her last name," José says in an offhand tone.

It's only an instant, a flash in Kim's eyes, that joins me to José.

"So that's your last name," he says gently.

"Yeah. You didn't ask."

"I was about to. Did people tease you when you were a kid? Call you Hershey bar?"

José jumps in. "No nicknames? Nothin' at all?"

I look at Kim. Don't tell him, I think. Because suddenly Sparkle Plenty has become poignant, as if she's a new part of me printed on the night sky, a reporter with a spangled wave of peroxided hair and angel's lips. A woman who looks like she has raindrops on her eyelashes.

Kim smiles at me. His hand at the base of my spine—it doesn't move—it fuses me to him. Oh my god, for a minute I want to be that woman so badly.

"My head's itching like crazy." José begins to adjust his bandages and all at once lifts the entire dome of gauze off. Looking around uneasily, like a gentleman caller who's not sure where to put a cumbersome new hat, he turns the turban upside down and places it in an empty plantholder near the window. "I hope you don't mind. I'll be real careful. I'm not gonna spatter blood all over your place."

He looks up at me, this bellicose, comical man, and the three of us begin to laugh. José stumbles backwards onto the couch, kicks his shoes off and wiggles his black socks in the air.

"Oh God, that feels so good," he moans. Then he remembers his promise, and removes his jacket, spreading it lovingly on the couch, smoothing out the wrinkles as if it were a silk pillow. At last he lies down.

Kim seems different to me now, this wound laid across his forehead. I like his face flawed, since his flaw is an invitation. I might find my way in through it. His eyes are closed. He could have died. I press my mouth against the neck of his white shirt and rest my head on his shoulder as if I've known him always and he is my protector.

Somewhere on the Hudson a barge groans. All across the city rain is falling, on the stainless spires of the Chrysler and Empire State, on the grass in Riverside Park, and the balconies of the Dakota, where John Lennon was killed and Rosemary's baby born. I hear footsteps and a garbage can clanging. In the city someone is always walking, while at a darkened window someone's surely listening. The cloak of sleep is never drawn, even when it's nearly morning.

EIGHT

We go to Camelot's, a neighborhood place every-body calls Joe's, even though when old Joe died young Joe spent an entire Saturday painting on the new name, and another Saturday rolling out spar-kling linoeum. It's the kind of place where Italian men in sweat-stained t-shirts play cards, tapping slow-burning cigars into tin ashtrays.

Slipping onto stools whose leather seats are cracked and warm from use, we joke with the grease-spattered owner. He rubs his hands briskly on his starched apron, peels hamburger patties from a stack and slaps them on the grill, then reaches for buns from a large aluminum drawer and flips them open with thumb and forefinger. "What's on the burger? Lettuce, mayonnaise, no tomato, no pickle, nothin' but coffee in the cof-fee?"

"You got it."

They chat, and I watch Kim let the conversation rock him, resting inside the easy banter. The owner talks about his fat wife, a wife he calls a "beautifulla mountain," a slow-grazing mama-bear with folds of flesh. He grins, laughs, squeezes Kim's arms. Between the two men is the sudden love of solitary drunks. I spin on my stool, alone and full of the cup of murder. Kim puts his arm around me, to draw me into the warmth of ordinary life. Oh, he never meant to make me fugitive. I wonder if I'll leave him soon.

NINE

"It's no use now," Kim says, half to himself. It's not quite morning; I'm lying beside him. "No use," he repeats. What's he trying to say? That he should sneak away while I still seem to sleep? That I can't refuse him now?

He shifts onto his side. I wonder if he likes my room. Thick cotton lace, creamy with age, hangs from twin windows; the floors are scattered with kilims. Across from us is a Newport bureau with fluted legs and swivel mirror, a blue satin loveseat fuzzed and frayed by cat's claws, and a scarred rolltop desk. It's a room of faded elegance; the worn antiques carry an air of the places they've been, of old clapboard homes and country inns.

"Are you sleeping?" he asks me now, touching my lips.

"You sleeping?" he repeats.

"I was dreaming," I say.

"Tell me about your dreams."

"I dunno . . ." My voice sounds distant, tinny. "I never remember my dreams."

He strokes my breasts through my leotard. I feel like I did last night—an animal caught in another animal's teeth and shaken gently and relentlessly, until some balancing center in the brain goes dumb and still, and the whole body relaxes. The prey just goes gratefully limp in the predator's mouth. So I turn away from him. Of course he doesn't understand. He probably thinks I'm frigid.

"Last night," I say, to fend him off with conversation, "you fell asleep right away . . . and I was standing here looking at you. I was thinking about why I called you in the first place. It was your face. It went right through me. You looked so innocent in that picture."

"Pictures lie," he says automatically, his hand still moving down my throat. I catch his hand.

"You were in love and your life made sense and all that showed in your face. Now you're—"

"I wasn't in love."

"Why did you tear half of the picture off then? Wasn't that woman in it?" Do I sound innocent enough? Does he have any inkling of my detective work? "You sent me a torn picture because you wanted me to know about her."

That's not what I want to say. I want to ask how much he still loves her. Maybe she's just the scar, the kind that tightens and hurts.

"No," he says, "it was torn for a very mundane reason. I didn't have a scissors to cut her out."

I laugh.

"Anyway, I'm not in love with her now." He looks straight at me. "What time is it?"

I crane my neck, squinting at a beige plastic clock with glowing orange dial. "Five-thirty. Why?"

"I have to make a call."

"At this hour?"

"I'm a factory worker, remember? I'm due on the early shift."

"God, how can you do it?" I brush his hair back lightly, only once. Do I want him to stay?

A minute later, having confirmed with his boss that he and José will take the day off, Kim stands.

"You're going—?"

"I need to take a shower and change this bandage. And it would do us both good to think a little."

"Think about what?"

"About whether we want to continue seeing each other."

"Why wouldn't we?"

"I like you, Lynn, more than I expected to," he says. "But you're scared of me. You think I'm going to hurt you somehow."

"Am I wrong?"

"Maybe not," he says bluntly.

"I don't understand you. I come down to the hospital, wait three hours to make sure you're okay, bring you and your friend up here for the night, and now you're walking out."

"I have to go home for a few hours." He starts toward her bedroom door, then turns around and asks curiously, "Why do I scare you? Am I so different from everyone else?"

"What kind of question is that?"

"One you probably can't answer."

"Sure I can." I stare at him. "But if I answer it, what will you do?"

"Listen."

"Okay. You're different because . . ." I smile. "In some strange way you've got a bead on me."

"Is that unusual?"

"Yes."

I put a detaining hand on his arm, and I can feel his awareness distilled to a funnel point. As if I alone exist.

"I keep coming back to you. You don't belong in that hotel room. Or that factory. You can't make me believe welding is a heroic act. And I'll never believe José's your type. It's like you dropped out of the sky and put together a life out of whatever was handy. A shitty hotel, a meaningless job, a crazy friend, and me from an ad in the paper. I don't get it."

"You'd have to live a little to get it."

He turns to go.

"See," I say quickly, "I shouldn't have said a thing. Now you're going to say thanks, you'll call me later . . . and you won't call me later."

"You're free to call me."

"Just stay."

His voice is low. "I'll come back. How about this afternoon?"

"If you go you won't come back. I'm sure of it."

"It's not you, Lynn. I just may not be fit for human consumption right now."

"You shouldn't have answered my ad, then."

"It was purely chance that I even saw it. Do you know where I found that issue of the magazine?"

"I couldn't guess."

"I was at Astor Place, where all the kids get their hair chopped off or shaved. While I was waiting for a cut I settled back to read a magazine somebody had left."

"That's why your letter was so late." I gaze at him, half-believing, then take his hand and lead him back to my bed. He doesn't resist, seems grateful, actually, and I'm surprised at the glad leap of hope in me. But I don't show a thing. I just add neutrally, "So if not for a haircut . . ."

"I read your ad while I was watching a kid get his head shaved in some kind of design he'd drawn on a torn piece of paper. You're right about one thing. Here I was alone, living in a shitty motel room, and instead of a sailboat for an office, I was cutting metal in a factory in Brooklyn. Then there was your ad. Crazy and touching. I kept going back to it. But you know, I didn't answer right away."

"Nope?"

"I kept it in my wallet another week. Now let me ask *you* something."

"What?"

"Where's the woman who wrote that ad? The one who wanted another Muhammad Ali."

"I'm not her."

"Not yet."

"I promise you that line was a lie."

He shakes his head. "And the pictures of girls in your front hall. How do they fit in?"

"You don't like them?"

"Oh, but I do like them."

"I used to like them. But not anymore. The paralyzed sluts, my friend Sherry calls them. Yeah, I know, I'm being sarcastic."

"Was anything in that ad true?"

"I don't know, Kim. I didn't *really* expect anyone to come along from an advertisement, especially you." A guy who keeps an answering machine in a hotel drawer and looks like a broken Adonis. "You don't even read books."

"Not your kind of books."

"What do you read?"

"*How Things Work*. Did you read that?"

"Nope."

"It's lucky we didn't meet in a bookstore. We'd have come and gone without even seeing each other."

"What else don't we have in common?"

"Metal," he says. "Boats. Islands. And our opinion of José."

"We can prick our fingers and become blood brothers and then it won't matter."

He presses my hand to his mouth, strangely tender. "Does it matter?"

"I know something we have in common. You're not close to your family, are you?"

He looks at me. "I love my old man. But I keep a distance."

"Because he wants you to be like him?"

"Right."

"So, anyway, you're not close."

He laughs in disbelief. "This is a point of common interest? Half of America's estranged from their families."

"Well, who do you feel closest to in the world?"

He shrugs. "A dead man."

"What's his name?"

"That's a joke."

His mouth moves to my wrist.

"Are we—?"

"What?"

"I don't know."

He stops.

"Why did you stop?"

"I go at my own pace. You're lovely."

"I'm lovely?" I hold out my hand again. "Show me."

TEN

It's past the hour when he told me of murder, how he went to kill a man with sun-darkened face and silver ringlets. Past the hour when he spoke of Old San Juan—salt-washed city. It's morning, and the cavalcade of hours roll on, and he lies in my bed and speaks. His speech is halting because he's not a storyteller. "You write it down, Sparkle," he says. He talks like a solitary camper lost in the mountains, in order not to be swallowed up by night, and to remind himself he's human. He talks to keep me, because he's beginning to love me.

He tells me something Nadal said: *In the streets here,* Nadal told Kim, *you see sometimes a kind of dog called, in Spanish, tuco.*

You think I don't speak your language? Kim retorted.

Forgive me. You know then, they call him that because he has no tail. Listen, tuco, you weren't made for murder.

How still the man stood in his green garden. Against the brick and flagstones of his green garden. He poured coconut syrup over queso blanco, a white, sweet cheese, and went on. *Sabes la pata que cojea? You have to know the leg that limps. You weren't made for murder.*

And you were?

But Nadal didn't answer. He didn't like to answer questions so much as leap from them into long tales.

Now he motioned to a ceramic bowl set on an oak credenza under a tree. A rainfall of moss fell from the lower branches, cordoning off part of the courtyard, and Nadal walked through it. Kim followed. They stood in shade; the bowl was jammed with dirt-caked tubers.

With a starched handkerchief the man wiped summer dust from his face. He folded the cloth a few times and fit it with care into his shirt pocket, so a gay corner popped up, as if he were about to attend a celebration. He said to Kim,

Why do I love Puerto Rico? Look at this yautia, red as a Pinot Noir. And this one from Vieques, pale velvet. And here's one, nothing but bristles on the outside, like a man with a new beard. I can cook them all so they sizzle in your mouth. We understand pleasure here. And why do I hate Puerto Rico? See this cassava, white with dark veins? It's poison. The Taino Indians drank it to die at their own hands rather than ours. But we learned from them. My father's father kept it in a blue jar in the back of his wardrobe, as a pious last resort. Does that tell you something about what beautiful cowards we are?

How do you live with yourself, anyway?

If I could, I would reduce my whole life to some hours. My real life, mi vida, is only a few hours. Maybe only a bug is as modest as I.

What were those hours?

I ask Kim that question. What hour or two lived on inside that man? And Kim says, Why do you think I'd know?

ELEVEN

I've lived too long where I can't be reached. I scare myself—never cry out at orgasm—hide inside my body as it shakes. Men move me, but not enough.

Now I might be in for a change. I don't know the man before me. He's saying my name in a hard, sad voice, shirt loose as a wet sail, so much sweat in the pits that the cotton bunches in accordion folds. When I pull down my leotard he looks as if someone slapped his face—and then he tells me he's going to protect me. He presses my hand against his jeans, and I unzip them, tugging at each leg, amazed by my own ineptness, until finally I'm kneeling before him holding his pants in a crumpled heap against my chest. His thighs are broadly muscled, smooth as flint, and shivering uncontrollably —a delicate, erratic flutter that mesmerizes me.

I look up. "Are you okay?"

"Not really," he says, roping my hair through his fingers with a sensual violence. My mouth is so close to his crotch it almost brushes his erect penis, which is bobbing slightly in the air, deliciously thick and broad. His pubic hair is pale brown, wiry, darkening to red near his testicles. Those testicles have the look of taut, plucked chicken skin—so vulnerable and ugly in a sublime kind of way.

As I stare at Kim, Stephen's elegant phallus flashes before me; it was too narrow, a long cigar with a welt of purple around the rim.

I could only come when he entered from behind, giving the illusion of a heft he didn't have. Before Stephen I dated a rabbi whose organ was like a fat little bullet, and an uncircumcised Swede with one tortured vein snaking up the side; and of course, before them all was my brother Cob, who one morning when he was eleven pulled down his boxer shorts and tentatively bent his flaccid penis in two—"Touch it," he'd said, "it's soft as a mouse."

Now I take Kim's milk-white cock in my hands, clasping him at the root, and sperm wells up like a tear from a shut eyelid. His penis is big and beautifully cleft, and yet all penises when engorged with blood seem raw, livid. I think of the ways men have asked me to help them come, touching the penis, licking the penis, letting them press their penis against the crack in my butt, between my thighs or breasts, inside of me, on top of me, just rub it, honey, just squeeze it a little. . . . and though some men howl and bellow with pride, when it's over all you're left with is a spoonful of fluid that looks like bird droppings. One guy liked to ejaculate on my stomach and tenderly swab me with Kleenex, cleaning me in long, careful strokes. When he finished he'd toss the damp wad in the wastebasket. The next day as I was dressing, I'd glance down and see it there, brittle and crumpled like an old flower.

I run my thumb along the fissure of Kim's penis, where the sperm-drop clings, rub the sticky wetness into the skin, stroke the satiny pulp of the head. Almost instantly another drop appears. He holds me back, twisting my hair tight as if it were a harness, though he's careful not to hurt me. He tilts my head so I see his face, and I'm shocked by the cannibal succulence in his eyes, so heavy-lidded; and the softness, almost slovenly softness, of his open mouth.

He's saying something. Asking me why I'm not in his arms. Telling me to stand up.

"No—I don't want you to have me yet."

He thinks I'm backing off again, but I'm not, I tell him. I just can't submit yet. "Let me be the explorer for a while."

He lowers my head and brings me close, pushing his penis down until it's mine for the taking. My tongue flicks out, shy, tentative, and I taste the drop. It's a pungent, salty semen. I kiss the lip of flesh where shaft meets head. And now he has that look of bliss all men seem to get when a woman blows them. Why do they like it so much? A mouth is no mystery. The mystery's between my legs —when I put a mirror there, part my vaginal lips and observe the buds folded on each other in secret conference, I'm awed. I can never quite know that silent and primordial part of my flesh. Sometimes I tighten and bear down until the buds expand into a many-petalled cup, and slide my finger up the spongy muscle. It hugs me as if lying in wait for an intruder.

He pulls me back—away.

"You like this?" his cautious voice floats above me.

"Let me have it again, you'll see."

"Mmm." A happy shudder. "You're surprising me, Lynn."

But he doesn't move, just strokes my hair gently. There's a quality to even Kim's lightest caress that's unyielding; he intends to comfort, but his touch seems an act of possession, a way of marking me as his. His hand moves to the nape of my neck, and he guides me toward him again.

Have minutes passed? I'm going to burst, collapse, scream. He's making me move so slowly and I love it so much—from the moment I saw him I wanted him to master me, and every small act of ownership thrilled me: when he guided me across the street, his hand resting at the small of my back or the nape of my neck; when he unbuttoned my blouse the other night, taking his time as if I were his property. I've always liked it when a man pinned me down, hands clamping my wrists, positioning me to heighten our pleasure. I remember the first time a lover swung my legs over his shoulders, and I felt pride in my body, so flexible and easily contorted, arranged like a dancer's in a crazily choreographed duet— and giving me orgasms anyway.

He guides my head back and forth, up and down, as if I were simply another part of him.

"I'm killing us both," Kim says suddenly, pulling back yet again and I groan in frustration, caressing his spit-slaked penis with my hands. His fingers dig into my scalp, forcing me to stop.

"We had better wait," he says with bewildering formality.

"Don't you like it?"

"I'm taking advantage of you."

"You're afraid of being selfish?"

"Not how you think. I'm usually good for a second round."

"Why wait, then?"

"I wasn't sure how you felt. Pretty soon I'm going to reach the point of no return."

I'm touched by his awkward courtesy. Tilting forward, I tongue the sprinkling of hairs at the base of his penis, and at last he lets go of my head. I sink my mouth into the muscle of his inner thigh, wishing I could swallow him whole, but I only graze there before sliding up to his tight, high balls—I like it when a man's balls harden and lift, a sign of urgency—popping each one in my mouth like candy, and finally I begin to blow him in earnest: in a rhythm of rocking need, like gliding along some primitive totem in an act of ceremonial worship. Baby, slave, siren, my lips a vise to grip his cock—cock, I say to myself and the word is guilty pleasure, almost an act of thievery. I hear him gasping and I'm glad—a cruel euphoria—I'd like to see his face when he comes, see those spasms that look like grief, derangement, rage, but are pleasure. Still, I'm surprised when he begins to utter words, phrases that sound hackneyed to any ear, *god, oh god, woman, oh Christ,* except I'm crazy for those lonesome words, want to hear him call me woman a hundred times, not Lynn, not darling, not baby, but woman, woman. The whole length of him stiffens as I suck, whatever way I want, I'm merciless now, I—slow—down—, he pleads, I stop, his hands slip blindly over my face, I take him all at once, half-choking but I manage it, until he growls in pain like somebody dying alone in the night, driving deeper than he should so I feel his penis bunting the small cone of flesh that hangs from the back of my throat, I'm pushing him away with my hands then breathing and sucking him in again when suddenly he cries *no*. And the *no* beats like drum-bursts under the rhythm of need until he takes up the cry again, a riotous, red-hot, convulsive cry he keeps hurling at me, he cannot move or master himself, he's lost and he loves it, and utters a low animal scream as his body starts to buck, arching, and I hold him so he comes in my hands.

Even though he's stopped ejaculating he's twitching with sensation, sweat dribbling down his legs.

He keeps moving.

Don't stop yet—Lynn, don't let me go.

Okay, shh, quiet, shut up.

I can't believe it. I've never blown a man twice in a row (and what will he do for me, I'm going to be crazed after this), but I'm tempted by curiosity and the nightmare sweetness of his body. Besides, I don't want him to make love to me yet. I don't want to be lost to him yet. I jack my fist up his penis and his head drops gratefully, although his face has gone ashen and he looks exhausted. We begin to move again, mouth and cock meeting and separating with a sureness of their own. He's less urgent now and I have time to notice the blurry ribbons of light flowing across my bedroom wall. . . . I didn't close the blinds completely. This time he reaches into the air as if seeking something, and his hands open and close, open and close.

"Is something wrong?"

"Yeah—I'm—dizzy again—" he mutters, and a moment later stumbles forward, and his knees start to buckle. Before I have time to panic, he steadies himself and lifts his head. I stand and press my hands to his burning face.

"You've got a fever," I hear myself saying. "Let me get a washcloth and cool you down."

He ignores me, won't look me in the eye. I guess he's frightened.

I go to get the washcloth; in the living room José has shifted onto his stomach, one arm curled around his jacket, which is balled into a pillow, and the other hanging to the floor, fingers splayed like a duck's webbed foot. He might wake and see me completely naked, but I don't mind—I guess if he did he'd just smile and go back to sleep. Last night's fraternity still holds.

Running the tap in the bathroom, I discover that the woman looking out of the mirror is not me: her face flushed and turbulent, lips swollen to an abnormal ripeness—she's brazen and uncouth, she licks the residue of semen, musses the hair he twined so tightly, laughs at me with radiant cruelty. I switch off the light, wring the cold cloth in the dark, and then, trying to trick or shame this other self out of existence—for I simply can't believe she's sprung from me—I flick the switch again. She gazes at me, self-absorbed and content, like a woman seen undressing before a window. I lean forward and breathe on the mirror until she's fogged out of sight.

I find Kim sitting on my bed, head in his hands. When I press the cloth to his forehead he thanks me in a voice devoid of expression.

"Lie down," I order.

"I'm fine," he says irritably.

"You need to rest. When you wake up I'll feed you. I've got sweet rolls in the freezer and fresh eggs."

"We're not finished. We haven't even begun yet."

I laugh uncertainly. "I'm not going to have you fainting on me again."

"I blacked out for a second, that's all."

We stare at each other.

"Kim, I'm not interested in making love right now. You've probably got a concussion. I mean, for all I know your brain is swelling or you're bleeding inside your head. I should send you back to the hospital but you wouldn't go, would you? So as long as you're here in my apartment you do what I say."

"If I lie down I'll be giving in to this thing. If I ignore it it will go away. Besides, I'm in good shape. I was running two hours a day in Puerto Rico. To Río Piedras, Santurce, Isla Verde. Anyplace as long as it was far enough and hard enough."

"What does that have to do with a car crash in Manhattan?"

"Hell, I don't know," he says wearily.

We're silent for a moment. "Why were you running? To get in shape for a marathon?"

"Nah."

"So—why, then?"

"Always asking questions, aren't you?"

"Only when you lead me astray with strange confessions."

"I was running for my life," he says lightly.

"Your life was in danger?"

He gives a short laugh. "I mean that I wanted to get in the best shape I could."

"Come on. What were you running from?" I feel like I'm banging stupidly against a locked door, but I can't stop. "Were you in danger?"

He doesn't answer.

"So what is it, did you kill somebody?" I joke. I don't know why I said it, but as soon as the words are out a sickening panic shoots up my spine, because Kim's face doesn't change at all, he just keeps on looking at me, the way I'd imagine a head looks after it's been guillotined; the blade whacks through the neck so fast the expression on the face doesn't change at all. *Why did I say that?* Fear. I'm on to something. I can feel it. It was like this over late-night dinners with Stephen—long before I knew there was another woman I'd imagine him into a betrayer, a man fucking women for kicks. He'd be talking about baseball (the clean green of the diamond and the way each man at bat was a hero facing Fate, tipping his team's destiny one way or the other) and I'd be flaying myself with the image of my boyfriend screwing some stranger.

"You killed somebody," I repeat. I glance up at Kim. He's still staring at me as if I hadn't said a thing.

No. Even bandaged in his bloodied turban he has a look of clean simplicity. It's not possible. Listen, I can close my eyes and feel the goodness in him, a hewn, hard goodness in him. He never killed anybody.

I press the washcloth over his whole face—to hide it? To wipe it clean? And why does he submit? Slowly I fold the cloth down, like I sometimes do with pictures of serial killers in magazines. I fold it down to show the eyes—inexpressible blue. No murder in those eyes. Down the pure slope of the nose, slightly flared nostrils. Okay. And to the mouth. There's pain in the mouth. But it could be any kind of pain.

"You want to know the truth?"

"Please."

"I was running because I wanted to stop thinking." He tells me the only time he could stop thinking was when he was hyperventilating, weak in the knees, sweating like a Sherpa, knots of pain in his back. "And running had the nice side effect of helping me to sleep at night."

Slowly I let out my breath. "And now? I mean, are you still running here in the city?"

"I don't need to."

"Why not?"

He shrugs. "It doesn't make any sense, does it? With all the noise and dirt outside my window, and a mattress worn down to the springs, I sleep like a baby."

"It was your girlfriend. She left you, and you couldn't sleep—right?—"

He lifts his hand. "Don't make it so simple. It was the situation she put me in."

"I feel strange."

"Don't," he says, and puts his arms around me. "You're taking me away from it."

My muffled voice: "But I want to know. That's me, that's what I'm like. I just need to know."

"And once you know, you'll need to know something else. You're a junkie."

"Okay, it's true. Secrets get stale once you learn them, and then you want new ones."

My flesh feels cool against his—his fever must be climbing. But he said to ignore it, and I want to rest in his arms. Tomorrow I'll ask him again, even if he gets mad; and if he gives that quiet stare I'll tell him to get the hell out. But let me have this hour. Let me watch his face.

"Lynn?"

". . . Mmm."

His voice is quiet. "Will you touch me a little?"

"Touch you?" I echo, dumbfounded. What's he trying to prove? "Come on," I admonish in an older-sister tone, "you really have to take it easy."

But it's useless, for now I feel the wombed warmth of the room draining, and though he hasn't moved, it's as if he's curled up in pain.

"I asked too much," he says finally, half to himself. "I've got to leave."

"Kim, you really *are* out of your mind. What's gotten into you?"

"You."

"Yeah, sure. Right."

He's silent, and I see that now neither of us will sleep. Oh hell, I give up. I guess he can't faint lying down. So I reach out, and to my surprise he's rock-hard—what other cliché can describe it? A boner, boys in my neighborhood used to call it, and that's exactly what it seemed like, a bone shooting into their soft penises. Rock-hard never fails to move me.

"Do you have a condom?"

"Yeah."

He waits while I open the night-table drawer and toss a few foil packets at him, and a tube of lubricant, and then, with a smile, a small, eggshell-colored plastic vibrator.

"How often do you need this?"

"I never use it. My friend Sherry gave it to me, it's one of her old ones."

He laughs. "That's like passing on the family heirlooms?"

"More like giving away an ex-boyfriend."

"You'll do the honors?"

"Sure." I tear open the sky-blue packet, and unroll the condom onto his penis, pulling at the tip to leave a little reservoir; it flops there like a deflated nipple.

And now I touch the coiled flank and haunch of him, legs and buttocks and the low saddle of muscle slung from hip to hip. He rolls to me with wary, stealthy grace, his mouth doing things to my neck exactly like our first night on the street at three A.M., and the same knot is unknotting in me, knot of a lifetime unknotting in me, skin-orgasms bursting under his mouth so I can hardly stand it and I try to force his head away, no such luck, he rolls onto me, his packed bulk a shock and a sweetness, his tongue on my nipple making lightning-flashes to my groin; his teeth, mouth, fingers stroking the lips of my vagina, lips folded like wings but he parts them, I think he whispered that I'm swollen, I heard him say it with a kind of divine bitterness, god you're wet and so swollen, he's licking my juice from his fingers now in the darkness, thumb on my clitoris, fingers inside massaging that place that seems the root of my clitoris, a deep embedded bundle of feeling, he's touch-ing me and I'm afraid because everything I know is changing, spiralling upward and jetting out of me as sound, the kind of sound I never want to make ever, not in front of anybody ever, a keening, a wail in my ears, a cry of oh Christ stop me because I can't stop myself, and now he grasps his cock and strokes it along my inner lips, marking and making me his, he hasn't even entered me but new sound keeps skittering out, and he's listening, a man I don't know is hearing me with his body until I half-say, half-sob, it's not me—between the sounds I sob, not me at all—and he pulls back as if leaving—

A pause. Thank god for the reprieve, I can breathe finally. This isn't foreplay, this is lurid, gorgeous smut that I'd love if only I knew him, but who is he? I've had men part my legs and slide inside, thrust for a while and then reach down to fiddle with my clitoris until I start to come, fuck me some more and it's over. Two orgasms. Three, if I'm lucky. But Kim is the kind of lover I always imagined and never believed in, kneeling on the bed above me, waiting, I guess, for me to beg. I won't beg. I'm glad my terrible noise has left and I'm still intact.

"Have you ever been fucked all day long?" he asks suddenly.

An instant ache between my legs. "No—have you ever done that to somebody?"

He laughs. "I want to make you stop thinking, okay? Just for the rest of the day."

"You can't stop me from thinking, not ever," I whisper, too late.

He lifts me by my buttocks.

I feel him waiting for me. Can't speak with this feeling. I'm seething, flushing, quaking.

"Talk," he says.

"Can't talk. Can't say a thing."

"What do you want?"

"I want you to fuck me."

"Let me hear it."

"For hours—"

"Like this?"

"I—"

"Or this?"

"Yes, like that—"

"This? Or this?"

"You know!"

"I know what?"

I'm already shaking with that sweet rage of the body. My pelvis a sponge of blood. The blood singing under my nerves. Nerves whine and shudder. It's as if he's stroking some primordial membrane.

He knows everything. "Dammit, how did I ever let you make me wait so long? You're perfect. You're amazing."

"Who taught *you* all this?"

"I'm not doing a thing. How did you get so wonderfully tight?"

"—Born lucky—"

"—Mmm. You're great."

"You're terrifying."

"Tell me everything—I want to hear it. Talk to me. You're the writer. Tell me."

He stops moving, and I'm rising out of bed like some rabid animal to beat the sheath of his chest. "Shut up, there isn't anymore to say. Just fuck me."

He laughs—a peculiar edge of desperation. "Quiet down, now. I'm going to stay with you for a long, long time."

You're making me cry. Can't think what to say. Love it, I'm in love with it. And all the crazy, stupid things in my head now, how his love is nothing but physical and I'll never tell him I love him but he'll lay claim to my body anyway, how he's fucking me inside my loneliness where no one ever trespassed, how these are body-orgasms, eruptions that have nothing to do with clitoris and vagina; violent and extravagant calamities of the womb itself, I'm girded round with muscle and all of it is clenched around him, dying and reborn in time to his thrusting.

I belong to him—my god I belong to him—

Still, I won't scream. The scream sticks in my throat.

Later, I don't know when, in the deaf silence between fuckings, I look down and see my breast floating, shallow and pale like a water lily, and on my breast his calloused hand: rock from a gorge. He's nothing but fugitive and I'm eternal mother, and I tighten in another spasm before I realize he's just slipped his fingers inside me.

"Again?" I whisper. My body's lost, I can see that.

"I want to."

"But why?"

"Can I turn on the light?"

"It's midday!"

"It's cloudy outside. I want to see your face better. Can we turn on all the lights?"

"What do you want to see?"

"Whatever you don't want to show me."

They say angels smile with pleasure when they harvest the tears of the dying from hell. What do angels do with tears—drink them, probably. And you. You smile like an angel when you touch me . . . and now you want to watch me cry.

TWELVE

The morning of the murder was warm and clear, a stripe of cloud on the horizon. He woke early and brewed a pot of Café Rico, unfolding the red and yellow bag, pouring the pungent black powder, and adding a few shots of cognac to taste.

For nearly an hour he sat in the backyard looking out through the fence to the sea, holding the gun in his hands. Then he fit it into his jeans and set off to visit Nadal. He did not want murder, but he felt murderous, so that every step thundered as if he were walking in seven-league boots. At the same time he was bereaved in a way he never had been, and that morning as he went to visit Nadal he felt like a tourist wandering the streets before the last flight home. He noticed everything. He walked all the way to Old San Juan, past the pink and cream of Condado, over the stone bridge with its rows of lanterns, where on weekend nights teenagers parked their cars bumper to bumper and let their radios blast American music up the bay. He walked the high paved road that turned to a kind of cliff by the sea, and finally reached La Plaza de Armas in Old San Juan. Vendors were cutting the skin from oranges so that sweet odors floated in the air; children turned cartwheels in the spray of a municipal fountain, Americans stood outside a china-blue pharmacy waiting to pay six dollars for the Sunday *New York Times.*

The old city. Talk as you might to American friends, no one was prepared for the beauty of Old San Juan: a slice of Spain baked to stillness by the sun, set on a hill in the middle of a blue, blue sea. As Katie had once said, its houses were the color of cake icing, pink, mint and cream. And parts of the city were in ruins still. On a single street you passed restored mansions, and crumbling, vacant buildings.

Kim stopped at La Bonbonera, a local hangout, and ordered *mallorca tostada,* sweet fried bread coated with sugar. It was slightly charred on the outside, sweet in the center. He ate it on the street corner, tearing off a few chunks for a stray cat. The city's totem animal should be a stray cat, he thought, since the place was crawling with them and they were all pitifully thin. Probably dying of leukemia, the whole lot of them. He tore off another chunk and another, and the cat crouched hungrily as bits of food came sailing toward it.

He went the long way, past Calle de la Luna, Street of the Moon, and Calle del Sol, Street of the Sun, walking up the wide paved avenue at the top of Old San Juan. There you can look over a precipice into that shantytown built outside the city walls, on the very brink of the sea. And you see the ghostly city minted out of vagrants sleeping in rutted streets and tin houses painted in the pure hues of the city above. La Perla. This was where Nadal had gone weekly to cut and bag cocaine. In a gutted building there his workers turned the snowy stuff back into rocks to sell wholesale.

Kim turned now onto Boulevard del Valle and

stood outside Nadal's green house. The gate was unlocked—did the man feel so safe, then, that he didn't bother to guard his own home? Kim lifted the iron latch and stepped inside. Before him was a room of white stucco walls and arched windows inlaid with wood in fan shapes. The floor was tiled in black and white and the high ceiling was crafted of ausubo beams, a native lumber nicknamed iron-wood because it hardens as it ages, until nails can't penetrate.

Kim hesitated before three different archways and went under the smallest, passing through a gallery filled with carved wooden *santos* and then into a kitchen where pinto beans simmered on the stove. A sparrow darted in through the open window. It lighted on a bowl of sugar, pecked at the granules, and flew off. He followed it. And suddenly he was standing in an open-air courtyard at the heart of the house. Creamy, crumbling walls molded of hardened mud and beach rock four hundred years ago. Flowers dangling from a sheet of vines. A blue tile stairway leading to another wing. And, under the shade of a furled banana tree, a man eating a breakfast of fruit and bread. Waxy, star-shaped *carambola,* oranges and papayas, and a heap of *parcha* looking like a bunch of wet, discolored rubber balls.

Again and again, it was the same, in memory as it had been in life. At first he was taken aback. There was no malice in this man; his face was mild and madonna-like. But when he got close Kim saw Nadal's fingernails. Bitten down so that they hardly seemed nails at all, more like pieces of wax stamped into his fingertips. Katie had described how Nadal, when he was angry, would reach into his shirt pocket, open his wallet, remove a double-edged razor and begin to pare away slivers of nail. The sliv-

ers fell as he cut, and he cut, Katie said, with a
perfect concentration. A man removing his claws.

Kim looked again at the face. It was soft. For just
a moment, his mind clicked shut. The difference
was too great—it was like playing with those ho-
lographic gizmos that changed when you tilt them
first one way, then another. The light hits the image and the nun's habit disappears, revealing a
whore with cherry tassles on her tits. Tilt her again
and the nun is back intact.

THIRTEEN

"I just might be crazy about you."

"Don't be," he says.

My hard, thin arms go round him in a suffocating grip, my head drops back, and with a helpless groan he slides his hands under my butt. Hours have passed; he's sated and exhausted. He shakes his head. I push myself up, legs sliding apart, lifting my pelvis; and pose for him, fingers folding back my lips, offering pink cunt slaked with milk. I'm still crying.

"You've had too much." Even so, his fingers greedily stroke my wet face, and he moistens his mouth with my juice. "You're like a drunk falling down in the street—"

I don't want to listen, and I make a sound, slurred and angry. We both look down at my hand on his cock, silenced by the pornography of the moment.

So he finds me. And almost immediately he begins to come. The fist inside him bursts apart, he cramps and burns. It's the shadow in him, the pain at his core, that is coming. Every little thing—his hand on the pillow, bitten lips, matted hair—stuns me as if this were love. I beat on his back, pelting him in triumph and exhaustion. Nothing left in him but dry heaves now. When he finally lifts his head I cover his eyes with my hand.

"I'm not falling in love," I say incoherently. "Bastard," I add.

He pulls my hand away.

Later we drag on our clothes, sticky with dried perspiration, and find José watching television in the living room. He rubs his eyes and grumbles about the sound effects of the last hour. We laugh. In my stained, old kitchen I whip eggs and cream, and José discovers a frayed spatula ("Look at this freak of nature, man. This spatula is bogus.") I toss the eggs in a skillet and bring out a carton of milk, and feel a wary bliss: the lull of playing girlfriend to these two blue-collar renegades.

"Call me," I say to Kim when they're leaving.

"When?"

"Before you drop off to sleep. As soon as you wake up."

"Tomorrow," he says. "I'll call you tomorrow."

For three weeks he calls as promised, and after work José drops him at my place. He takes the stairs instead of waiting for the elevator. I'm out in the hall in my bare feet, leaning over the banister to watch him. He's wearing a gray cotton coat, a faded fabric bulked up with some kind of goose down, hip and raw at the same time. I think that coat alone could make me love him—

But when he stands near me I stiffen; I'm newly afraid.

He swings me into his arms, and I wrap my legs around him as he carries me inside, kissing my frozen mouth, and it opens, and I sink. That's what he loves. He bites, eats, strokes, and I disappear farther and farther from him into an oblivion of feeling. He's blotting out my virginity. Each night there's a little less left.

"I'm addicted," I announce.

When he comes, just at that shuddering suspension of self, his cry of release is a cry of rage. I wait for it, all day, that primitive yowl, that proud, tribal cry. I want the cry, that's the strange thing —I coax it, pull him into me, ask him to rip me apart and fuck me all the way up to my heart.

He sleeps, but I can't; and in the morning he wakes a few minutes before the alarm rings. "What are you looking at, Sparkle?" he asks. He brushes my hair back. " 'Nightwatch' is over, the reporter can sleep now."

Neither one of us mentions the word love. One night I caress the back of his neck, and sniff.

"What's that?"

"Baby powder."

"Baby powder? Why?"

"I got a haircut at lunch."

I close my eyes, smile. There's a new carelessness in me. "My blue-collar baby. That's your cologne. Metal dust and baby powder."

Sometimes he pauses at my rolltop desk, drumming his fingers across my computer keyboard. It's a notebook, made of plastic, and it fits into a black foam travelling case so small and light that when I take it to interviews I feel like a kid carrying her lunchbox. It's like Bonsai trees and paperweights—a whole world funneled into miniature. Kim presses his thumb against the malleable plastic screen, making prints that melt away. He stops to read a page of writing I've left there, some prose about double helixes or black holes.

Occasionally we crawl out of bed to order pepperoni pizzas or open a bottle of red wine, and sometimes we go to a bar. Kim shows me how to tie a cherry stem with his tongue: eyebrows rushing together, his face contorted with a kind of comic fury as he twists his tongue rapidly around the stem. I laugh until it hurts.

Then we go to the supermarket and fumble with pints of gourmet ice cream in the freezer.

"Chocolate?" he suggests.

"No, only primary colors."

"Blueberry, then."

Back home: "Will you feed me?"

"Within an inch of your life. Maybe two inches. Eat this."

"What is it?"

"An airplane."

I squint. "It looks like a snowmobile."

"Okay." He digs in for another spoonful.

I taste. "And this, I bet, is a 1947 Batmobile."

"Yes, forty-seven was a good year for Batmobiles. Here's a bathysphere," he says.

"I don't eat words I don't know."

"It's a glass chamber that's dropped into the ocean. Usually for research. I've seen them in the Caribbean."

"What's it looking for?"

"You." Suddenly he shakes his head, and his light mood seems to fade. "It's just ice cream," he says, and falls silent.

He takes me to see his friend Richard Thompson, a broadcaster and radio talk-show host nicknamed "Cheeks" because as a kid whenever he smiled his cheeks popped out like a hamster's. He and his wife own a tenement in Hell's Kitchen. Kim met Cheeks' wife his first month in New York, in a ramshackle theater bar. He was sitting alone when he was spotted by an elfin woman with short, raggedy hair and a bright slash of mouth. Ginny. She was hemmed in by friends at a red-checkered table, looking like a bored kid, hunting for diversion or even danger.

"Their marriage is big enough to hold the world. I think it's because they never had kids. Cheeks always wanted to be a father, but Ginny couldn't. She kept having tubal pregnancies, and last time she almost died."

"How many times did they try?"

"Seven."

"My God. He must have really wanted it."

After each failed pregnancy, Kim tells me, Cheeks nursed Ginny back to health, and had the same heart-to-heart with her: "All the egg has to do is roll down the other tube. Now why can't it do that? Why can't we try again?" The seventh time scared them both, and splintered the marriage. Then one October day Cheeks brought home a handblown green glass jar with a copper lid. He found Ginny in the kitchen, and held it to the light.

"I'm just crazy about it," she said.

And he began to collect things. Their marriage danced and breathed again, because of his collector's passion. When Ginny was mad, all she had to do was examine his latest found object, and say, "No, I don't think that *lives*. I think it's ordinary." And he was dashed; he fought to regain her favor. Their home filled up like an ark, with everything from barber's chairs to the innards of a grand piano—this last mounted on the wall like a harp. One day he shoved a toy carrot, vinyl with green felt leaves, between the strings. Ginny said it was just the right touch of kitsch.

"They collect people, too." Kim explains. "It just means they consider you family."

"Forewarned," I comment.

Cheeks turns out to be a silver-haired man in baggy khakis, with a friendly face that crinkles up when he smiles. Ginny serves a dinner of steak, potatoes with caviar and sour cream, and a salad of bitter greens. She can't sit still, but keeps darting into the kitchen, bringing out condiments or ice or another bottle of Pinot Noir. She's a small, light-fingered urchin with a crop of shaggy hair, wearing nothing but dancer's leggings, a faded men's dress shirt, and beach thongs.

"This paean to a cellblock," Cheeks is saying, "this four-story tenement, is now worth a fortune. This is prime real-estate. When are you going to move in, Kim? We want you back."

"I'll think about it."

"We've been seriously dreaming about renting the top floor," Ginny says.

"Think about it," says Cheeks.

"I'll think."

"We should rent out the whole building. I could quit my job while I still love it." He turns to me. "I want to remember it as the best fun on the planet, being a late-night deejay on talk radio."

"So what'll you do instead?" I ask.

"Bum around the Eastern hemisphere. Go to Nepal or Lhassa and get hit over the head with enlightenment."

"We'd never actually sell this place. I'm certain we're going to die here," Ginny interjects. "But Cheeks could start that newspaper he always talks about."

Cheeks nods, eminently pleased, as if Ginny just made it happen. "Politics and art. I'll start local. A Hell's Kitchen rag." He looks at me. "I'm not really a broadcast journalist. I don't have a massive enough ego, I promise you."

"Me neither. I write about science."

"Science?" Cheeks echoes. "You look like somebody who should be gardening by the sea."

"It's her eyes," Ginny agrees. "Sad eyes. Like a basset hound."

"Why science?" Cheeks asks.

I shrug. "I want to know why apples fall and stars burn."

"She likes mysteries," Kim interjects.

Cheeks tilts his head at me. "So why didn't you become a scientist? Why just write about it?"

I tell them about my favorite Calvin and Hobbes cartoon, where little Calvin with the shock of feral blond hair and the broad smile complains about the big bang. How can scientists take things of such unimaginable wonder, and give them such mundane names? He'd call it "the horrendous space kablooie!"

"They need writers," I conclude, "to explain their miracles. Otherwise nobody else would be interested."

Cheeks laughs. Kim is watching me, contemplative, his arms crossed at his chest.

"And you don't write about anything besides science?"

"Only science."

"Me," Cheeks says humbly, "I'm just in love with news."

"He reads seven newspapers a day," Ginny comments.

"I was a reporter before I produced my talk show. I got bit by the riot bug. I was even ready to try a war or two, but then I met Ginny. But I'll know I'm dead when I want to stop hearing news."

"I'm the backstage girl. My friend Sherry calls me a hunter-observer."

"Wonderful."

I lean over to Kim. "Have I been collected yet?"

"Collected?" Ginny reaches into the pocket of her shirt, pulling out a cloth pouch of tobacco. With jabbing movements, she rolls a cigarette, licks the end and holds it to the candle flame. Kim tilts the candle toward her, and in the warm flutter her face looks unbelievably young and vulnerable. She might have looked at him with this mixture of tenderness and affection years ago. She smiles, and he goes on holding the tilted candlestick as if he might affix Ginny's face there forever.

"Collected," she muses.

"I told her—" Kim starts.

"I figured." She turns to me. "We don't take hostages."

"How about applications?"

Ginny smiles. "By the way, Kim, you're not collectible."

"What is he?" I ask.

She observes me through a veil of smoke. "A discovery. I discovered him, and it's usually Cheeks who discovers people."

*   *   *

One Saturday afternoon we're eating mandarin oranges and spitting the seeds into our hands as we walk up Broadway. The street vendors have spread their wares along the sidewalks, and at the corner we see a boy with a featherduster. His father is watching him, approving and stern, as the boy dusts a table of gleaming hardcover books. Kim reaches out to tousle his hair and, without slowing his pace, tosses the handful of seeds into a garbage can.

The boy smiles.

"Basket," he says, without looking. The boy runs back and checks—the seeds are clumped on a wedge of *The New York Times*.

I pour my seeds into Kim's hand. "Again," I say.

He smiles down at the kid. "My dad would do it like this," he says, and tosses them over his shoulder. And he smiles at the father.

"Basket," I say as we walk on. "Hey, you never told me what your dad is like."

He thinks for a moment. "The kind of teacher you hate when you're a kid and love later for teaching you the right things."

"What does he teach?"

"I don't mean that's his job. He's a pilot." But, says Kim, he was born to teach. "He gets crazed with it sometimes." His father, he tells me, was a completely physical creature—tight-bellied, loving and hard. If there was wisdom in him, it was the wisdom of motion and the thrift of grace.

Kim grew up in a four-bedroom house on an acre of land outside St. Paul, Minnesota. He says his street was shaped like a horseshoe, the homes set back on wooded land. He had three older sisters, and he was fond of them, but they moved in their own feminine realm. Occasionally they babied him, sometimes they flirted with him, but usually they left him alone.

He found typical boys' pleasures: riding dirtbikes with friends, smoking pot, lying between the tracks when the train was coming, so it clattered over him in one obliterating roar. And a girl named Rachel who he'd known since nursery school, where one day he'd peed proudly down the cracked wood of the teeter-totter, while she sat astonished, staring at the urine dribbling toward her. "Jump!" urged Kim. She leaped off at the last minute. Kim leaped deftly, too, and when Rachel began to cry he felt strangely stirred. After that he used to come sit near her, quiet and protective. Seven years later she turned into a shy slip of a girl, whose body he explored in the basement all summer. She lay on the orange vinyl couch and solemnly peeled off her undershirt and pulled down her cutoff shorts, hemmed with a thick band of lace.

Rachel was one of his secrets, and Thursday nights were another. Each Thursday night when he was twelve he snuck out. Wearing black Levi's and a cotton turtleneck, he moved like an intruder among the light and shadow of his house, down the polished staircase and along the pine planks of the hall, until he was out the door. Then he broke into a run, passing the swing his father had cut and hung ten years earlier. Its weathered seat was warped, the ropes slick and hard. Kim gave the swing a tug, as if saluting his old man, and always he glanced back to be sure his mother had not, by some alchemy of intuition, opened the door and seen him go.

By the time he reached Moon Park he was free to race like a whipped dog, and he did just for the fun of it, tearing across the football field, careening around the jungle gym and vaulting into and out of the sandbox, up the hill and over the railroad tracks, kicking up gravel as he went, until he reached the neighboring town. There he caught his breath and sauntered, half-boy, half-man, past liquor stores and restaurants. Tucked at the end of a small alley was a bar where Kim joined a group of adults dancing the shag, somehow transplanted from the south. They were fanatical about it. This ratty blue-collar bar meant everything to him; adventure, rebellion, and a woman named Teddy James.

Teddy was forty-five, a tiny, skinny, bristling blond who dressed like seventeen, in miniskirts, open-toed pumps, and stockings that almost hid the cord of veins on the back of each knee. Her freckled arms were long and expressive. One night her partner was sick, and she approached Kim. After a few months of partnering Teddy, he became a bonafide and capable shagger.

Kim practiced the shag daily, dancing with the doorknob to his bedroom. Once his mother caught him humming and swinging the door back and forth, and she looked at him strangely but said nothing.

Patricia Beckett was nearly six feet, with sheaves of coppery-blond hair hanging halfway down her back, broad hips, a man's hands, and a musical, bounding voice. Kim's father said that when he met Patti she was the best-looking thing in the state: wide-boned, with a powerful sway in her hips—the only woman strong enough for him. The night he proposed he'd taken her flying in a small plane as far as the Canadian border, and made a surprise landing in a deserted field. They walked for a while, and when she said she liked the tall reeds by the moonlit stream, he took out a pocket knife and cut her dozens. With every protest of "That's enough," he laughed and cut more, snapping them at the base and whipping the knife through the stem. She stood there, her arms full of the crude bouquet.

But Nick was a man of military spareness. He'd unwittingly make his wife cry, and then, seeing tears, walk away with a sense of confused outrage. By the time Kim was born, Nick was sleeping with another woman. And Patti acquiesced, her great tree of a body gone still. Even so, Nick's physical nearness made her glow in a gloomy way, like beaming a flashlight into an attic—she saw him and suddenly her face became brilliant, eerie and shadowed.

Patti nursed Kim for three years. Even after he ate solid food, she'd put him to sleep with the breast. Uneasy relatives protested, but Patti claimed her boy would have nursed longer if she hadn't forcibly weaned him. The truth was that one week she went to a friend's wedding in California, and the night she returned, she opened her shirt as usual for him. Instead of sleepily suckling, he turned away from her. She tried to lift him and he turned his head. She must have sat there for a few moments, then hooked the clasp of her bra, buttoned up her shirt, and left the room.

His whole childhood he tried to repair that rift. Sensing his mother's loneliness, he'd go to her and sit, cross-legged, almost oblivious, and let her hand steal out to stroke his hair. Or he'd bring her his torn clothes, skinned elbows and knees. And then the music—the sound of cymbals—came back in her voice for a few days.

It was his father Kim loved. Nick had left commercial airlines to fly private jets for the wealthy, but was more a friend to his clients than a chauffeur. He emulated these men, with their Bally shoes and Sea Isle shirts, immodest lies, easy drinking. He'd return from his trips with too many presents, elated as a conquerer, but a day or two at home and his mood would blacken. Sitting in a silk robe at breakfast, turning the pages of a newspaper, he'd light on Kim. And, mouth suddenly twitching with a smile, he'd lean over to his son while both hands would become Hanskim and Leggo—two animals trotting on the table. Hanskim climbed a bottle of juice and wobbled on top, the middle finger waving in the air like a head, sniffing the butter, salt shaker, and open jar of marmalade, while four finger-legs moved in unison. Leggo watched from below, envious, afraid to take a risk, and then shook with laughter when Hanskim fell. Then they marched on in easy symmetry, until Hanskim met with another challenge. It was a feat that took Kim months to master himself.

Like his father, Kim found release in the physical world. He let Nick teach; rock climbing, sailing, skiing, and—the year he turned fifteen—flight. Nick took him flying in a Bonanza. They'd walk on the low wings, climb inside the austere four-seater; and Kim, with his own controls and wheel, got to be co-pilot. Before him was a constellation of dials, and at his feet two rudder pedals that made the plane's tail wiggle to the left and right.

Sometimes his father flew crazy, like a stunt pilot: the plane looped and rolled and cartwheeled, dropped spinning and rose spinning, and just when Kim thought they would breathe, Nick turned and dipped, his face tight with joy, eyes fixed on the nothingness before him as if it were a beloved enemy. The Bonanza shuddered and whined, and they dove until treetops were rushing at them.

"Watch everything I do," his father would shout as the plane rose with a roar. "One of these days I'm going to take my hands off the wheel and you'll have to fly." He would shout that same thing every time, and Kim waited in terror and excitement for an initiation that might come at any moment.

The summer Kim turned sixteen, they flew every night his father was home. Once Kim learned to handle the plane, his father placed a hood on his head so that part of his vision was blocked. It gave the feeling of flying in clouds. Nick would stall the plane and make

Kim recover, covering up the dials on Kim's side one by one, giving him less and less information. Kim always recovered.

One evening when wispy clouds fleeced the sky they hit a wind pocket and the plane went into a steep turn, so deep that one wing was pointing at the earth. His father looked painfully excited and grinned, leaning on the wheel so the wing tilted further and the plane went somersaulting. Then he pulled the throttle and they began to spiral downward. And Nick took his hands off the wheel. Didn't say a thing, just placed his hands in his lap.

"Recover it," he ordered, as always over the scream of engines and wind.

"Don't know how—"

Sick from the plane's plummeting spiral, Kim pulled at the throttle, tried to lift the nose. The machine spun like a piece of paper. A strange brightness made his father's face glow. He was going to let them crash.

"Neutralize it," came his father's voice, at last. Somehow Nick had leaned over, grabbed him, shouted into his ear. How else had he heard words?

"You've got to be kidding," Kim screamed.

"Do what I say."

He obeyed.

And then Nick let him go, reaching out for his own wheel and throttle and, as they plummeted toward a windshield filled with rock, he too neutralized his own controls.

A few seconds later, the craft began to recover.

When they were finally coasting, Kim spoke in a low, unbelieving voice. "You'll do anything for a lesson, won't you?"

"Maybe."

"I don't want to be like you," Kim said.

Nick laughed angrily. "This happened to me once when I was flying alone. I figured I'd lost it so I gave up and prepared to die. And I didn't. Since then I haven't been scared of dying, so I haven't been scared of much of anything, really." When Nick finally looked at him, they were circling the airport. "I don't know, I just wanted you to feel that."

And though Kim told himself he didn't believe it, a part of him must have. Somewhere inside there would always be the memory of that moment of collapse before he neutralized the plane—and the miraculous calm that followed, when the world was his once more.

When Kim turned seventeen and graduated from high school, Nick drove him out to the airport one evening, and as they walked toward the Bonanza, he tossed a bunch of keys at Kim. Parked next to the plane was a gunmetal-green two-seater, a reconditioned fighter.

Kim looked at the plane with a polite, stupid expression, but his father could see that his look was studied, and instantly protested:

"She didn't cost much. A favor from a friend."

"Pop, what do you expect me to do with her?" But he knew. If he took this plane, he would become a pilot.

His father said, slow, uncomprehending, "I thought you'd want a plane of your own."

"I don't want to fly for money. I never did. If those are the terms, I can't take the plane."

"Please take the plane," his father said, showing a weakness that hurt them both. When Kim failed to answer, Nick walked away.

Kim never flew the plane. He left it in the lot. He took the keys with him to New York, in spite of the fact that they were keys to a life he didn't want. But what did he want? Like his father, when he pitted himself against the physical world, he could almost feel who he was. He got close, strained close, but always fell back with the mystery unsolved. So he carried the keys to each new city. They're in his drawer now.

FOURTEEN

Kim was there in his house at last and Nadal, amaz-
ingly, was acting as if he'd been expecting him.

"No need to introduce yourself," he said, "since
I know who you are. Why don't you join me?"
Passion fruit. Loaves of warm bread. Coffee in a
pitcher. What was this, Spanish civility or something?

Kim didn't move. Nadal asked Kim to frisk him.
To show he had no gun. Got to his feet, clumsily,
since he was a big man. Kim had one hand on the
man's shoulder, his shirt, it was soaked in sweat and
it smelled. He thought but didn't say: My woman,
she can't get over you. I could stand it if she
stopped loving me, but I can't stand seeing her
broken like this.

"I want to talk to you," Nadal said. "You will
listen?"

"Go ahead, if that's what you want. Talk."

He talked a long time, until clouds rolled in and
the sky started to spit. His talk made Kim dizzy, he
was almost keeling over from this mountain of talk.
*What a fucking magician. I held the gun steady. I let
him keep talking because if I shut him up he'd see I*

was soft, and he wanted to see me soft. Wanted that triumph.

The things Nadal said about her. Like they were twins. The things he said. Kim was hanging onto his words, as if he might finally explain what Kim had never understood, why Katie was unhappy.

"Why didn't you let her come back?" Kim asked.

"I have a better question. Where did she run to that evening?"

"Not to me."

"She went straight to you. And that night. She talked to you, didn't she?"

"I'll leave San Juan. If you give me your promise—"

"You trust my promise?"

"I don't have much choice."

"Then you should trust it less, *compio.*"

"Even murderers must have a code of ethics."

Nadal took out the razor blade Katie had described, the double-edged blade that not only cut cocaine but cut his nails, and he put it on the table between them. And, in that single motion, he seemed to render them equal, as if somehow the blade were lethal and not Kim's gun.

Nadal said, in a companionable tone, "Do you know why I left my gate open?"

"You were waiting for somebody."

"You." Nadal squinted up at the sun. "The walls, you see how at the top they glint? You see the pieces of glass? We broke glass in a thousand pieces. We sunk the pieces in wet bricks. Nobody climbs over the walls unless they want to bleed. Nobody gets in or out unless I want them to."

"Why did you let me come?"

"Because I knew you wouldn't kill me. Now listen, I have something to tell you."

FIFTEEN

"Let's talk about penis size."

It's eight P.M.—Sherry and Dana and I are lingering after dinner at a Thai restaurant on Columbus, waiting for Kim to stop in. As he was leaving this morning, I asked him to meet us here at seven-thirty. "I haven't seen my girlfriends much since I met you. Anyway, I wouldn't mind showing you off."

"What time?" He was staring at my body, the shoulder blades visible under a thin nightshirt.

As he was leaving, I called him back to my bed. "Hey."

"Yeah?"

"I want to ask you something."

"Don't you always?" But he smiled.

"The sex," I said. "It's not the same for you as it is for me."

He sat, patient and just a little irritated, on the bed. "I guess not. How could it be?"

"It means too much to me. And you, it's just who you are."

"I need to be physical. You can't fuck a scientific equation."

"So I can't be your fate. I never will."

He was silent. "Jesus, I'm really worn out. I can't even think straight. Can we talk more about this later?"

It's already eight P.M.; he hasn't arrived. This restaurant is a popular hangout for Lincoln Center dancers, pretty girls in leotards and floppy cotton sweaters, hair pulled into golfball buns.

Dana is peeling open a moist, chewy dessert I've forgotten the name of, wrapped and tied in a stiff leaf, and the three of us keep ordering drinks served with halved oranges and tiny, colored umbrellas. We toss the umbrellas at each other until a confetti of pink, green and blue covers our table.

I've realized I actually like Dana, her powdery skin and jet-black crewcut, the sisterly affection with which she greets me, stroking my hand as she talks, and above all, her breathless, tawdry gossip. Just now she finished recounting the saga of Ray, a designer in his fifties. "He gets plastic surgery, gets all his fat sucked out, and it really works. Any time he gets sick or has a problem, he's got his plastic." Lifting her sunglasses, a new design studded with white eyeballs mounted on bouncing wires, Dana grins at me.

"Penis size?" she echoes me now. "Let's talk plant size instead. Norman, my avocado plant, got down to a leaf on each branch. For weeks it was like, uh-oh, my neighbors gave me this dying plant, and then by some miracle he started growing back. Anyway, yesterday I ate a delicious avocado, the small creamy kind, and put the pit in a glass of water. I'm thinking of making a friend for Norman." She giggles and lowers her sunglasses again. "Okay, Lynn. You've been gooey and spacey all through dinner. The only thing on your mind is sex, right?"

I nod, swallow the last of my fourth drink and tell them, in a sincere haze, how for weeks this man has poured honey into my body, and I guess I've become a complete degenerate but I've been thinking about his penis, how thick and beautifully carved it is.

Sherry puts her hand on my forehead. "You *are* sick."

"Yeah, but the question is, are all penises born equal?"

"When you're in love with a guy, his penis becomes the Ur-penis."

"What's that?" Sherry questions. "Like Nietzsche's Ur-mensch?"

"Uh-huh," Dana says casually. "I've been checking pricks out since I was fourteen. They all have their endearing qualities. My favorites are the uncircumcised ones. They look like little wrinkled sacs, and then the skin starts folding back all by itself and out comes this head. I even liked my ex, Tom, and I used to call him pencil-dick to his face. But he knew how to use it. He did his belly-dancing in bed."

"I can't even remember what my old boyfriend felt like. I can hardly remember what we did."

"Yeah, but Stephen was a preemie," Sherry reminds me.

"Well, I *thought* Stephen was premature. He was convinced he was normal." I turn to Dana. "The textbooks say most men last a few minutes."

"That isn't enough time to get wet."

"Stephen wouldn't make a sound, he'd just shiver and all of a sudden you knew it was over. He'd collapse like a busted balloon and plop out a few seconds later."

Dana peels open another dessert. "Did you ever try to slow him down?"

"He said he got sore if he went on too long. So I learned to sneak my orgasm in right at the beginning. He'd work me up before, and then it was like a 100-yard-dash, whoever got there first." I laugh, a little bitterly. "But neither of us let out a peep. And he wouldn't take his glasses off."

"I've worn glasses in bed. Cat-eye sunglasses and a garter belt."

"The first time we kissed I started to take Stephen's glasses off and he said, 'You're taking away my eyes.' He let me do it, but . . ." I tell them how Stephen had penetrated me from behind, and after a minute reached for his glasses and put them on. And took one look, I suppose, at the rear view, and came. "He tried to make up for it with his tongue," I conclude, "but that's not my drug of choice. Actually, after Kim, I don't care if a man ever goes down on me again."

"You *are* seriously ill," Dana protests. "When a man puts his head between my legs I own the world. And the ultimate test is blood. If he'll eat my blood, he's a hero."

"Cunnilingus is a consolation prize," I insist, and they both shake their heads as if humoring a petulant child. All I want them to do is sigh and cluck over Kim's magnificence, but they're chipping away at every outlandish compliment I give him. "When I put my hand on Kim I felt rooted to the center of the earth."

"Not earth—Neptune, maybe," says Sherry, and they both start laughing.

"Don't be shy," Dana says. "Videotape it next time."

"Yeah, you can use it as a teaching tool."

"I'm sure neither one of you needs it."

"Don't bet on it." Dana shrugs amiably. "Listen, I don't mind hearing your maudlin sex stuff. Y'know what my favorite lines are? From a Prince song." She pauses, then leans forward dramatically. *"We can fuck until the dawn, making love till cherry's gone.* Right? Every woman knows it takes a long time and a special man to fuck all the cherry out of you."

"Exactly," I say, but without much enthusiasm. I don't want Kim reduced to a pop song.

"I wish I knew what they say about us. Did you ever ask a guy what it feels like to be inside *you?*"

"Yeah, they say warm."

"Oh, it's warm all right, it's nearly 100 degrees in there! It must feel great. I wish I could be a man just once."

"What if you were the kind of man who always got rejected? I have a friend who reminds me of the Pillsbury Dough Boy—"

"—kind of plump and white?—" says Dana.

"—and I adore him," I continue. "But the thought of sex makes me queasy."

"Sure. How can you make love to cold cookie dough? Or maybe you have the woman's version of a Madonna-whore complex?"

"Easy on her," Sherry warns gently. "By the way, Lynn, I know you're going to roll your eyes and say, 'Don't give me the mother bit,' but you are using a condom, aren't you?"

"Latex," I affirm, touched rather than annoyed. "But I gave him a couple blow jobs. That's a little risky, I guess. You know what I showed him? Your old vibrator."

"My first erotic bauble?" she says, casually.

"Remember you dragged me to Eve's Garden last year? You bought yourself a new vibrator and gave me that little white one." I turn to Dana. "I don't like vibrators. Too intense."

"What's Eve's Garden?"

"A lesbian-feminist porn shop. Actually, it's very tasteful, on the fourteenth floor of this art-deco building across from the Russian Tea Room. They've got the typical stuff, like body paints and Astroglide, but that's not all." I tell Dana about the latex underwear, gloves, dental dams, and rubber finger "cots"—toys for the age of AIDS. About the collection of sculptured penises in lavender, purple and pink. They're pliable and sticky to the touch. They've even got pink lesbian dildoes called two fingers.

The funniest toys, though, are the vibrators. The Eager Beaver, a black rubber penis whose head has a solemn face, has a rubber beaver mounted on its shaft. Turn a switch and the penis revolves, like a frantic caterpillar at the end of a leaf. Turn another switch and the beaver's lips jiggle, in the most servile, distracted parody of clitoral stimulation you've ever seen.

"Sherry bought one," I conclude. "Now, Sherry, aren't you ashamed?"

"I bought a kangaroo. With a baby kangaroo in her pouch. But I don't really use it. I take it out to scare Kyros sometimes."

"When I was married," Dana confesses, "I used a Hitachi Magic Wand. I'd go into the bathroom, turn on the water, and plug in my vibrator."

"Do you still use it?"

"These days it's getting dusty under the sink."

"Speaking of marriage . . . Kyros proposed to me again last night," Sherry says.

"Is he the one I saw you with in the lobby? He's wonderfully handsome in a droopy kind of way."

"He's got a face like a friendly Labrador," Sherry agrees.

"Why do you sound so sad?"

"Because I'm seriously considering saying yes."

"You don't love him."

"I do love him."

"If she marries Kyros she'll lose her other men," I explain, "and they're like alternate personalities."

"It's like giving up travel before you've seen Greece and Bali." She adds thoughtfully, "I met a man on the courthouse steps yesterday, and asked him to recommend a restaurant in the neighborhood. When I got there the waiter came over and said one of their customers had phoned ahead and the meal was on him. It was like a dream."

"He's probably married," Dana retorts. "A man's most interesting when you can't have him."

Sherry throws her a wary look, and Dana smiles. "Don't I know, with my two married guys?"

I've been wondering about Dana—Sherry says she divorced an artist two years ago, and since then she refuses to sleep with any man who's available.

"Do they promise to leave their wives?" I ask.

"If they do they don't mean it. Not the ones I choose, anyway." She pauses. "They have wet dreams about me. I have romance and no hassles."

But I know she's lying. She goes to bed alone every night. Brushing her teeth. Turning down the covers. Switching television channels. Making lists for the morning.

"I know a woman who was seeing a married man for twelve years," says Sherry, "and she only found out he'd died after the funeral."

"What in the world do men mean when they say you're the one?" I muse. "When Stephen met me he said, 'You were made for me.' A year later he was having an affair."

"What they really mean," Dana shrugs, "is you're *one* of the ones. It doesn't mean you're not a terrific one, but there have been other ones before and there will be ones again."

"And the ones keep getting younger."

"Yeah. Do you ever read the personal ads? A forty-year-old man advertises for a woman who's under thirty-nine. She just has to be a year younger."

"My own father," says Dana, "claims to look twenty-eight, so he thinks there's no reason to date a woman old enough to be his mother. One of these days he'll end up in bed with a fifty-year-old who's had a face lift. And he won't know until it's too late." She laughs. "That's how you screw the patriarchy."

Kim is so late that Dana, giving her regrets ("Lynn, I know I don't know what I'm missing") kisses us both and leaves for Brooklyn to deliver sunglasses. I no longer feel pleasantly drunk; my head is pounding and I'm thirsty. We order coffee and ask the waiter to bring the check.

"You're too quiet," Sherry says.

I nod to the clock on the far wall. "It's nearly nine. I'm afraid he's not going to show."

"Another car accident?" she quips.

"I'm going to check my answering machine."

"No message," I tell her when I return to the table.

She stirs her drink. "You're making too much of him, Lynn."

Stung, I say nothing.

"If I felt what you're feeling, the first thing I'd do is find myself a buffer. I'd run into the arms of another man, and make sure I wasn't putting all my orgasms in one basket."

"Right now it's the only basket there is."

She laughs. "I've got a few years on you. Some people are sexual athletes, that's all. It's a talent."

I remind Sherry that she's a sensual gourmand. She's done threesomes, foursomes, danced in strip joints and made love to women and taken Betty Dodson's classes where feminists learn the joys of masturbating en masse, and all of it has left her somehow polished, a fine erotic instrument.

"That's the whole point. I don't have vaginal orgasms, Lynn. I'm a completely different animal than you are."

We stare at each other like two fighters in a ring.

"Bullshit!"

"Right. Bullshit."

"But I thought—"

"Oh, once in a while. But basically I need to reach down and touch myself. It's been that way since my first boyfriend." She shakes her head. "That was twenty-four years ago. Do you think I'll ever settle down?"

"Didn't we just go through this with Dana?"

"My father wants me to marry Kyros. He called me today. He keeps talking about grandchildren."

"He already has grandchildren. All of your brothers are married."

"I'm his only daughter. He wants my children." Suddenly she looks perplexed. "Kyros wants children, too. I told him last night about my baby, how I was living in Seattle being a vegetarian artist and I got pregnant and gave her up for adoption."

"What did he do?"

"He didn't say much," she admits. "I asked him if he thought it was wrong, and he stroked my hair very gently and said, 'Yes, it was wrong.' "

"Jesus, Sherry, you were only twenty. How could you keep her?"

"I was so sick after I delivered. A twenty-six-hour labor. But I held her for a few minutes. Why are you looking at me like that?"

"Like what?"

"Like somebody staring into a coffin at a wake."

"You never told me that part before."

"I did tell you."

"Not the part about holding her."

"Oh well." She opens her purse. "Let's pay and get out of here."

"It's on me this time."

"It was on you last time."

"Yeah, but Kim didn't show up and I feel bad. So the way to make me feel good is to let me pay. All right?"

She tilts her head in her familiar, endearing way, as if she's going to nuzzle me, and then she looks past me. Almost magically the pain in her face recedes. And I think to myself that her peasant cheer—that warm good earth of Sherry, and her husky night-voice —is a brilliant, if noble, lie. Well, then, we are all liars. I love the lie in Sherry.

On my way home I wander in and out of late-night shops, wanting Kim. One store has a wall of scarves. My favorite is a red shawl, feral and lush at the same time, knitted of heavy wool with a halo of fuzz. It looks like a Victorian mohair sofa. It's the kind of thing a harlot would wear. I take it into the dressing room.

There a woman is staring into the mirror. Her face is bonelike and spare, and blanketing her head is an opulent fur cap. Her cap reminds me of my scarf. She removes her clothes one by one, hangs them on a hook, until she's wearing only bra and camisole. Then she pulls off the cap. Her head is completely bald. She holds her hat in her hands as if it were some miraculous and foreign thing.

She must have had cancer and lost her hair from the drugs.

Maybe she doesn't have breasts. One of my friends had both her breasts lopped off, and somehow I imagined her like an eleven-year-old, flat-chested with pink nipples. But then one summer day she undressed in front of me, and I saw a battered runway of punched, dented skin. It was as if she'd been dug up and torn apart. She pulled on her bathing suit, with its foam boobs, and later as she was climbing out of the pool she squeezed her water-logged bosom, like a female Tarzan who really wished she could beat her chest in pain. "I'm the only woman here who can squeeze her tits dry," she joked, and squeezed again.

She had silicone sacs put in her chest and new nipples sewn on, but the sacs hardened and when her lover's tongue touched them in the dark she didn't feel it.

And yet there's this amazing ingenuity we all have, this ability to find ourselves again. Her lover stayed. I don't know if he took her from behind more often, or if he began to feel desperate over the swell of her thighs or the flesh on her neck, but one Saturday afternoon she stopped before a rack of silk undershirts in a shop, fondled them thoughtfully, and dropped a few in her basket.

I buy the scarf.

When I turn into the courtyard of my building a slim-hipped man steps in front of me. He's dressed in a black suit with delicate brocade, and a thin cotton shirt faintly tinged with lavender. A tiny diamond glints in his ear.

"Please don't be alarmed. I need to talk to you for a minute."

Warily, I step back onto the sidewalk, so I'm in clear sight of the doorman across the street.

"I'm looking for a friend of yours," he says. His English is perfect, though the rhythms are Latin. He's about twenty, his eyes soft as olives, and he has a fine, lithe grace to him.

"What friend?"

"Kim Beckett."

He can see I'm taken aback.

"Who are you?"

"My name is Popi Clemente Nadal," he announces, with subtle pride, as if he were the son of an ambassador or financier.

"Are you a friend of Kim's?"

"Actually, I've never met him. But we have a mutual friend in Puerto Rico."

"He's not with me, as you can see. Why don't you leave a message at his hotel?"

"He never seems to be at his hotel. And I don't want to leave a message, I want to see him."

"Well, I have no idea where he is." I cross my arms. "How did you know who I was, anyway?"

He lifts mournful, dark-lashed eyes. "Just a guess."

I laugh, incredulous. "Who told you about me?"

He doesn't answer, just fixes his stare on me.

"What the hell do you want?" I say in a low voice. "Do you want me to tell Kim something?"

"Actually, Kim doesn't even know I'm here," Popi says.

I cross my arms over my chest and edge slowly toward the street. "Please don't mix me up in this."

He looks perturbed. "But you're already mixed up in it," he says softly, then seeing my expression, blurts out, "How can I convince you to talk to me? The truth is it's you I want to talk to. I didn't even try to get hold of Kim tonight."

I stare at him.

"You want to know how I found you? I knew Kim had gone. A cousin of mine in New York City has been watching Kim here in the city. He told me Kim comes to this address every night. Sometimes you and he go out together. My friend described you to me. Not many women have such beautiful hair."

"Please."

"Please?"

"I *don't* want to talk to you."

Neither one of us moves. For some reason I feel dead calm, my senses sharp and still, knowing already that this boy with soft eyes is part of the dark eclipse of Kim's life.

Slowly I let out my breath. I have to ask. It suddenly seems to me that if I don't ask I'll regret it forever.

"Did he hurt somebody?"

Popi just looks at me, soft, almost reproachful.

"Would you answer me?"

"I was going to ask you a similar question."

"But instead you're staring at me. Why are you staring at me like that?"

He looks away. "I'm sorry. I learned it from my uncle, and it's second nature. *La mirada fuerte.*"

"Which means?"

"Strong-gazing," he says simply. "Like the gaze of a *curandera*, a witch doctor. My uncle thought you could possess somebody that way. Not all of the person, but enough to get what you wanted."

"I asked you a question. I can ask the same question ten different ways."

"I'll answer. But can we go somewhere to talk?"

"Why? What could I tell you?"

"You could tell me if he cares for you a little."

I drop my head.

"Or if he's mentioned the woman he used to live with."

"You mean the woman in San Juan?"

"Yes." He hesitates, then says warmly, "She was my friend."

"Katie?"

"Katie," he echoes.

"Kim told me she left him and had an affair with someone. Was it you?"

"No," Popi says with reluctance. "It was my uncle. She was crazy for him. But they parted ways. So. I will ask you one more time. Would you sit down for some coffee with me?"

And say what? That I'm only a little intoxicated? That I awaken at three A.M. and see him in my dark living room, listening to my Walkman and smoking? And I wait, in the slow-blinking light of his cigarette. He stands by my bed, the cigarette an eyelet of red, the man all shadow.

"All right," I tell Popi, "Coffee. We can go to a coffee shop near here. But when we get there I'm going to call my friend Sherry. I'm going to ask her to meet me there in an hour. I want her to know what you look like, and I want her to walk me home."

He nods sadly. "One thing I've never done is lay a hand on a woman. But you may call your friend if you wish."

He offers his arm, bent at the elbow, for me to take.

"No thanks."

"But I want to," he says, a note of courtly entreaty in his voice.

"I'd actually find it insulting." We start to walk toward Broadway. "So, shall we talk?"

He nods, but for the moment is silent.

"Tell me what it's like to be a Puerto Rican these days," I say.

"Every Puerto Rican is born a refugee," Popi says.

"From what?"

"I will tell you."

SIXTEEN

Ahora tu estas como la caña en febrero. Nadal's
voice had been beautiful, like deep drumbeats.
He'd been talking most of the morning, it seemed.
At last he folded his napkin, placed it on the glass
tabletop, and pushed his chair back. He no longer
watched the gun in Kim's hand, no longer seemed
concerned. Instead he seemed expansive. Something was changing.

You're like the sugar cane in February, Nadal
translated, needlessly. It was an old Spanish cliché.
But the man seemed to enjoy the English, as if it
gave him an excuse to say the same thing twice.
When it's ready for cutting, Nadal added.

*Why do you keep telling me what I am? You do this
to everybody?*

No one ever talked to him like Nadal did, it was a
kind of singing, like a tribal chief intoning stories in
a sweat-lodge ceremony.

*Don't you think every man has that moment in
him? When he's ripe for cutting? I spent my life making such moments in men. Is that creation?*

I'm not ripe, Kim told him.

I will be, soon, the man had answered. Then his

mood changed. He laughed. He said to Kim, *It's a joke. I could not resist a joke because you are so serious, and I'm afraid I might fall into your seriousness like a pebble into a pit. One of us must keep joking. You came here ready to sacrifice everything. But how can I take you seriously?*

Kim shrugged.

It seemed there was a long silence. There was peace between them. It had begun to drizzle, and the man looked up quizzically at the blue sky. *Están casando las brujas,* he said to himself, another bit of slang. *The witches are marrying. I mean it's raining at the same time the sun is shining.*

A clock chimed on the balcony above. *I think we have an hour left. Then my nephew comes home. I made sure he would be detained most of the morning.*

So what have you planned for this last hour?

SEVENTEEN

"Every puertorriqueño," says Popi, "is born split in two. He's like the *yagrumo*, the tree whose leaves turn from dark to light in the wind. Every one of us is born with this divided self."

"Divided between what?" I ask, watching him pour milk into his coffee until it's the color of butterscotch.

"Latin and Anglo," he says quickly, as if pleased at my indulgence. "Being part American and always the poor cousin. And you know what's hardest? Talking in English when your hands are moving in the rhythms of Spanish."

"But lots of people are bilingual. Why should that make you feel split in two?"

He stops, just a touch annoyed, and then laughs.

"Listen." He leans forward, slender face flushed. "When I came here to school, in upstate New York, I was a boy, *un chico*. Do you know how my mama used to make love to that word? I was her *chico*, and when that wasn't enough, her *chicito*, little boy, and when even that couldn't hold her heart in it, *chicitito*. But I lost that in America. You can't put love into "boy," because you don't think that way."

"I think you're still very *chicitito*. How old are you?"

"Twenty-five."

"So you went to school here? Didn't you go back home every summer?"

"Not a chance. I was sent around Latin America, the whole southern half of the globe, Colombia, Chile, Brazil, and one summer to Portugal," Popi boasts, so ingenuously I can't help smiling. "I came home when I turned eighteen, and then I was king. When you're young you have to serve the grown-ups, but as soon as a boy turns eighteen even his own mother won't sit unless he sits first."

"And do you like it? Being served?"

"Not really. I prefer a little pride in others." He grins. "Especially girls."

"You like the ones who play hard to get? Are you really that simple?"

"I'm not talking about the pride of a virgin or a girl who's beautiful. No. I'm talking about a girl who won't abandon herself to anyone." He smiles, and his eyes half close in memory. "The girls who give themselves so completely, you hate them for no reason, because they laugh too easily, or wait for you to call, or allow your cruelties."

"And the other kind of girl?"

"She gives herself drop by drop. You suffer from the first kiss. The moment your lips touch hers you can taste her pride."

"You know from experience?"

"Oh," Popi warns in a friendly tone, "that question's forbidden."

"Then don't answer." I pause. "So. Let's start at the top. What brings you to New York?"

He says instantly, "My uncle. He's the reason I'm here."

"He sent you?"

Popi lifts his sleek, dark head. "That would be impossible."

"You ran away from him?"

"No, of course not."

"So, what is this, a guessing game?"

"He's not alive any longer."

"Oh—I'm sorry."

"Last month he was shot through the heart."

I look away, as most of us look away from another's loss, because we can't endure it unprotected. Popi waits until I look back, and now his eyes are shielded. He says politely, "You know nothing about it?"

I shake my head.

"Whoever shot him knew him," Popi continues, "because the gate to our house was open and the killer left half-eaten fruit and cheese on a plate."

Early that morning, he explains, his uncle had sent him on an errand in Arecibo, a coastal city two hours away from Old San Juan. When Popi finally made it back, mid-afternoon, the house was empty and Nadal lay slumped against the stone wall of the inner atrium. His gun was still upstairs, laid at the back of a drawer. "Who could he have trusted so much that he put away his gun?"

I murmur my condolences, but Popi waves them down. "I was not so close to him," he says suddenly.

"He wasn't cruel?"

"Oh he was cruel, but it slipped in like velvet. But what I felt doesn't count. He was family."

"All right." I lean forward. "What's Kim got to do with this?"

"Do you need to ask that question?" Popi waits expectantly.

"Why else would you chase him up to New York, right," I say dully, and spread my hands on the plastic table, staring at the broken nail and bloody cuticle of my index finger. When did I bite it? It makes me want to cry. It's ugly. Is it possible? I've been fucking a murderer.

"He was seen in the old city the same morning my uncle was killed," Popi begins.

"Is that a big deal, that he was seen?"

"Maybe not."

"What was your uncle's business, anyway?" I counter.

"He owned a quarter of Old San Juan."

"That's not business, that's investment. You don't want to tell me what he did?"

"Importer."

"Right. Maybe there were reasons for people to want to kill him."

"Oh, there were times even I had blood in my eyes for that man," Popi says instantly. "But nobody could get close enough to do it. He was obsessed with his safety. This didn't happen because of business."

"That's hard to believe."

"Believe it," he says, with another little flare of anger.

"Well, I don't have any information at all. I told you I only just met Kim."

"You certainly know more than you realize." And once again his doe's eyes lock with mine. "Besides, I didn't expect this, but I like you."

"Popi, *don't* flirt with me. It's really unnecessary."

"I don't mean it the way you think. I simply like you. I can talk to you."

I say lightly, "Journalists know how to listen." I stretch my legs out lengthwise along my seat, even though my head feels packed in ice and my hands are trembling. "If you want to quiz me about Kim, you've got to give me something first."

He nods. I wonder what in the world he thinks I can actually do for him.

"What can I offer you?" he asks.

"Tell me what your uncle was like."

And he speaks.

Rafe Nadal was the dark savior of his family—a fallen saint from a clan of proud, pure-blood blancitos who, for centuries, operated sugar mills. Restless Spaniards with a barbaric streak, the Nadals were one of many clans who emigrated and planted sugarcane in the early sixteenth century, and their crops multiplied until half a million tons of cane were being crushed each year. The stately white mills dotted rural Puerto Rico, built in the style of colonial homes—and in their vaulted, musty interiors the sugar lived a life of its own: stiff reeds smashed, spittle of juice running wet down wooden troughs, vats of cane juice percolating. And in every generation, each father showed his son the same little miracle: together they rode to the mill, and once inside he shook a drop of amber syrup onto a square of glass, fumbled for a magnifying lens in his pocket, and held it to his son's eye, so he could see the universe in a drop of sugar. The brown liquid spiked in crystals like a hard flower, and at its heart was a staff of rum.

Outside, the leftover husks of cane were heaped like rotten hay, and the odor of sugar—a fermented perfume—soaked the hills. Poor caneworkers lived in thatched-roof shacks patched with packing board, cardboard, Coca-Cola signs, and in the morning they tied the cuffs of their pants to their ankles with cords, hefted their machetes over their shoulders, and trudged into a sea of cane twice as tall as themselves. Their shirts hung loose and wet with sweat, and the sharp hairs of the cane pierced their necks and backs. At noon their women came with pots of hot taro root and fish broth. The congregation of pots hung on wire frames under a blistering sun. After harvest time came *el tiempo muerto,* the dead time, and to make money they bottled *cañita,* the little cane—white rum.

The landed aristocracy of Puerto Rico was, in its own way, gentle and easygoing. Life was celebrated with fiestas, horse races and lavish meals; fertility was prized, and the men left behind as many bastards as possible, hiring them as mill workers. Any occasion, from a wedding to the death of a child, was celebrated with a dance. In the evenings families gathered on wide porches to eat bowls of bread pudding washed down by *aguardiente.* It was a modest paradise—no palaces of Peru, no pyramids of Mexico—but when the men looked out into the warm night with its carpet of moonlight, they were pleased.

"I don't want to tell you the part of the story that my uncle always emphasized," says Popi now. "About the Americans coming, and how the Spanish gave us only machetes to fight American rifles, and how a long-lost relative of mine went running into the streets to meet the army with a whip, calling out the nickname of her husband, 'Tito Caliente.' My uncle had the whip framed in glass in his bedroom. It's a joke in our family, whenever we see somebody making a fool of themselves by fighting an impossible battle, we say 'Tito Caliente!' "

When American industry came to the island, oil refineries and factories replaced the sugar mills. Fish were poisoned, soil near the factories turned the color of ash, and men's hands were swollen from mercury poisoning. But the women no longer cooked over kerosene and charcoal in concrete kitchens. The streets of Ponce were paved. Hundreds of schools opened. The children learned English.

The Nadal clan decided to commit a kind of wild and celebratory suicide. They refused to sell their property, or to finance their dying mills with Northern money. Instead they ate, drank and partied. Let fate take them in the middle of a dance, breathless and proud. Then came a time when they realized they *had* to sell, but still they couldn't, because they loved their pride too much. The more status they lost, the more wonderful their pride became.

"I think," says Popi, "pride is an obsession with us. But it means self-respect. To honor yourself. It isn't arrogance, as you might think. We are an unusual family. Most Puerto Ricans are comfortable, not so proud."

And Rafe Nadal? Who knows what he was like as a child? No one talks about it. Something went wrong there, in his childhood.

His mother sent him to a monastery when he was eight. She died when he was eleven. He grew into a mulish, barrel-chested man with thick legs and black hairs bleeding down his back like an inkblot. The same hair inched down his arms and sprouted on his hands. He hated his hands; they were the beast in him. He used to whittle away at his nails with a double-edged razor, and he used to do it in front of people, but only because he hated his hands. Even as a young man he dressed exquisitely, in silk and linen, and his clothes gave him an almost monstrous elegance.

He believed in God, but a tormented God, a misanthropic deity who randomly picks off lives the way tourists shoot down metal ducks at a carnival.

He never married; he was always carrying on the search for a wife.

He kept horses—if you were poor in Puerto Rico, you kept them in homemade stalls as pets; if you were rich you boarded them in stables on the island or in America, and paid for jumping lessons for your children. A child trained in dressage could gain a foothold in the social web of America's prep schools. Nadal bought horses for his nieces and nephews.

He owned two ranches in the middle of the island, along its lush, volcanic spine. He liked things in pairs—he installed double nineteenth-century mirrors and double marble tubs in his San Juan bathroom. And he kept two sisters as servants. He'd found them in a public housing project when they were fourteen, and taken them from their roosters and pigs. The first week they worked for him he discovered one of them crouching on the toilet as if it were a hole in the ground. Why did her care and coarseness make him feel so tender? He never corrected her.

He lived in a sea-green house at the top of the old city, a few houses from a convent, overlooking La Perla, the ghetto that was practically in his front yard.

"Why did Nadal live so close to a ghetto?" I ask Popi.

"My uncle always said living right above La Perla was like standing behind a horse's tail, so if the horse kicks he doesn't really wallop you."

When the nuns sang, Nadal stood in the street throwing bits of chocolate to the pigeons. Popi watched him from the window as the flock settled around him, and Nadal stood there, head bent, silent, birds leaping and pecking at the pieces of chocolate melting in the sun. He only stood there when the sisters sang, and Popi knew he would rather be seen doing something foolish like feeding pigeons chocolate, than be discovered outside the convent listening to the sound of woman's love.

On Sunday mornings, instead of going to church, Nadal walked down into La Perla, when its streets were quiet and smelled of Clorox and frying sausages. He'd pass the cemetery, a crypt of white and gold. Horses tied to the gate. Chickens running free— they ate them at Christmas. Flowers tossed on fresh graves. Slabs of marble in the sun.

He'd walk to a yellow and rose *capilla,* and stand there while the wind blew through the open dome, waiting for a woman named Doña Nilda. She was a seer. She would come, a stunning black mountain of a woman in a homemade green caftan, wearing sapphire-flecked reading glasses.

After her sermon and prophecy, he'd follow her back to her small house at the top of a road. He'd enter a little foyer with a couch and two chairs, an orange curtain hanging. A boy taking a shower peeked out from behind a towel and giggled. And Doña Nilda would cook a meal in big aluminum pots. Rice, beans, sweet fried bananas and corned-beef hash. From the living-room couch he could see her bedroom, with plastic bottles of baby powder on the dresser, and an open closet rod where half a dozen dresses hung.

"Buen provecho? Buena?" she'd ask. She'd open beers and when they were empty she'd go to her little balcony and toss the cans into the street, like a bride tossing wedding garlands. "For the poor," she'd say, in complete innocence, as if she were not poor herself.

It was Doña Nilda who told him *La Americana* was coming, or so Nadal boasted to Katie, who later boasted to Popi. As Doña stood in the yellow *capilla* one morning, she closed her eyes and "saw" a woman kneeling in the sand at the bottom of La Perla, against a night sky, washing out bloody linen.

"Always one woman or another." Nadal shrugged.

Later that day, as he was waiting in the lobby of La Concha, Katie came in from the sea, and stood there shaking out her hair.

The first time Popi saw Katie was on a Friday evening. Until that evening no one in the family even knew a woman named Katie existed, but they did know Nadal was throwing *una fiesta* in the old style, to honor a mysterious friend. Guests were invited to dress in traditional costume. Two hundred friends and relatives showed up, and every room in the green house on the hill was lit—except the courtyard inside, which was purposely left dark.

Nadal had picked Katie up as usual in a limousine; she wore a simple t-shirt dress and her brown shoulder-length hair was pulled back in a ponytail. A smudge of orange lipstick and a faint sunburn brightened her cheeks, rendering her hard face almost beautiful. Instead of escorting her to dinner, Nadal brought her to his house, and she said frankly, "You've got the wrong idea. I'm not fucking you, Señor Nadal. Not tonight or ever." He laughed and he led her past the gates, through the wide rooms with their beamed ceilings and slow-whispering wooden fans, into the inner court-yard, where candlelight flickered in the darkness. And she looked up into the cavern of space, at the night sky above, and saw faces peering out of the dark, on every floor.

Following the old Creole tradition, the guests had circled the staircase that wound around the four-story courtyard; they filled the steps and balconies. Katie stared up at them, her small mouth half open, as Nadal walked around the dark courtyard, lighting glass-enclosed candles. Musicians began to shake their maracas and gourds, and song ballooned around her. Everybody sang along. Everybody, that is, but Popi. He stood staring down at this girl— *Americana! Coño!*—His uncle always called them silly little canaries!—this girl in a green dress and sandals. How old was she anyway? From his vantage she didn't look more than seventeen.

And yet he saw something surprising in her face. His fingers brushing the balcony railing, he descended the stairs to take another look. Yes, it was there. A tropical *dolor* he'd seen only in the heavy-lidded eyes of Latin women. It was a sensual sorrow, gloomy and irrevocable, made of the monotony of island life. The dolor of the old man who sits on the plaza and from time to time sings his song of death: *The people laugh, and dance with joy. I drink a little beer, and if there is a guitar I play it. I get a dime, I spend it on cards. I may win or lose, but the way of life is easy and it loves me. But wait. Enough of poetry, for tomorrow they bury me.*

"You want to know what they were like, those two lovebirds?" Popi asks, stirring milk into a fresh cup of coffee.

I nod.

"Typical," he says shortly. "*El blancito y la Americana.* After all those years of cramming Spanish pride down my throat, he went for an American. It's so simple and stupid. The Puerto Rican male wants a lady who is a shade lighter than himself. Look at me, for example, compared to you I'm dark, right?—"

"—Dusky."

"But in Puerto Rico I'm considered transparent. I'm so white you can't see me! And so was my uncle." Popi shrugs. "He had no choice but an American." Popi starts to laugh. "You see what I mean?"

"No. It sounds like he went against all his instincts."

"That's funny, very, very funny. She represented nothing but instinct to him."

When the guests were done singing, they began to chant the word "danza." The lady must dance. And the old tradition, of course, was that her man danced in one place, legs rising and falling like jackhammers, while she herself made love to the whole floor. Dance was a woman's way of showing love.

That night most of the men tried to prove their admiration for Katie, and finally one had the courage to remove his hat and put it on her head as she danced. By the end of the evening, Katie had so many hats that she was carrying them in her hands and under her arms, until there were only two she hadn't obtained: Nadal's, because he wasn't wearing one, and Popi's, because he didn't dare.

That night Popi thought to himself, "These men have the eyes of fish who have been frozen, all they can do is look at her. I will be something else to *la Americana*. I will become her friend."

Popi looks at me now. "I became her friend. It was simple. And that's why, when I had to tell her to leave, I thought I would break." He pauses, and says softly, "I didn't break. I carried it off quite well. Not a drop of tenderness."

"I don't understand—why did you tell her to go?"

"I was my uncle's messenger. My uncle wanted her to go."

I can't help laughing in bewilderment and contempt. "Come on. He loved her. Why did she go?"

"I'm utterly exhausted. I'm not usually such an eager storyteller. I think I'll stop now."

"Why?"

"I told you, I'm exhausted. Like a man after a night of love."

"I have one more question."

He stares at me. And yet the cold fury I was afraid I might tap—the fury of a liar, or a killer—is not there: his eyes simply smolder. He looks hurt and tired.

"You asked about my uncle, and I told you."

"But just one more question."

"What's that?"

"He never loved another woman besides Katie?"

Popi folds his hands on the table. "Always there is one love when you're young. Isn't that what they say?"

I flush. "I never had one."

"It wasn't easy for my uncle to love," Popi says. "He did it against his will, and so it took everything out of him."

"But he threw Katie out?"

Popi nods.

"And you know why?"

"Yes, but you can't expect me to tell you everything."

"All right, you've been more than fair, you've been wonderful, in fact. What do you want from me?" I ask gently.

He shrugs, spreads his hands. "Whatever you have to give."

I smile just a little. "You make it sound romantic, Popi."

But I find myself leaning close to him across the scarred formica table, almost like a woman longing to be seduced. Under the fluorescent glare—stirring a cheap spoon in my cup of tea, trying to ignore two Columbia University students discussing computers at the next table—I give him the poetry of Kim: tell him how little I know of the man, and yet how blighted and strong his face first looked. I tell him Kim came to me for release from some unendurable secret, and I don't know what the secret is. I know none of his secrets. Neither, I think, does his friend Cheeks—but Cheeks is scared. I had dinner with Cheeks and Kim, and what I saw was an easy, loose and lucky man struggling with suspicion and fear.

What's the secret Kim carries? It could be murder. I think maybe it is murder. For instance, he cries out in his sleep sometimes, not a cry of guilt or shame, but simply bewildered pain. I think I know why he cries. I think he's the kind of man who was born innocent, innocent enough that life never should have led him to murder. And out of his innocence he loved something, and surprised himself because he was able to love it completely. And it turned out that thing was evil. Then he had no choice: he had become that thing, it was part of him.

"What was it he loved?"

"He loved Katie. It's just a guess, but—"

"She's not evil," Popi says flatly.

"I don't know. Maybe she is. Let's say Kim killed your uncle. Do you think she put him up to it?"

"They would have left together," Popi says instantly. "But she stayed behind."

"She called him a few weeks ago."

"He told you?"

"Not exactly. I overheard him telling Cheeks."

"What were they saying?"

"I only overheard him mention the call. That she'd found him.

That he didn't think she'd come up here. She wouldn't like New York City."

"She wouldn't," says Popi, sitting up straight and pushing his coffee cup away. "So, he still loves her."

"Popi, are you planning to take revenge? I mean, in some old-fashioned Latin sense of the word?"

He shakes his head. "I need to talk to Katie," he says. "Where could she have gone?"

"Why didn't you talk to her before?"

"She gave me the slip."

We're silent for a few moments, then he says, "Help me."

I'm already ahead of him. "You want me to tell Kim I saw you, right? Shake him up a little. You need to buy time because you don't really want to hurt anybody. I know. And I'd help you, Popi, I really would, because why should I be loyal to him? It isn't me he loves. Except the thing is, I think if I see him again something stupid will happen like my heart will break. I don't want to look at his face again knowing what I know. I'm going back to my books and my writing. I mean, my hands are dirty enough—" I notice that I'm crying, but I don't care, in fact I think it's making Popi like me more, and even in my heartsick fury I can feel the flutter of vanity. "I'm finished with him, Popi. I slept with him for a few weeks and that's all I want to remember."

I slept with him. It was a gorgeous mistake. It's over.

"I understand," says Popi a moment later. "In case you need me, I'm staying at the Royalton."

I barely have time to nod to him; I'm pushing myself away from the vinyl seat and moving out the door, moving in a rage, like an orphan headed nowhere.

EIGHTEEN

I open the door for the man I love. He's beautiful and his beauty is my cure, the first I've ever had, the last I'll ever need. It's night and he has brought his friend along. He sits between us without vanity, sits between us almost unconscious of himself.

They've come straight from work and their jeans and flannel shirts are streaked with grime. I called him at his factory this morning and demanded he come as soon as possible.

"I've met someone who told me about you," I said.

"I'll be there," he answered.

His friend promises to stay for only a few minutes. Now the two men are joking and I don't say a word to José. I don't remember why I begin to run both hands down his leg and up under his jeans, but I feel a knife, a shiv, strapped to his calf above his ankle.

"Stop."

"Let me feel it."

"Lynn—"

"Let me see."

I shove the jeans up, an accordion of cloth, and

close my hand on a leather sheaf strapped snugly against his skin. I kneel. My hand stays there. Neither of us is surprised. Kim leans back and looks down as if I'm blowing him and he's slightly bored but curious and maybe in a few minutes he'll get into it, and his friend watches. I unsnap the sheath and pull the knife out.

"It smells like your cologne," I say.

"Keep it," he says. "I don't need it."

Soon his friend goes. I unbuckle the leather casing and lay knife and sheath on the table. They don't frighten me. I almost think he wore it on purpose, because he knows what I'm going to say. I won't see him after tonight, but for now I'll tell him what I know.

NINETEEN

"So you tell *me*," Kim says, watching me cross my legs Indian-style. I've retreated to the far corner of my couch, and he's in a chair. "Why are you sitting here with a man who's killed somebody?"

"Well, did you? That's what I'm asking."

"You already seem to know."

"I can't believe you're saying that."

"If you didn't believe it would you have called me at work at seven this morning?"

"I tried to call last night. What did you do last night, anyway?"

"I don't want you mixed up in this, Lynn," he says.

I'm silent for a moment, head lowered, pulling at the cotton cowl of my sweater. I'm wearing no makeup except reddish-brown lipstick smeared sloppily over my mouth, but I don't care.

"You shouldn't have ever laid a finger on me," I say grimly. "And you shouldn't have stood me up last night. You gave Popi his chance."

I face him now, and feel a strange shock of pleasure at my strength. Doesn't he like it? There's a quiet thrill in being searched like this.

He submits to me, half-curious, half-hardened against my stare. I can't really violate him. You can unravel a man for a lifetime and still not loosen the knot of his mystery. But as I look he bends forward a little, unconsciously, as if to assist me, as if he were a maze of tunnels in a miner's shaft. With the lamp of my gaze I'm crawling to him.

"Your curiosity's going to hang you," he says suddenly, and the spell is broken.

"Look," I tell him, "I know Popi left out a lot of the story."

"I have nothing to say."

"Yes you do, or you'd walk out. I don't know you well but I know that much."

"I didn't kill anybody. And if I did kill somebody, there's no point in asking questions."

"Then there's no point in my seeing you."

"That's probably true."

I frown. The phone rings but I don't move. "What could make you joke like this?"

"Only callousness," he says.

"Would you hurt me?"

"I doubt it."

"If you thought it was necessary?"

"Maybe." Then he shakes his head in exasperation. "What kind of answers do you expect? I'm not going to say anything you might tell Popi."

"What—I'm getting this information for Popi?" I say incredulously.

"For yourself, then."

"Yeah, and the magazines I write for are really interested in a drug blowout in the Caribbean. You're just a guy I was sleeping with. That's what I told Popi."

"I wouldn't trust a woman who asks as many questions as you. Neither would Popi."

"He told me much more than he needed to."

"You shouldn't be talking to either one of us," he says almost absently, and walks to the window. "I guess he has me on twenty-four-hour watch now."

"You're glad he's come, aren't you?" I ask incredulously.

He shakes his head, but with a certain hesitancy.

"Look at me."

"I'm looking at you."

"Kim, you wanted me to know from the start."

"I don't need that kind of company. I never wanted you to be part of this."

I laugh.

"You were my refuge," he says. "I thought of you as the place I could go and forget."

"Just what I always wanted."

"I told you that night in my room," he reminds me.

I look at him blankly. "But that's not what you've done. You've tried to wash your hands in me. I'm part of it now. And it could have been anybody. Any woman."

"It was you," he protests, his voice harsh, and reaches for a brandy snifter on the table. I filled it earlier, but neither of us drank. Now his hand, grasping the glass, knocks it accidentally to the floor.

"Oh great," I say.

He crouches and moves his hand over the fragments of glass, as if his flesh could magnetize them, retrieving each shard, even the little seeds wedged in the floorboards. Kim pours the glass from his hand into an ashtray, and for some reason it reminds me of William Burroughs, who killed his wife, and I tell Kim about it. One day at a party Joan Burroughs put a wine glass on her head and lowered her arms and her husband went into the bedroom to get his gun. They were playing *William Tell*. He missed the glass and shot her through the head.

"Was he convicted?" Kim inquires in an even tone.

"They were living down in Mexico and nobody investigated. But the important part is it made a writer out of him. That's when he started to write novels. Rich as nightmares. I wonder how much he suffered over her. She was drinking herself to death. Maybe she wanted to die."

He says nothing.

"Do you think it was a mercy killing?"

"There's no such thing," Kim says. "What could—"

I'm sitting forward on the edge of the couch with knees pressed together and hands on my knees, biting my lower lip, with a kind of palpitating emotion.

"What could—" he continues.

"What could. What could. What could what?"

"What could make you compare me to him—Burroughs?"

This man, this room, this moment, has taken on a hallucinatory purity, and I'm beating with my own animal strength—I feel like a woman who's about to lift a diesel truck.

"Tell me who killed Popi's uncle."

"You think it was me."

"Tell me."

"That I'm the one who did it?"

I nod.

"Isn't the possibility that I did something enough?"

"I want to hear it in your voice. It's my only way out."

"Out of what?"

"Us. This. Oh, I know, there's not much of an 'us' yet, but . . ."

"You want out?"

We face each other openly now. "Remember a few weeks ago? When I thought for a second maybe you'd killed somebody. Remember?"

He's silent for a moment. "You're perceptive."

"Shouldn't I be afraid of you?"

"Probably."

"Should I stop seeing you?"

"I don't want you to." He leans against the wall, closes his eyes. Agony of indecision makes his legs buckle slightly.

Now he stands before me, hands hanging at his sides, feet planted a few inches apart. A penitent. And then, almost imperceptibly, he nods.

"Yes?" I murmur.

"I killed somebody," he says slowly, practicing the words.

Killed a man, he tells me.

TWENTY

Shot him in a clear kiln of summer light. And shot him again, too. His head sort of stuttered, snapping forward and back as if he were falling asleep in public. He was dying, and he fell with a thump, a sickening whonk, on the paving stones of his court-yard. Dying, and he reached up his hands and asked me to move him against the wall. Under the shade of the banana tree. He didn't like the idea of his corpse cooking in the sun?—or was it some foolish attempt at dignity?—death would find him sitting here, just so, under the tree, just so.

His arms went around Kim, warm and loose and unbelievably heavy, like a sleeping bear's. He seemed twice as big then, and Kim hauled him over to the wall, propped him there, and held his head until he was gone. He asked only that Kim look at him. It was like a lover's stare.

And he looks down at me, and I don't tell him to go. I don't tell him to go. He sees that I want something from him.

"Why?" I ask.

TWENTY-ONE

Because his whole life seems filtered through the dark glass that is Katie. He remembers her sitting cross-legged in a church courtyard on San Sebastian. First date. He'd asked her to meet him there, planning to take her across the street for a drink at Amadeus, a restaurant with ceiling fans and open windows. He describes it in simple, groping sentences, and I can feel the languor of San Juan: the easy informality of the place, the way local men kiss their women's cheeks in greeting, the croissants wedged with melted Brie and served with tangy guava butter.

He had told Katie to meet him at six, but he was delayed and arrived forty minutes late, hair still wet from a cold shower, spattering droplets of water across his starched shirt. She didn't budge from her spot, didn't even acknowledge the steel-gray Jaguar. He started to open the door and call to her, thought better of it, parked and got out. The heat hit him like a wall.

When he approached he saw she was crying from pure frustration, her scoop neck t-shirt was drenched with sweat, clinging to an indecently beautiful body. Katie was tough, muscular and sensual, she looked like a deliciously fuckable tomboy. Her thick reddish hair was cropped in a blunt cut at the shoulders; she had heavy-lidded eyes and a small, full mouth. He'd met her the week before—she'd come on to him at a beach party in a way he'd liked but hadn't thought much about. She'd given him the number of the print shop where she worked in Old San Juan. Almost as an afterthought he'd called her.

She couldn't—or wouldn't—stop crying. She just stood there on the plaza, rubbing tears from her face with her fists. She didn't pretend her weeping fit was all his doing; apparently he was the last straw in a long day of disappointments.

"Let's get you home and changed into something dry. And then—"

She gave him a hostile glare. "Who says we're still going out?"

"I don't think you have a choice. I could never leave you like this."

She said nothing, but greedy pleasure tightened her mouth. He saw her wondering how far she could push him now, this stranger who'd almost stood her up. He watched her hesitating, saw her eyelids go heavy, sleepy. Suddenly he decided he'd give her everything she wanted, at least for tonight.

"If you're up to an adventure," he continued, running his thumb down the slippery nape of her neck, "we'll drive to my favorite restaurant for dinner."

Her mood lifted a bit. "Which one?"

"Su Casa."

"At El Dorado? You're a member?"

He nodded. "We can swing by your place first, if you want to change."

She was quiet on the long ride out, quiet as they drove into the resort, with its vast lawns, and its nets of hanging vines. But she agreed to walk on the beach before dinner. Of all the beaches in Puerto Rico, Dorado's were the most primitive, where sea smashed into breakers of volcanic rock before it lapped the shore. Katie hitched up her skirt, tugged off her shoes, and ran on the wet rocks. "Come on, get me," she kept yelling at the waves, but she stayed out of their reach. And then it began to rain, one of those torrential rains where people were shouting, *"La lluvia, la lluvia!"*, and Katie stopped running. She lifted her face. "Oh shit, shit, shit!" But she was laughing.

"You wanted to be soaked," said Kim, as they stood under the umbrella at an outdoor table and waited for the storm to pass.

"I did. I was."

And she tilted her head and stared at him so provocatively that it knocked the air out of him. That night they stayed in a beachfront suite, and sometime in the night he woke to find her masturbating next to him. He started to say something and she put her hand to his face and slid her fingers over his mouth so he could smell her.

"Why were you doing that?" he asked.

"I dunno. I was turned on before. I couldn't sleep and I didn't want to wake you, at least not until morning."

"You wanted to wake me," he said. "You want me to watch you make yourself come."

"And if I do that?"

"How fast can you be?"

"With you watching?" She grinned. "Medium fast. Why?"

"I'm not sure I want to wait."

There was no tenderness between them then, though the whole bed floated in moonlight. Katie touched herself. It took a long time. Kim had given her everything she wanted that night, trying to prove something to her that he hardly understood himself, and now she was rebelling. *Nobody owns me.* And he reached down with his own hand to stop her.

Katie lived in a loft on a tree-bowered street named Calle de Caleta. They spent mornings on her roof drinking café con leche and listening to Spanish guitar. She told him how the summer she turned twelve it was so hot in Galveston that she and her friends took turns standing on a footstool and licking cottony ice from the freezer in her kitchen. Katie stayed too long with her mouth pressed eagerly against the roof of the icebox, and the ice fastened to her lower lip so that she began to scream and tore the skin trying to get free. "It was awful, but then I got a great big blister," she told Kim, "and I was tickled, I was so proud."

"And you went back and did it again."

She flashed a triumphant smile. "I had to. One morning I woke up and there was this crust on my mouth and chin because the blister had popped in the night. So I stuck my mouth up on the ice again to make it come back, but that was only for my cousin Liza who was coming that week. I had to have something to show her," she finished in her throaty tenor and rubbed her heel against his thigh. "But aren't you a smart boy to figure it out."

He said what he was thinking, as he often did with Katie. "We've spent every night together for the last—what is it—five weeks? You're practically transparent."

"Don't get cocky," she said in her rough, flirtatious tone. "The next summer I outdid them all, anyway. I shaved my head. I told them it was to keep cool. Liza was devastated. I'd really trounced her! There was no way she could outdo me." Katie laughed. "I ruined August for the local boys. They were damned if they were going to woo a bald-headed tomboy."

In their first months together, she took Kim every Sunday to El Parque de las Palomas, Park of the Doves, a cobblestone courtyard a few blocks from her apartment. Pigeons nested there in the honeycombed ancient walls, and swarmed in a beelike mass on the ground. She'd buy a brown bag of corn for a quarter, and toss it like a tourist while the birds flew toward her, so dense and powerful they stirred up a genuine wind and her hair whipped across her face. Then she knelt in front of a small chapel outside the park, built in the 1700s, and prayed. Kim watched cruise ships docked half a mile away, hands in his pockets, ear tuned to catch her plea. It was always the same: she prayed to be lifted out of pain.

"You're unhappy?" he asked once after her prayer. They were eating at an outdoor café whose tables were set in the middle of a quiet street. He'd ordered a croissant, and she'd ordered coffee cake with walnuts and raisins, explaining that she needed food with lots of surprises.

"Who said I'm unhappy?" she retorted.

"Just a question."

"Hey," she protested, "this is the easy life down here. Who'd have the balls to be unhappy? When I first came I was a rebel and an exile but no longer. I'm head over heels for this place." Then she sighed. "Anyway, you know why I came."

Her family had left Galveston when she was thirteen, moved north to Boston, and the next winter she contracted a cyclical form of arthritis. Every winter it flared. "I used to pretend my bones were joined by red hot coals, and I'd keep trying to pull the coals out with my bare hands, but they'd be too soft and break off and then the pain would go into my hands, too." She'd paused, added with grim pride, "The doctor said a warm climate would help. I decided why not leave the whole country behind. I wanted to cut my life off like a bad arm, and I did, and Christ I was proud of myself, but you know how they say an amputated arm aches? Well, I ached for my old life. I always seem to be aching for something."

"I can make you happy," he replied, and then seemed astonished at his offer.

"You're not the first who's tried," she said. "Maybe I enjoy being a malcontent. Besides, happy people are the ones who expect nothing, Kim. Don't you have expectations?"

"No, I have absolute certainties."

Her eyes narrowed, and she leaned forward and said in a smoky voice, "Such as?"

He looked down at the cast-iron café table where they sat, and without thinking lifted the jelly glasses, printed with Daffy Duck, in which they'd been served ice water. "These glasses," he said, clicking them together, "painted green and yellow, and which used to be filled with mint jelly, which is the worst-tasting green muck in the world, these glasses are my morning's absolute certainty."

He set the glasses down and instantly her hands closed around them both.

"You silly boy." She was laughing. "You want to make me happy, huh? Then you're going to have to steal these for me."

"What for?"

"Now that I know they're one of your absolute certainties, I'm going to display them on the mantel in my front hallway."

"I've got another absolute certainty," he said, finding her hand under the table.

And she smiled. "Kim," she said suddenly, "when I was fifteen I used to sneak out in the middle of the night and play basketball at the high school in the dark with my friend Sarah. So dark we didn't know *where* the fucking ball was going. It was fantastic. Will you do that with me tonight?"

"Yes," he said.

That was when he began to love her. She stirred in him a sweet and futile instinct, a soul-lust, almost—to be her keeper. The calling of those who have no calling.

* * *

When he was first dating Katie, Kim divided his time between her city loft and his rented house in Condado. In the mornings he'd drop her off at work, though she usually insisted on stopping first at a bodega that sold sodas and beer. A noisy metal fan was propped in the corner, and men leaned on the worn wooden counter smoking. Katie would buy a six-pack of root beer and a bag of ice. She would hug the ice to her chest and nuzzle her cheek against the plastic. "I have a thing about ice," she'd remind him. Once she ripped open the bag (he had never seen her open any bag by loosening the tie), wrested a few cubes from its bulk, and lifted her arms, rubbing the cubes against her armpits. Water dribbled into her shirt. He licked her, tasting water and the shaved stubble of her skin.

In the early evening he'd pick her up at the print shop. The shop was warm with light, and the shouts of the street rolled in as she smoothed one last print flat on wax paper and matted it on cardboard. They'd wander down the roads of Old San Juan, narrow roads built to fit Spanish colonial carriages, stopping finally at Amadeus. When they left, it was late, and a crisp moon lay like a disc of white paper in the sky. Under cover of darkness the island frogs called to each other in their two-note song, co-qui, co-qui. And it seemed, as he walked the streets with Katie, that all of life wanted only to hear and be heard.

He'd sleep, but wake before dawn, turning to feel the muscle of her leg or buttock. In his bed she seemed a primordial animal— most dangerous when asleep, when its limbs go soft and doughy. At first his touch woke her and they'd make love, but once she became accustomed to him his fingers drove her deeper into what seemed a dreamless sleep. He'd watch her eyelids and they didn't make the spasmodic flutters of the dreamer. They were thick and still, those covered eyes.

"You're taming me, you bastard," she said. "I'm gonna leave you before you rub the spark out of me."

"Nobody could do that."

"Don't you know one person has to be sacrificed for love to survive?"

* * *

Kim tells me he knew Nadal through Katie's stories. According to Katie, Nadal despised America. His hundred-mile-long island was a country of its own. All the island's miracles, its massive spine of volcanic mountains, thirty thousand acres of tropical forest, hot springs and night-blooming orchids, subterranean caves, carved colonial city—all this Nadal called his *patria*. "I am born an American citizen," he said. "Now I ask you, what about me is American? I have no voice in your world. You don't count my vote. You order me to fight your wars. Now I know what you're going to say. My people welcomed you. Yes," he concluded bitterly, "we ran to meet our chains. Every day we're more American."

"What would make you happy, Rafe?" Katie asked him.

"To have been born centuries ago," he answered.

"He *was* like a man from a different time," Katie told Kim in bewilderment, as if that could explain Nadal's change of heart, why he had spit her out.

Katie had met Nadal by accident. She told Kim he'd asked her out a few minutes after he first saw her in the lobby of La Concha.

"I've got a fiancé," she said, watching Nadal's colleague, whose smile was frozen on his face.

"Will he mind?" Nadal asked.

"Will you get the wrong idea if he doesn't find out?"

"Where is he now?"

"He'll work until sundown." She hesitated, and then said bluntly, "Are you two looking for sex? You like to fuck Anglo women or something?"

Nadal didn't laugh, as she expected him to. He answered seriously, "I'm breaking my rules for you. I never date American girls."

"I'm always in the mood for breaking rules," she echoed.

At first Katie felt no desire for her Puerto Rican suitor—she always insisted afterward that he wasn't her type, she liked men as smooth as hard apples, and he was massive, fleshy—but she continued to accept his dinner invitations. In each restaurant he was treated with a solemn politeness he hardly seemed to notice. Katie was intrigued. Two or three times a week she walked to La Concha, where Nadal picked her up in his limousine. She was home by midnight. Then in the third week something happened that made her want him physically. She later told Kim that things just changed, but never explained why.

For a time she was moody and displayed an uncharacteristic sloppiness, dropping clothes on the floor, misplacing her keys, cooking dinner and forgetting it midway through the recipe, so that Kim would come home to find a cold stew diced with raw meat. She banged into things. In her sleep she twisted away from him. Kim kept a fixed course, working, eating, sleeping, waiting for the tumult to subside. One Thursday night she finally cracked. She came into the room where Kim was reading, stood by the bureau and ran her thumb around the lip of one of the jelly glasses he'd stolen from the restaurant. Suddenly her face crumpled and she threw the glass at the wall over his head. It shattered.

"I thought maybe that would catch your attention," she said.

"You have my attention."

"Then you've noticed how I'm going out of my mind?" She added, half-aloud, "I can't believe I did that. I loved those glasses. Well, there's still one left."

"Why did you smash it?"

"It was irresistible."

"What *is* going on, Katie?" As soon as he asked her he was sorry. He'd broken his rule of careful waiting.

"You want me to tell you?"

He closed his eyes. "Yes, I do," he said finally.

A moment later she was at his feet, legs crossed, hands twisting and untwisting, as she let her sins spill out, and then, mortified and belligerent, announced she was leaving.

"I've done some checking on Raphael Nadal," Kim told her a week later, the night she split. She was dumping her drawers into suitcases, literally turning the drawers upside down so that perfume, clothing and papers tumbled out, and when her set of stout tweed luggage was stuffed full, she came back with garbage bags from the kitchen, pulling blouses and dresses off hangers and shoving them into the bags. "He's a drug dealer," Kim announced.

"You think you're telling me something I don't know?"

"He has the slickest operation on the island. That's the kind of man you lose your head over?"

"If I want to destroy myself I'll fucking well destroy myself, all on my own without any advice from you."

He watched her pour a handful of prescription bottles on the bed and go through them one by one, packing Valium and codeine and Dilantin, discarding aspirin and antibiotics. The empty bottles clattered on the floor. And as he watched, a new feeling beat in him. Somehow he found himself fascinated by the sheer betrayal he was witnessing. It was a ghoulish fascination, the kind an army cadet might feel if his leg was blown away by shrapnel and he happened to look down at the bone and blood before he lost consciousness.

"Anyway," Katie was saying, sullen and a little uncertain, "you don't understand. It's just a business. Like any other business." She bit her lip and for a moment looked miserable. "Shit. I don't know how to do this at all. I don't know how to do it with lies or how to do it nice and easy. I'm fucking this up totally and I don't want us to end like this. Goddammit, Kim, couldn't you go out or something? Do you have to watch me down to the last minute?"

"You'll be back," he said suddenly, surprised that he could say it, and a minute later he left the house, the screen door banging lightly behind him. He glanced through the window once before heading toward the beach and saw her standing in the bedroom, clutching a bundle of brassieres. She looked terrified. It was the last he'd see of her for nine weeks.

Katie returned as tired as a person who has been physically ill for years and finally gives up the fight. She didn't talk about the fact that her life was in danger. She talked about the man, Nadal. She told Kim how she'd come down one morning in a cream silk sleepshirt, and found Nadal eating fruit in the sun. Soon they were laughing and they started to wrestle, and he began smashing berries against her shirt, with a kind of violent sensuality. He was slow, hypnotized, grinding the smashed skins into her shirt. "I was laughing. I couldn't stop laughing. I felt so free." She told Kim how Nadal had taken her down into La Perla in a silver Lamborghini. They walked on *la calle mas caliente,* the hot street, and stopped at a sea-green house like his own, except it was sheathed in battered tin. Just inside the door a young man in a black satin tuxedo stood guard. Inside were marble rooms, skylights, and an indoor pool. They went out the back door and she followed him along crooked steps, where sewer piping was laid as a banister, down to a shack by the sea. There she'd witnessed a drug murder; when the shots burst she'd pulled off her high heels and run barefoot, screaming, up the slum's streets until she reached the city. She'd wandered for hours, shivering and crying in the heat, and that night when she came back to Nadal's house the gates were locked. She banged until his nephew Popi appeared, and he stood on the cobblestone steps, and refused to let her inside. He kept shaking his head. *"¡Vaya! Vaya o él va a matarlo."* Go or he'll kill you. "But why? I came back. Tell him I lost my head, but it's okay now." "Go," said Popi. "He made a mistake, and now he's through with you."

Kim took Katie back, though not as a lover. She lay around for days without eating and then one morning she got into her car and drove to Río Piedras to see a Puerto Rican *bruja,* a *curandera.* She came home with a bag of herbs and roots that she simmered in a cast-iron pot until the house stank; she drank it and a few hours later got sick. She lay on the floor wailing, said her skin was peeling and she could feel blood burning in her throat. Kim held her most of the night, drifting in and out of sleep. Once, in a forgetful moment, he moved his hands sensuously down her stomach. She rolled away and began to hit herself, and he pinned her wrists down to make her stop.

"It hurts when you touch me," she cried, indignant and bitter. And he thought to himself: that's the only time I've hurt her. She must have been frightened by the defeat in his face, because suddenly she grinned cruelly. "Nadal held me down like this."

He let her wrists go. She lay there watching him, the brief brightness of her malice flickering back to pain.

The next day Katie went back to the *bruja,* but the woman refused to give her an antidote. Katie was dying of grief, she said. The only hope was poison, since maybe one poison could chase another out of the body.

Was that when he became a murderer? While he stood in his quiet room on his quiet street, where white houses gleamed in the tropical night? Or was it many weeks later, after the threats from Nadal?

Two weeks after Katie came back, they heard someone moving in the house, and a spray of bullets went singing through the plaster wall of their bedroom. A bullet had lodged in a leather recliner; Kim dug it out. "Hollow point. Does more damage," he commented, and explained how a hollow point explodes into the body and why it was illegal. "They weren't trying to kill us just now," he said. "Just trying to scare us."

"It's his way. He'll drive us to the breaking point, and then he'll kill us." Katie lowered her head, and added dully, "Oh, who knows. Maybe he won't. Maybe he can't decide."

It seemed they were under siege. A week later four men came to the door while Katie was taking the dog for a beach run; two of the men held Kim down, pinning his arms across his chest, while the other two put him in a restraining blanket, a plastic sleeping bag tight as a vise. They left him. He tried to move and movement tightened the bag painfully; the material was so thick and poreless that the bag roasted him. His heart began to skitter. He couldn't catch his breath. He reeked of sweat. It was incredible—his own body heat was destroying him. Just as he began to believe the four men had gone after Katie she walked in the door; it took twenty minutes to free him and he gasped as he rolled his head against the floor.

He went to the police, but they put him off. Nadal, he soon inferred, was tight with local cops, and the city government. He took Katie to Saint Thomas for the weekend but as they were disembarking from the small plane, a young Puerto Rican with the soft eyes of a deer nodded at her. "That was Popi," she whispered to Kim.

"If they're following us, then we're probably safer at home." Nonetheless, he moved Katie to a condominium in Isla Verde, with a view of supermarkets and high rises; he told her it was to keep her safe, that maybe Nadal would think they'd split up. Was that the moment his whole being shifted from wanderer to murderer?

Or did he change on the day when he called her at the condo and she didn't say hello, simply, "Is it you?"

"Who else would it be?"

There was a pause.

"I don't know," she said tiredly. He could hear the falsehood in her voice. "I was half-asleep," she lied, "dreaming I was a regular person who could get phone calls from friends."

For the first time he understood that Katie might be stupid enough to give Nadal her phone number. He hired a retired Puerto Rican chauffeur to watch her, and the man reported that she'd left work at noon and sat on a bench near a group of old men playing checkers.

"At the top of the old city?" Kim asked him, "Near the entrance to La Perla?"

"Sí, acá. It look like the lady waiting for something. But nobody come, and she finally gone home."

Kim didn't buy a gun until a chance meeting with Popi. Coming into his house the back way one afternoon, he paused before the sliding glass doors: there, in his bedroom, a pale, dark-haired youth knelt, twisting two copper wires. He was planting a bug. His face was solemn with concentration.

Kim half-expected him to pull out a gun or knife, but instead the boy got slowly to his feet. His silk shirt hung loose on a slender frame. Finally Kim slid the door open.

"Are you one of Nadal's lackeys?"

"He is my uncle," the youth replied in perfect English.

"Katie's not living here anymore. Why does Rafe Nadal care what I mutter to myself alone in my bedroom every night?"

Popi thought. "He is obsessed," he said finally, and though he shrugged, all that was unsaid showed in his face: how he feared more than loved his uncle, and obeyed him reluctantly. "He can hardly think about his business, it doesn't interest him anymore. Only this. He thinks of a thousand different ways to kill her."

So Kim bought the gun and sat in his yard, turning it in his hands in the midday sun.

TWENTY-TWO

Murderer, you call yourself, the sound succulent and hideous. You're pacing back and forth and saying once more that you did it out of love, maybe out of need. And then you say, "But the good in it, nobody knows. There was good in it."

And you stand there, your story told; head curled, shoulders rounded, like an animal dying out of its natural habitat.

You can't bring yourself to leave. I can't bring myself to touch you.

TWENTY-THREE

"So why didn't you just leave her to her fate?"

"I won't even answer that."

"If he intended to kill her he would have," I protest.

"You didn't live through it, Lynn."

"You said she sat outside his house. No woman would actually sit outside the house of somebody who was getting ready to kill her."

"She was in love."

"Even love draws a line."

"She hadn't drawn it yet."

"Kim, don't use love as an excuse. How many love affairs end up in murder?"

"I'm not making excuses for myself. But Katie . . . she was like a little kid with her fists in the air."

As if to prove it, you tell me how Katie was once attacked in Old San Juan. Something about her insolent walk infuriated a drunk in a doorway. He came after her, and instead of running into a store or bar, she turned and insulted him. When he grabbed her, Katie put her hand through a window, breaking off a spear of glass and jabbing it into his arm. She was holding the glass so tightly it gouged her fingers. "She called me, I took her to the hospital, and there were about twenty people ahead of her in the emergency room. But she told the doctor she was a concert pianist and he had to save her hand. He did, too. He worked on that hand with the care of a heart surgeon." It was a triumph, you explain, and she would have lived that night all over again.

"Does she know what you did?"

"I'll never let her know."

"You're still protecting her."

"No," you say in a weary voice, "I'm protecting myself."

"I don't get it."

"From Katie's eternal wrath." And you smile a little, as if that wrath was something that once pleased you.

"I care very much for her, I want to say as a friend, but I really don't like her. It's all in the heart."

"You want her back."

"There was a time when she had this incredible hold on me. Now I feel sorry for her. She's like a sister to me more than anything."

I used to picture a boa constrictor wrapped around my heart. It fed on the sterile core of me. I might have slowly died, but you reached me. Was it just your body?

Now you say it as if you were puzzled. "Murderer. Why did she love a murderer?"

"You mean Katie?"

"Why did she love him?"

"What did Nadal do?"

"I told you. A wholesaler. Cocaine."

Your gaze moves slowly, with the effort of someone deeply drugged. It sweeps the room slowly, and rests at last on me. "Do I look different to you now?"

"Yes."

"You could never make love to me now."

"Maybe I could."

"I wouldn't even want to."

* * *

I lie on the bed. "Go ahead," I say.

You undress me like someone walking the plank. As if I'm going to shame you. I want to.

"What's this?" You turn from the open drawer of my nighttable, foil packets of condoms in one hand, Xeroxed pictures of Katie in the other. I'd taken them out last night, and put them in that drawer unthinkingly, sure I would never see you again.

"You shouldn't be so foolish," you say, putting the pictures away and closing the drawer.

I'm numb. My body is a tongue that's been cut out of somebody's mouth; it lies on my mattress, thick and warm and senseless.

"You're not responding."

"Sure I am. Look, I'm shaking, I'm hot, too."

"You're not responding to me."

"So get out of my bed."

"Really?"

"You're crazy. I'm responding. You must be blind. You must be crazy."

You're right. It could be anybody's mouth. It doesn't matter. You moved me so—just two days ago?

"Oh, you're just crazy," I repeat, as you leave my bed.

But you don't leave the room. Once you leave I'll gather the bits and shards of my strength and build a perfect wall. I'll never let you near. Leave me and the gavel bangs, guillotine slams, hope snaps and all that's left is stubborn, irreducible evil. I won't mention your name again. Except the truth is you fucked me into being.

"Do you want me to go?"

"I wouldn't dare ask. I'm scared of you now," I mock.

And you stand in the middle of the floor like an orphan. Still, the line of your body is proud.

After you killed him you walked in the rain, and stopped by the marina. You said to yourself, "I need somebody, and there's nobody but me." It was not murder you regretted, but the fact that you could not bring him back to life. You wanted him alive so you could tell him the simple, obscene fact that "I need somebody, and there's nobody but me." He'd know what you meant because the same thing had happened to him.

After you killed him you held him. You hoped somebody would find you and snatch the burden of your secret before you could begin to bear it. But the courtyard was all emptiness, not a living thing stirred, not the broad leaves of the banana tree, not a blossom, not a shadow.

After you killed him, the rain soaked your shirt and skin. It was a typical island squall, clouds tumbling out of nowhere, then disgorging water. Rain fell on you as it fell on all of Old San Juan, on Nadal slumped in his courtyard, on Popi coming up the steps. And you could say the rain was merciless, because it fell on murderer and murdered and made no distinction. And you could say the rain was merciful, because it fell on you.

Yes, what you say is true. It's your story. I can never live inside it, and I won't die from it. For instance. I don't flinch when I touch an orphaned child. Tell me the child is dying of AIDS and I'll bear it with grace. And I've done that, you know, I've gone to an orphanage and smoothed the scabbed scalp of a child, and looked into a puckered, gnomish face so resigned to pain that it seems evil. Is there always a difference between pain and evil?

I can choose the timing of my heartbreak. I have the luxury of grief. I take pictures of these children, and I hold such children, and then I go home.

I suffer, yes, but lucidly, reflectively, elegaically. A writer whose books I like wrote those words. Don't ask me who. You've never read her. Edith Wharton. Yes, her book is on my shelf. I know you aren't interested. Besides, there's no way you can be part of my world.

You can love, but only to a point. The rest is silence. Then the muteness we all live with.

* * *

I can't stop myself. Quoting writers, making images. I need my veil. But this is real.

Blood brother. Track star. Murderer.

Paperboy, patriot, sailor, welder, drifter, son of a father you never speak of. You're starting to be mine. Because I have your secret. I don't know what to do with it.

It hasn't made a mark on your skin. A fine sweat glows on that body that has so much hope in it—no one can see the pain incubating. I don't know love but I love your lashes when you close your eyes, the pleats of flesh when you cup your hand, the blue tattoo on your leg where factory piping smacked. And I love the *noli mi tangere*—the don't touch me—of your face.

"Nobody will hurt you," you say awkwardly. "They have to go through me first."

"They might do that anyway."

"How much are you going to tell Popi?"

"Nothing."

"You mean that?"

"When I was a kid," you tell me, "I was always the backbone of the team, never the star. I was the one who made the catch. I don't know what I'm going to become. I don't know what's left for me."

You say it in a hard, clear voice—you keep the plea buried.

"Did you want to make love before?" I ask.

You smile and shake your head.

"But you went ahead anyway?"

"I'm not hard to persuade."

"Hope is all you've got?" I mock.

"That, and whatever else is in my back pocket."

"So. Make love to me now."

* * *

When you come to me I won't be looking. When you touch me I won't be touching you. When you fuck me I'll cry. Will it be from pleasure?

Matted hair, tender mouth. It's the mouth I love, swollen with unseen milk like a child that just suckled. I never really looked before: milky blossom in that cliff of face. I'll keep looking.

See the hollow of your cheek? There's sorrow. And the way you hold your shirt in your hands, sifting it through your fingers like an old man. How strange that in some way you seem to accept your fate.

Don't move. I lift my palms to your face. Just a touch and you come to life.

Exquisite panic. Touching your face now that I know what you are. But I can't do more.

But you don't need more.

I can give more.

I can't touch you enough. This night will never be enough. I need to caress you out of life, so that you never lived and I never knew you. I stand outside you looking at love. Nothing will beat back the tides in me now, I need the unthinkable, to be in you, of you, under you snuffed out—but where

Heart-pounding sickness
I'm in love with a murderer
Voice hand mouth cunt flood

Knees just a little bent, cheek against the pillow, arm flung over your head, you sleep for a few minutes at a time, and then shudder awake.
Soon I'll tell you to go.
I'll tell you to go.
"Kim."

"What?"

"You're falling asleep."

"Oh," you say, eyes still closed, a half-smile on your lips, "you think I don't love you anymore."

"You don't love me, period," I protest.

"Only because you don't want me to." You open your eyes. "That wasn't fair, was it?"

"I don't want your love."

"I won't force it on you."

"Do you believe in the devil?"

"How could I? You let me stay here tonight."

"Seriously."

"Okay. Seriously." You turn onto your back. "The devil's not the point. That's like saying, do I believe a voice in my head made me kill?" You reach for a half-smoked cigarette in the ashtray on the night table, and light it again. "Lynn, I did it myself. Of my own free will."

But then you turn to me and promise, "I'll keep you out of this."

"How?"

"I'll tell Popi to leave you alone."

"He won't if he doesn't want to."

"I'll take you away."

"My whole life is here. Besides, you don't need to save another woman."

TWENTY-FOUR

Hold me. Only you can protect me from what you are.

For months nobody could see you—the killer, the penitent. You walked in eclipse, killer and penitent. I see you. And you take a shocking pleasure, don't you, in being seen. You taste your own muscle and fiber once more. You love living in your skin for this honeymoon moment in time.

Suffering—I never knew it could be this voluptuous. You have finally made me love you. But why are you shaking? Lying on your back, skin as feathery as a burnt leaf, body fluttering as if it were paper, not bone. You can't exist, two men in one. Knees against your stomach, you rock beside me, and a sound of shattered gears, an unholy grinding sound of grief at last.

This thing pours on our hearts, drop by drop. Is there any wisdom to be had from a life gone wrong?

TWENTY-FIVE

Toward morning he swings his legs over the edge of the bed, and for a minute doesn't move, as if he's forgotten where he is. I follow him to the bathroom, where he fingers the scar on his forehead. It looks like red ants have been stitched into his skin, a mean and lacy chain. He splashes cold water on his face again and again, for ten or fifteen minutes, and I stand there in the silence, watching this ablution that washes nothing away.

"I know you haven't told me everything."
"I'll never tell you everything."
He shrugs on his jacket.

At the door, he seems unable to go. "Look at me," he says.
I look at him.
"No, look at me." He seizes my head, and I stay, caught, but my gaze wanders uneasily away—into the hall, up at the ceiling, down to his scuffed high-top sneakers. "You can't look at me now, and you really think you want to know more?" he says, and I stand transfixed. I look at him.

He relaxes. Then he says my name, half to himself. I know—he can't help it, sometimes he thinks I can actually save him.

*   *   *

He tells me, then, that Katie showed up the other night, when he couldn't make it to dinner with my friends. She was there, curled in front of his door. Lying on the stained carpet, butt against the wall, head against the jamb, arms wrapped around herself like a hibernating animal. When he was within a foot she looked up. Sullen and without a trace of shame.

He told her he'd been hoping she wouldn't come.

"Aw, come on, you were waiting for me." She sat up, wrapped her arms tightly around her knees and stroked her arms as if she were her own lover. She used to stroke herself like this to make him jealous, shutting him out and flaunting it. Inevitably he'd come to her.

"Where've you been?"

"I just had dinner, and I was coming back to get my suitcases."

She stared at him suspiciously. "You're not living here anymore?"

"You caught me by my coattails. You're like one of those trick toys, Katie."

"Yeah? Where's the trick?"

"I was about to tell you. They're over on Eighth Avenue, these woven bamboo things shaped like a thimble. Stick your finger in, and the thing just grabs you. The harder you pull the tighter it grabs."

"Fuck you," she said evenly. "I can see you have no idea why I came here."

And then, with a resentful pride that was typical of Katie, she flexed her foot so the thigh muscle swells, and she went on flexing with the violent, stubborn concentration of a dancer, as if nothing mattered but the stretch, as if she hadn't been hurt. She was a lonely warrior, this tomboy in Spandex tights, denim miniskirt, and suede loafers, her ponytail twisted tight with a Day-Glo orange headband. Finally she lowered her leg, and covered her face with her hands.

"Why did you disappear?"

"How else was I going to stop us, Katie?"

"Who says we need to be stopped?"

"We were just great together," he said. "All we talked about was

who was following us and whether we were going to get killed.
Not much of a life, is it?"

"Why didn't you tell me you were going?"

"I didn't tell you and you're here. If I told you, you'd never let
me leave."

"Kim, you've got to help me. I'm not going back there. I'm out
of San Juan for good."

He laughed in disbelief. "Maybe I'll move back, then."

"You think I'm lying," she said flatly.

"San Juan is your second skin. That place healed you."

"It hurts me now. So I have to do something, so I'm moving to
the States."

"Anywhere north of Florida and your arthritis will come back."

She rubbed her eyes dispiritedly. "My arthritis," she muttered.
"Well, it's not winter yet." She slid up the wall until she was standing. "Kim, I have to talk to you. Will you let me stay tonight?"

"I was heading over to Cheeks's."

"Don't." She looked up at him, her face hard. "Stay."

"I'll help you. But I can't stay with you. I just don't want to."

She leaned against the doorjamb. "I'll sleep in the hall, then."

"All right," he said, suddenly bitter. "I'll find another room
tonight. Around three A.M. when you get tired you can come in
here and lie down."

He swerved past her.

"No!" she screamed in a high, crushed voice. Instantly a door
cracked open, a head peeked out. "Shut your goddamned door,
this is private. He deserted me and I followed him anyway. So shut
your goddamned door."

The door shut.

"I don't get it, Kim," she said, more quietly. "You keep dicking
around with me and you never did that before. You hole me up in
a condo in Isla Verde and split town. You call me every day and
then suddenly don't call anymore. I don't know what's happening
'cuz I'm not supposed to call *you* in case my line's tapped, or so
you say, so I'm waiting thinking maybe Nadal got you, maybe
you're stuffed in some garbage bin or washed up on the rocks of
La Perla, and I'm thinking this sitting in a two-room apartment
that feels like two boxes stuck together. You say you're doing it all

to protect me. And then you just split!" Her head dropped, and she concluded wearily, "Oh, fuck. Forget it. You could have told me you were going, that's all."

"I was trying to hurt you," he said, surprised at the discovery.

She rolled her eyes. "That's news? We're re-discovering the wheel here."

"But it was the first time," he said, still wondering at himself.

She shrugged. "You never had to hurt me before. You thought you were pulling the strings."

"Even you, you're not that cynical," he said slowly, but some long-held sense of himself was cracking, and in a few more beats he'd be raging mad.

"If you'd touch me—"

"Don't ask."

"If you'd touch me, I wouldn't feel cynical. You're still my friend. I swear if you'd hold me I'd forget what you did."

"Just what did I do?" he snapped.

For a moment she seemed bewildered. "I already told you. Before."

"Katie, why did you come?"

"I couldn't get hold of you. Your phone was off the hook, or there was no answer. And Cheeks and I talked again last night. He said you missed me."

"That man's getting to be my nemesis."

"Besides, I had something to tell you. I came to tell you something. I couldn't tell you on the phone. When I tell you what happened, you won't believe it."

He put up a hand. "You don't need to tell me."

"You think it's going to be some more stuff about death threats? No, I came to tell you that—"

"I already know."

"You know crap. You *know*," she mocked. But he didn't protest, and now she gazed at him doubtfully.

"Why do you think I really left, Katie?"

She stared past him. Her face clouded, then hardened. "I didn't think you knew. But," she said with sudden suspicion, "who told you?"

He said nothing. She was staring off into space.

"I guess I found out kind of late," she said in a dull voice. "I guess everybody else on the island knew, but I hadn't been out of the condo much, and I hadn't seen a paper in weeks. You knew?"

He nodded impatiently.

"So we're really over," she said, half to herself. "So what I'm gonna do now is—what I'm gonna do now is—" Then she looked at him, confused. "Kim, I'm dead tired and fuzzy, and I don't understand. You knew. I flew 1,600 miles to tell you, and you say you already knew—"

She was close to the truth, circling it dizzily, a punch-drunk animal, but her sight stopped short of murder. Kim was not a murderer; therefore, he didn't murder.

Her face tilted up slightly as she rested against the wall, arms spread, hands splayed.

"Nadal," she said, half to herself.

It was the slightest of pauses. Her face was lifted like a child's, and Nadal's name was the only name in the air, and he was not prepared: Nadal's name in Katie's mouth, Katie shaping the whole man with her voice, until Kim was a man rocking on the edge, his need simple and Katie's silence terrible.

He spit out the words: "Nadal's dead!"

Katie's heavy lids closed over her hazel eyes, and she slumped against him. He felt the physical shock of this woman: in spite of the ruptures between them, his body still believed she was the beloved.

The door locked and the window shut firmly against the world —Kim tells me he didn't stay long with her, maybe an hour, but he listened.

"He hated me for what he did to me. So if he could let me forgive him we'd have been okay. I'd picture it, how his face would look when he knew he was forgiven. That was my power over him that he never knew, that I could forgive him. Except now I can't 'cuz he's dead."

"He didn't hate you, Katie."

"I keep trying to imagine his body dead," she mused. "So big. So much flesh and hair. He never liked me to see it. He used to make me wait to come into his bedroom at night. He was already undressed. But the day before he took me down into La Perla he let me undress him in his room. And I told him he was beautiful, even though he was like a walrus." She touched his hand. "Kim, do you still want me?"

"How could I not?"

"I'm dying," she whispered, and put his hand against her groin.

"It wouldn't mean enough. Not now."

"Well, who cares. Let's pretend for a while."

He shrugged. "Your move first."

"When did you get such self-control?"

He didn't answer, and she said softly, angrily, "Lie down. Just lie down next to me and that'll be good enough."

He went to the dresser. "You want a beer?"

"A warm beer? I'd rather know why you're playing monk here. Some woman's been taking the edge off."

"More than the edge," he said.

She stared at him.

"Can I ask you something, Katie?"

"More than the edge?" she repeated.

"Did you notice me trying to change the subject? What did the papers say about Nadal?"

"Nobody can make you forget me."

"Not even myself," he agreed.

"Oh hell," she said bravely. "Let her have the edge, and the buffer zone, too."

He laughed grudgingly.

"The papers talked about his horses," she said, "and his ranches and the buildings he restored and his family name. All kinds of bullshit about one of their most respected businessmen. Well, I guess it was true. He used to say there was more money selling a twenty-minute high to *los americuchos* than all the oil companies combined. Anyway, the detectives figure it's a family feud, or some lunatic who waltzed up from La Perla. They didn't even mention drugs. You know he had police protection."

Kim twisted open the beer bottle and settled himself on the bed next to her.

"It's been hard?" he asked suddenly.

"The last few weeks were," she said. "I'd turn on the air-conditioner till the room was freezing, and then hold a heating pad against me until my skin hurt and then I could finally fall asleep. And I'd dream it was you I was holding, or him. I haven't felt this bad since I was thirteen. I've even been playing my old trick."

It was a trick she taught herself when she was thirteen, after she'd gotten arthritis. She hated sitting in the classroom or the lunchroom inside a jail of pain. One day she made up a game.

She'd picture a thousand cameras blazing their hot lights on her. All aimed straight at Katie Gonne. Black cans with white bulbs hanging from the sky. On the bad days she'd walk into places—restaurants, galleries, banks—and illuminate herself. And it worked. People came to her.

"I'll do it right now," she offered. "Turn out the light."

"You don't need to," he said gently.

She took his hand. "Why did you disappear?"

"I don't know myself." He removed his hand, but she took it back. "You're incorrigible."

"I haven't changed," she admitted.

What had Nadal told him? Katie and Nadal would wake up in the morning, and they'd say the same thing: *Oh God, too much light, demasiado. I want a dark pillow.*

Was that who she was?

Had he tried to bend her into something else?

Con permiso, Nadal had told him. *May I tell you what you did wrong?*

Don't bother. I won't believe it.

I will tell you anyway. You cannot take another person's night away.

You're talking crazy again.

So, Kim says, he put his hands on her small, heart-shaped face. "Katie," he said, "if I take you to the airport, will you go home?"

"Not now."

"When?"

"Soon."

"Soon," he affirmed. And he held her face as if it were a curious rock washed up by the sea. He didn't kiss her.

*   *   *

He didn't kiss her.

"Promise?" I ask.

He smiles.

"I don't need to promise. But I didn't kiss her."

TWENTY-SIX

Say this: He killed a man. Say it. Say something else. The air feels cool today. Now say something beautiful about love, like this: Even though you've done terrible things, I can still see the world in your face. Take these sentences and make a story.

No, I can't. I love words but they lie. Just because you tell a story, does that make it bearable? Say holocaust. Say Dick, Jane, holocaust.

I can't write a thing. Strewn on my desk are research papers about eggs. I'm supposed to write about rotten eggs. Not really. Eggs are only the image, for I'm writing about resonance, about the way all things in this world vibrate at a certain frequency. A physicist has found that pristine chicken eggs sing a sound of 830 hertz, while eggs infected with salmonella vibrate at a higher frequency.

I can't. Can't build a bridge between a sea of singing eggs, all rolling majestically forward on a conveyor belt, and the songs of sunspots, galaxies, single cells.

There's no song for Kim.

He left three hours ago. I can't feel the murderer. He feels innocent. I'm blind.

TWENTY-SEVEN

"**D**on't you ever *work* anymore?" Sherry asks when I show up at her door, bearing a bag of chocolate croissants and a bottle of raspberry seltzer. It's late morning. "Weren't you supposed to be writing something on scrambled eggs?"

"My deadline's tomorrow."

"So?"

"I interviewed the researcher yesterday, believe it or not."

She looks doubtful, but takes my offering of food, finds a blue earthenware plate on a shelf, places a linen doily on top, and warms the croissants in the microwave before arranging them in a starbust design. She pours the seltzer in wine glasses, and we sit at an oak table under her window.

"You broke up with him," she says, looking at my face. "Didn't you? You look terrible."

I shake my head.

"Is it just lack of sleep? You've just come off a sex marathon?"

"Nope."

"So what is this, Lynnie, a nonstop monologue?"

"An interior monologue, and it's going so fast I can't interrupt it."

We're silent for a minute. I eat.

"I tried on wedding dresses yesterday," Sherry says finally. "The last time I did that I was twenty and pregnant but I knew it was wrong because the better the dress looked, the sadder I felt. I was about to marry the wrong man. So I didn't. But yesterday all the dresses made me happy. They've got these short ones now, so you can show your knees."

"Have you told Kyros?"

She shakes her head. "I just wanted to see how the dresses felt."

"You didn't have to go to a store. Just say the word 'bride.' "

"Bride."

"Come on, get into it. Say it like a fiancée."

Sherry lifts up her mass of hair, shakes it out, places both hands on her breasts and pushes them up. "Bride!"

"Now. Do you feel as if someone just plastered your face all over the wedding pages of the Sunday papers? That your smiling picture is forever pasted over a headline like, 'A May Nuptial for Miss Sherry'?"

She laughs. "I say 'bride' and feel nineteen again."

"Then you're really thinking about it."

"No, I just found a dress I like."

I feel sentimental and strange. So many afternoons I've sat at Sherry's table while we bartered stories, and it's been delicious, even the misery, because it's part of our shared adventure. I want to put Kim's name in our quilt. And the way I feel, his name is going to be big and uneven, in block letters, the writing of a bewildered child.

I think of the time Sherry sat in the Museum Café on Columbus Avenue waiting for a diplomat she loved. Afterwards, I met her and we went back to the same restaurant and table, and she was dazzling. I gave her a Chinese accordion, a toy that's made of squares that unfold endlessly, and I told her it was for all her lovers. The affairs didn't last, but the accordion is still on her nighttable.

"It's just the dress," Sherry repeats, half-teasing. "If I go back and feel happy in it next week, and it doesn't need alterations . . ."

"You won't be faithful to him," I warn. Sherry's timing is too perfect, as if we're in some sardonic soap opera: Lynn goes out with murderer, Sherry gets married.

Tearing a piece of croissant, she pops it in her mouth. "Boy.

Maybe you didn't break up, but you look miserable." She touches my hand. "Talk to me."

"I don't know how to say it."

"Say it badly, then."

I look out the window, at the green wedge of Central Park, and drop the words as casually as possible, "He killed somebody."

There's a silence. Her chair creaks. I keep looking out the window. Finally she says, "Of course."

I turn to her. "You're joking, right? I mean, *I'm* not joking, but you can't have expected that. You're not supposed to believe it."

"But I do believe it."

"Why?" I practically shout.

She hesitates. "You were scared of him."

"That was *me*. You said so yourself. Because he's so sexual."

"Yeah, but you were terrified. Anyway," and this time she takes my hand in both of hers, "when did he tell you this?"

"Last night." I briefly reprise the facts, beginning with Popi's visit.

"So what are you going to do?"

"Stop seeing him."

"Have you told him yet?"

"Why do I have to tell him? He'll know when I don't answer the phone."

"Lynn," she says, "you don't talk like it's over."

"Is there a special way I should say it?"

"When's the last time you made love?"

"Five hours ago."

"After he told you?"

I nod.

"Did that give you a kick?" she asks quietly.

"A kick?"

She shakes her head. "Sorry."

"Sherry, it was like when you make love with someone you just broke up with. It was like an act of mourning."

She pushes her chair back. "I don't know. You're talking about him like we talk about guys who've cheated on us or lied to us or whatever. This guy is not normal."

"Hey, didn't you go out with an ex-Marine two years ago?"

"He didn't kill a drug dealer, Lynn. He never killed anybody, in fact."

"He never got the chance. I remember that guy."

Sherry shakes her head impatiently. "Don't try to drag me into an argument. You're not going to end up with this man. What would make you put yourself in danger for him?"

"I'm not in danger."

"You're being followed by the dead guy's nephew."

"Popi likes me."

"You can't be that naive."

"You're on the outside and it looks different."

"If Kim told you he'd done IV drugs, would you sleep with him without a condom?"

"Bad analogy, Sherry."

She seems gratified by the tightness in my voice. "Would you sleep with him, though?"

"Nope."

"So if you feel like you can't stop yourself from seeing him, move in with me for a few weeks. I'll be your prison guard."

"It won't work," I retort. "I'd just sneak out for a newspaper and jump bail."

She stares at me. "I've never seen you like this."

"Maybe you should meet him," I say, more humbly. "His face would change your mind."

She goes over to an antique wall mirror, framed in brass, and stands frowning, pulling bobby pins from her hair, lifting and twining the mass of it, and then sticking the pins back at new angles. It's like meditation and preening at the same time.

"I wish I'd met him already. The problem is now I don't want to meet him. He'd know that I know."

"Yeah, but he wouldn't show it. He wouldn't even mention it to me afterwards."

She shakes her head. "What is this, murderer's manners? The etiquette of the ex-con?"

Against my will, I start to laugh.

Sherry adds, "I *really* think you should stay with me for a few nights."

"I'll consider it. You know what I'd like?"

"Nope."

"To lie down for a while. I'm a walking sleepless automaton. Can I?"

"Of course," she says instantly, relieved.

Once I'm on Sherry's white featherbed, she sits beside me and strokes my hair.

"Sherry, I want to tell you . . ."

"Tell me later."

"No," I say sleepily. "I forgot to say the most important thing."

"Okay."

"It's like he's my happiness. I need a few days to give up my happiness. Do you understand?"

"Slow withdrawal never works. Did you ever hear of someone who's half alcoholic?"

"You want me to give him up," I murmur. "Next thing I know you'll be asking for his number."

She smiles, then stands and closes the blinds, adjusting a few stray panels so that darkness reigns. The door shuts. My body grows heavy, and the world begins to bury itself, and for a moment I see how life is. For I have put my eye to the kaleidoscope—a cardboard kaleidoscope painted shiny red on the outside. And inside I have only the colored pieces that are me. Turn. Turn. And each turning is a truth.

I leave Sherry quietly in the late afternoon. For the first time in our friendship I deceive her, and with ease; I say I'm going straight home. She hugs me.

I'm back inside the glass envelope. I turn south and walk to Kim's hotel, thinking he can crack the glass.

In the lobby of the hotel people drift past me, while I observe a young woman. She has the face of a boy Lilith, primitive, illiterate, canny. But she's not boy, not girl—her bones are hard, her mouth soft, her voice hoarse with a secret something that's all smoky androgyny.

I don't want to say her name.

She's leaning against the reception desk talking to the clerk. "Any messages, boy scout?"

"Sorry, girl scout," he shoots back, with the cheerful certainty of a man performing a daily ritual. Has she been living here?

"Hey," he calls after her as she walks away, "how do you keep in shape?"

"I was a gymnast."

Her gaze moves over me, and I burn, shamed—but invisible.

She's wearing a cream t-shirt dress, unbelted, and pearl earrings.

"You coming?" she snaps, impatient. I follow her into the elevator. "What floor?"

"Ummm . . ."

"Why are you looking at me like that? What floor do you want?"

"Your floor."

"My floor?" She crosses her arms. "Okay. This hotel is full of crazies. You press the button, since you apparently know where I live."

Where I live. I'll punch her. I press seven. The door starts to close and her hand shoots out, banging against the edge so that it stops and slides open again.

"See ya later," she says, pushing past me.

I grab her arm. "I know you."

"In your dreams."

"No, I do. I do know you." Her name is going to cut me, just saying it. "Katie." Having said it, I say it again. "Katie."

"So," she replies flatly, "say it one more time. Just so we can be sure."

"My name is Lynn," I offer.

"I don't know you."

"No, you don't."

"Well," she replies, "it's a thrill and a half to meet you here in this elevator. It's a little cramped, but what the hell. Can I see your invitation? We ask all our guests."

"I'm a friend of Kim's."

Her eyes lock with mine, she drops her hand and lets the door close. The elevator lurches and begins to rise; we get off and walk silently to his door. Once there, she turns around and crosses her arms as if to bar my way.

"How do you know who I am?"

"I came across some photos of you."

"Here?"

I nod.

"He showed them to you?"

I shake my head.

"You went through his things?"

"Did he tell you about me?" I counter.

"Why should he?" She opens the door. "Am I gonna have to wait for you again? It seems like I keep holding doors for Kim's girlfriend."

"So he did tell you."

"Not really." She shoves the window open and tosses her purse on the dresser, where a clutter of compacts, rouges and lipsticks lie half-open. "Well, there's only one chair in these luxury digs. I'll take the bed. Or do you want it? You take the bed, then."

She pulls a beer out of an ice bucket, opens it in the sink, kicks off her leather flats, turns the chair so the back is facing me, and sits on it the wrong way, her legs wrapped around its legs.

I retreat to the bed, cross-legged, pulling the pillow onto my lap and holding it tenderly as if it were a stuffed animal. The whole cotton spread is scented with Kim—cologne and cigarettes. Without thinking, I lift the pillow to my face. I have a friend who, late in her pregnancy, buried her head in her lover's jacket. And breathed in his smell. And her breasts started leaking milk.

"You're pretty," Katie says suddenly. "I can see why you'd take the edge off."

"Take the edge off?"

"That's how he put it." She rocks the chair forward a little, balancing it with her feet.

"Maybe I don't even want him."

She goes on rocking the chair.

"That's what he told me," she answers finally, her tone softer.

"Fine. There are probably things both of us want to find out. Can we talk to each other?"

"What do I need to know? He's in New York. He's fucking you."

"You're in New York, too. He let you move in with him."

She gives me a strange, almost contemptuous look, steadily drinks her beer until it's empty and aims it at the garbage can.

"Basket. I learned baskets from Kim. God, I just want to lie on the bed with the lights out and get a slow buzz going."

"I'm not stopping you."

"You'd better join me. Can you open me another one? You're probably a three-bottle drunk, aren't you?"

"Much less."

"I don't drink like this usually but I've got this mad going and it seems to burn up all the alcohol. Sip yours slow 'cause I want company." She lifts her legs, pressing her bare feet together, then swings them over the back of the chair, holds on to the sides and leans back. "How'd you meet Kim?"

"At the Algonquin. That's where I first saw him. How'd you meet him?"

"At a private beach party." She tells me he was wearing cotton khakis and a blue t-shirt, she says, and she followed him into the house where, thinking he was alone, he slipped off his clothes. He had great lats, slim hips. When he turned around, she blurted out,

"You're fucking beautiful."

"You're fucking outrageous."

"But," she concludes, "everyone went skinny-dipping anyway, since it was nighttime. And he's not the kind of guy who makes much out of a comment like that. I had to ask him out."

"I know what you mean. He's not shy, but he's careful. At first anyway."

She regards me. "He's easy. He was always easy."

"Easy."

"Yeah, he makes life simple without trying. He's my lion tamer. I'm growling and he coaxes me to leap through this hoop, and the whole time it looks like he was just standing there. He's good at that."

I must look perplexed, because she tilts her head and says cooly, "Yeah? What's wrong?"

"To me he's one of those still-waters-run-deep guys from the Midwest. He looks calm but . . ."

"Maybe it's New York." She shrugs. "He was relaxed in San Juan."

"When did you fly up to New York?"

"A few days ago."

"And you came straight here?"

"Hey, grill me."

"I'm sorry. Sometimes my questions tumble out too fast. Occupational hazard."

"What do you do?"

"I write about science."

"So what do you talk to Kim about?"

"We don't always talk."

"So you're slumming? You come to this room and . . ."

"Jesus. I give up." Turning on my side, I stretch out on the bed.

"What are you doing now?"

"Waiting for him to get here." I shrug. "He can battle it out, because I don't want to fight with you."

"You might have to wait a long time."

"He gets off work at four."

"He's not coming straight home."

"I'll decide when it's too long."

I close my eyes. The least I can do is humiliate Kim for lying to me. I suppose that will be delicious triumph for Katie, but she's won anyway.

When I look up, a few minutes later, she's standing over me. Her auburn hair hangs down, swinging with a slow hush. Her eyes, thick-lashed and hazel, gaze into mine. Her lips move but no sound comes out.

"I don't know when he's telling me the truth anymore," she says finally.

"What did he say?" I murmur.

"He said he'd send for me. Said he'd find a place and send for me."

"So you think he was lying?" I remember the snippet of recorded conversation on Kim's tape; he said he'd send her to her mother's. Was that a holding pattern? Was he planning to hook up with her again?

"I came too soon," she says, finishing her second beer and aiming it at the garbage can again. "Basket. Anyway. Yeah, I came unannounced but I thought what's the big deal? But I didn't know he had a distraction here. So I guess it was a kind of bad mistake."

"That's all? You don't care that he's sleeping with me?"

She shrugs. "Men are loyal, not faithful."

"Why did he want to leave San Juan anyway?"

Katie sits next to me. "I had a jealous lover," she says. "Jealous to the point where somebody was gonna die sooner or later. I left the guy but it was just to teach him a lesson. I was gonna go back."

"This lover—he wanted you back?"

She stares through me. "After I left him it was like he wanted to wipe me off the face of the earth. But . . . he'd been so crazy about me before that it didn't seem real. I knew there was a switch. A trick, some kind of something that would make him love me again. Oh, I'm not gonna even *try* and explain it."

"I understand." It's a breathtaking, satanic alchemy that lovers make when they shift to hate. Yet even in hate the whole person is turned toward you.

"One thing you can say about me is I don't scare. And he scared me. First time ever. It made him insane to see me scared, to see how he broke my fight. 'Cause he loved my fight."

"So what happened to him?"

"He went and got himself killed."

Don't look at me, I think. *If you look at me now you'll know that I know.*

"The worst timing," she says in an acid tone. "I'm wasting my life waiting for his change of heart and he goes and gets himself murdered."

"Who did it?"

Her voice is hard. "Why do you care? You're thinking maybe you just stumbled onto a front-page story?"

"I'm not that kind of reporter."

The phone rings and we both stare at it. After three rings Katie picks up the receiver and holds it, listening.

"Yeah, okay," she says after a pause. Her voice softens and drops. "Oh. Nothing all day . . . I went for a walk . . . Now I'm just drinking the beer you bought and trying to fall asleep. Closing my eyes and counting cobblestones on San Justo Street instead of sheep but it doesn't work. I just count cobblestones and end up at the bottom of the street." She listens for a minute, turning her face from mine so her hair slips forward like a shield. I'm alone in this room.

"I just might show up," she says in a low voice. "He has no idea why I haven't visited." There's a pause. "All right," she says resentfully. "All right. Talk to him as long as you want. Yeah, okay. It's okay. Later."

She holds the receiver for a few moments, then replaces it and says without looking at me,

"There's no point in waiting for him. He's going over to a friend's for dinner."

"Cheeks?"

"You know him?"

"The radio man. We ate dinner over there. I never saw a house with so much stuff."

Her face flushes. "Ginny met him first, actually, years ago. She used to call Kim her discovery."

"Yeah, she told me she bought him a drink in a bar and then when he walked over she realized he was only eighteen."

"She's a funny bird. But I like Cheeks." Katie takes a breath. "He plays therapist to us all. I call him the armchair exorcist. He just sits there in his big old armchair and gives advice."

"What's his advice now?"

"I can't ask his advice about Kim," she says shortly. "Look, this is getting boring. You and me. Can we stop? I just want to rest till Kim gets here."

"Do you mind if I beep into my machine?"

"How come? To see if he left you a message?"

"Maybe."

"Why don't you just come out with it? You want to know what Kim's deal is? He *doesn't* like me anymore. But he's in love with me. I had this hold on him. I'm not bragging. I don't know why it was. It just was. It's all still in his heart. And he's not in love with you, but he likes you. Not that he said much about you. But . . ." She pauses. "I usually know what he's thinking."

I sit up, hug my knees to my chest. "Maybe you're right. So what are we going to do?"

"Well." She taps her foot slowly against the bedpost. "I came up here to be sure."

"Of Kim?"

She nods.

"And now?"

"I'm going home."

"But—home to San Juan?"

"So he'll send for me. I'm in the mood to be sent for. You know, like the heroine goes home with her head down and vows next time she comes back to this city it'll be in style."

"That's just crazy. That's more like dropping out in the middle of a race."

"I swear it. I'm flying home tonight."

"Why did you tell me this?"

"So you don't come visiting me tomorrow," she jokes.

"Katie, do you still love him?"

" 'Course I love him. I was happy with him. It's just that I couldn't stay away from this other guy. He was the kind of guy you don't run across again. I could make him feel things. Shit, I made him feel things." Her jaw tightens. "I do love Kim."

"But not as deep?"

"Different," she says flatly. "Different. Not deeper, just different. It's the same for him, I guess. I can't stop him from seeing you if he wants."

"I can stop it."

"Why? He's a good sex machine."

My face burns.

She smiles. "Yeah. I understand you a little."

For the first time in my life my questions seem utterly superfluous. I'll go away with these broken bits of confession, but it seems that Katie just slugged me and stands triumphal, like a pint-sized prizefighter. I don't know if she's got Kim or not, but he lied to me and slept with us both.

I sink back onto the bed. When I feel like it, I'll stand up, say good-bye, and leave.

Last night when Kim was making love to me I thought, "He's drowning." He had killed a man, left a woman, answered my ad, and each act was a drowning man's gasp for air. His mouth was pumping mine. I thought, "I know he's drowning because I'm no longer breathing." It seemed in that moment we were one.

TWENTY-EIGHT

In the Mayan ruins at Copán I once crawled
through a cool and moldy entrail of stone until I
stood before a carved alligator tail and waved a
lamp—a bulb with a hood of aluminum—over its
scales. The tail was all that had been excavated, and
yet it bore the whole malevolent calm of this back-
water spirit. I was standing, an anthropologist explained, in the eleventh temple built on this site.
Mayan tribes perpetually tore down sanctuaries and
erected new ones on the same sacred spot, and the
remains of ten other temples—their foundations
packed in the earth—were under my feet.

But I never thought one had to travel to Copán
to feel that. Each place is deep, and for me now
Hell's Kitchen is deepest deep. Forty-third and
Eighth is my corner now, I don't care if Indians
were buried below me or George Gershwin stood
here with a headache, this is the corner where,
hand on the receiver of a public phone, crying, I
don't call Kim.

I placed a jar in Tennessee,
And round it was, upon a hill.

It made the slovenly wilderness
Surround that hill.

That poem by Wallace Stevens. Certain places
make you want to build temples on them. And certain men make a wilderness of you.

TWENTY-NINE

The Royalton Hotel is plush and stark, a cross between a space-
ship and a museum, and a perfect slap in the face to the comfortably aged Algonquin across the street. Popi is waiting for
me in the lobby, engulfed in one of the more memorable Royalton
chairs—all white, and pieced out of a hassock, a mammoth curving
back, and a single armrest.

Most of the chairs in the lobby are covered in white duck cloth,
a few crafted of enormous velvet seats impaled by tiny silver backs.
Waiters and bellboys in black samurai suits glide by. Four crystal
fishbowls, each containing one tiny Siamese fighting fish, rest on a
glass shelf.

"I thought you really would give him up," Popi says as I reach
him, "when you rushed out of the restaurant. Why did you see him
again?"

"I had to know."

"So now you deliver him into my hands?"

"I won't tell you here—"

"Of course not. Would you feel dishonored if we went up to my
suite?"

From one hotel room to the next. "Not at all."

It's like irresistible Chinese boxes. Can't stop opening them.
Still, it hurts.

Once inside the suite, I sit in a stark, blue-black velvet chair.

Popi pours cognac and joins me. How young he looks, slender and languid, wearing a black t-shirt and black European jeans. The whole mantle of family honor has settled on his shoulders, and he seems both determined and a little uncertain.

"So," I say, "Kim did it."

Popi nods.

Are betrayals so simple? I can't even taste this.

"I got him to tell me," I add.

He says quietly: "You're a good reporter."

"And Katie is in New York."

"Yes, I know."

"She's staying in Kim's hotel room."

He leans forward, as studious and earnest as a young scholar. "How long does she plan to stay?"

"She says she's leaving tonight."

He sits back.

"You knew she was there, Popi?"

"I did."

"You knew they were still lovers?"

He shakes his head.

"They're lovers."

"That doesn't mean they will stay together. Or that they're together even now."

"He was planning to send for her."

"I don't believe it."

"That's it. That's all."

"*No esta matadero,*" he says softly.

"Translate."

"This isn't lovers' lane you wandered into, is it?"

"I don't want your pity."

"Or my politeness?"

"Or your politeness."

"Just this . . . simple exchange?"

My head is waterlogged. Sitting in this lavish yet monkish place, I flash on Kim's room. Katie on the sagging mattress. Kim coming through the door.

"Do you want to go?"

"Where to?" I joke half-heartedly.

Popi's looking at me intently. "You wonder why he had anything to do with you."

"Yeah. Of course."

"Maybe he knew he was being watched."

"So he had to look like he had a girlfriend?"

"Yes, like he was here to stay."

"But he got into it," I protest.

He didn't just want to fuck me.

He wanted to taste innocence after he'd murdered.

He washed his hands in me. I feel so unclean.

I feel impregnated.

Stop thinking. I shake my head free of thoughts.

"Lynn, do you know why I'm really here in New York?"

"To find out if Kim killed your uncle. And then, I guess, to hold
your own private family tribunal."

He sighs. "Katie returns to San Juan tonight?"

I nod.

"Well." He moves restlessly to the fireplace, removes a steel
poker that looks like a spiralling shish kebob spear or a giant sperm.
He laughs. "Look at this. Crazy, huh? Listen, I will tell you something."

"Okay, tell me something."

"I came here for her."

"*For* her?"

"I'm following her."

"Then why—why did you bother with me?"

"I need to know something. I don't know how to find out. So I
wait and wait. I'm like a little Puerto Rican Hamlet! I know, you
smile at me because only a child could say this. But it's true. I
come up here and pretend to be a good soldier, and I surprise you
in your doorway. I hope you'll tell me something illuminating.
Except instead I tell you stories. How can I ask you to help me?"

"But—Katie? What could you owe Katie?"

"I need to know if she was involved."

"But why should you care?"

"Now you play the naive reporter."

"My God. What is it about this girl?" I feel sparks of fury. In the middle of this ashen hour. "She's mean. And she's kind of hard. And slutty."

He shakes his head. "She could never survive alone."

"She doesn't have to, that's pretty obvious. Anyway, Kim said she had no idea."

"He would protect her."

"But even so—"

"Listen, my uncle is dead."

"Yeah," I say dryly, "and he was living out the cliché of the times. Cocaine and the cartel."

"Nobody could reach him," Popi insists. "And it looks to me like suddenly he opened all the doors to his death. How did that happen?"

On the morning of August 24, Popi says, his uncle received a phone call and sent him on a fool's errand to Arecibo. The servants were at church. Nadal was alone in the house, and yet he unlocked the gates and put his gun upstairs.

That phone call must have warned him Kim was coming, and he must have concluded that he could beat Kim with talk alone. The almost sexual pleasure of a textile merchant when he fingers fine cloth—you could see it on Nadal's face when he shaped a man by talk, by the soft insinuations of a voice. A gun held little satisfaction. And he entered some unknown place when he talked like that; he was so highly concentrated that nothing existed but the limitless calm of the present, of a man's question and his own answer. There was only awareness. The greater the risk, the greater the awareness.

"My uncle could talk a lame and deaf burro into walking up a hill backwards," Popi concludes.

"You really believe he had second sight?"

Popi shrugs. "I'll tell you, my uncle was a big man in Puerto Rico, but he was dwarfed by the Colombians. He needed some weapon. They believed it, anyway." Nadal's "business associates" were ghostlike autocrats, says Popi, who never openly displayed their power. If they asked for something, you simply gave it. "My uncle had his informers, and his hunches. Maybe it was nothing more. But it worked."

"So what about Katie?" I walk over to the white bed and flop down on it. There's a round alcove near one of the pillows, a porthole with a vase and one exotic lily. "This is the kind of flower that would be poisonous if you stuck it in your lover's ear."

"I think Katie showed up," he says obstinately. "After Kim got there."

"*After* Kim got there?"

"Yes. He never would have left the doors open for her. She would have come later."

Katie, in t-shirt dress and sandals, her burned brown legs and dark orange lipstick. Nadal would have stood there, unable to say a word, and his witchery would have unravelled.

"Then Kim shot him?" I ask. "That's what you think?"

"Perhaps she expected him to. He may have promised her."

"I just can't imagine a man who loves to talk so much he'd risk death for it."

Popi comes to the foot of the bed, watching me. "Only my uncle wasn't like anybody else." He sighs. "And he put away his gun!"

"Your whole family thinks this happened?"

"They are letting me do the thinking."

"Okay. What happens when you're done thinking?"

He smiles, amused and irritated. "You ask awkward questions."

"I do."

"May I have the same privilege?"

"Why not?"

"Do you want to be accomplice to a second murder?"

"Good question."

"I need an answer."

"I don't think you're going to kill anybody."

"You don't know what you're playing with."

"No, I really don't. I feel absolutely crazy this evening. I'll tell you, I'm in danger now of picking up this phone, calling Kim, and telling him where I am. Would you stop me?"

He shakes his head.

"I have no idea how I could love someone I hardly know. My friend Sherry says it's sexual awakening. A belated sexual awakening."

"He's such a good lover?"

I just stare at him.

"*Me caigo en diablo*. I have to protect you. I see it."

"You can't. I already came here."

"You are right, after all," he says softly. "I don't kill. I tell someone in my family what I've discovered. Then something happens now, a year from now, I don't know and don't ask."

We're silent. "But that's just as bad," I murmur finally.

"Yes." His tone is softly surprised, as if he didn't expect me to understand. "Klimt," he says, pointing to an art postcard stuck in a steel holder. "The whole fate is mine. My uncle resurrected our family, and this is my inheritance. *Maricón*. What would *anybody* want with such a choice?"

"Nothing," I admit.

"But—Katie. Katie's the difficult part."

He describes once more how she came to the front gate that night, still carrying her high-heels—her index and middle fingers crooked over the backs of the shoes, so they dangled from one hand—feet dusty and black from walking on the cobbled streets. She just stood there, remarkably chastened, and bit her lip.

"My face was stone. It was my face that sent her away."

"All right. So at least one thing makes sense. You just don't feel she'll talk to you now. So you're tailing her."

"Will you help me?" he asks suddenly.

"How?"

"You're a woman."

"What's that supposed to mean?"

"Katie might not be honest. But she might talk to you. She's so alone now—I know. She might tell you something. If she was responsible for my uncle's death, well . . . it's honor, then, and she has to suffer."

"Talk to Katie tonight? That would finish me off."

"It's impossible?"

"I'd have to trail her down to San Juan," I joke. "Get an assignment about Puerto Rico."

"Perhaps about our cuisine?"

"Forty ways to fry bananas. Very amusing."

"But listen, there *is* a fantastic cuisine. My uncle had a chef, and our family still employs him. I could introduce you."

"A joke, Popi. A joke."

"Our food is so misunderstood," he insists. "Americans think of it as peasant food but really it's so inventive. We have African, Spanish, Indian influences—"

"You really want to keep pushing this?"

"But what will you do?" he inquires. "Wait in New York until Kim leaves you?"

"I don't believe you said that."

"What will you do?" he presses.

What?

Become very quiet. Rest in the quarry of myself.

Say good-bye. Watch, from an unbridgeable inner distance, the troubled look on Popi's face. I'm leaving him alone with this.

In the lobby, sit. Count the Eurotrash. Notice the horn motif: glass horns with flowers, lit horns over the elevators, and a steel horn stuck high on the wall. Drink Dry Sack. Observe emptiness.

I've lost words. It reminds me of what Popi said about Nadal. I feel like the narrator of that old nursery rhyme about a rabbit in the woods—*Help me, help me, help me please, 'fore the hunter shoots me dead. Little rabbit come inside, safely will abide.* Gestures accompanied the rhyme—the little rabbit made of two bent fingers hopping in the woods, the A-frame house shaped by arms and hands. Sentence after sentence was snipped off each time the rhyme was repeated, until the whole song became only silence and moving hands.

Popi comes out of the elevator about half an hour later.

"You didn't go home?" he asks.

I shake my head.

"Come with me, then. Please. A car is waiting outside."

He takes my hand in his.

"For a few hours we'll forget. We'll have a taste of Puerto Rico."

THIRTY

There is a tarot card of a man standing at the edge of a river. His back is to the viewer. You see the sorrowful curved scythe of his shoulders.

The river is sadness, and one of his cups lies smashed at his feet. Three more cups are set in the bright sky.

You know he will turn from the river and take those three cups in his arms and carry them. The lost cup is pain, the others gold. Love is that way. A part is broken, but the rest remains, and you want to carry it carefully. My moods change by the hour. I don't want to hurt Kim. I don't. I don't.

THIRTY-ONE

A white Cadillac carries me and Popi up Avenue of the Americas, into the lush den of Central Park, and on to the South Bronx, where taxicabs refuse to venture and children set fire to homeless men for the fun of seeing a human do a jig of terror inside fire.

We are going to a pig roasting at a *casita,* Popi says. Nearly fifty *casitas* have been built in abandoned lots in the five boroughs, all of them illegal, painted in the Day-Glo colors of the tropics.

"People get the lots through Operation Greenthumb, but they're only supposed to plant gardens. Instead they construct little houses like the ones in the mountains back home. And they cook native food on an outdoor *fogón.* It's their way of telling the city, 'Hey, you can take our island, our money, our citizenship, even our language, but you can never have us. We're still Puerto Rican.' "

The *casita,* a Latin gingerbread house, is painted a brilliant pink with blue trim. Even in late November the abandoned lot is thick with cauliflower, cabbage, beets, greens and carrots. In the summer months, explains Popi, they grow corn, and the children make themselves clearings in the midst of the stalks, where they often curl up and fall asleep.

"Popi, what ever would connect you with a place like this?" I whisper.

"They are my friends," Popi says calmly.

"What could you have in common?"

"Everything. You can go to Oxford to study, but when you get there, you will still crave your plate of rice and beans. Don't disappoint me, *hermana mia*."

An old albino with black eyes and crippled fingers comes down a brick path, opens the gate for us, and embraces Popi, touching cheeks. He's carrying a small machete in one hand, a bag of just-pulled carrots in the other. We follow him into the little house, with its simple wooden floors and open windows. Salsa blasts from a radio, statues of the Virgin Mary are stowed away under the sink, and industrial-size aluminum pots of rice and pigeon peas simmer on the stove.

"We start cooking the pig before dawn," the old man explains. "We find a long stick, put in his mouth all the way out back. And we use a big gas can, we build our own grill." A little boy runs by, touching everything as he flees, the albino, Popi, me, the table, hammock, porch railing. "The children pinch the crunchy part. All day they pinch a little here, little there. Come."

He pours rum into paper cups and toasts us. Outside, a few dozen people are gathered around the open fire, turning the charred hunk of pig. Over another grill a young woman stirs a pot of soup with a sweet odor of fruit, rum and cream. Popi stops to talk in Spanish to an obese couple, the woman's bare feet bound in gauze, the man smoking a cigar. Finally Popi turns to me and says softly,

"He was a trucker for the same company for twenty-five years. Now his back is bad. His company won't pay for sick leave. She's diabetic. Her feet are bad. They have nine children. Two of them they sent home to Puerto Rico to help them get the old values back."

The man nods at me as Popi translates, his face regal and enormous, and he goes on nodding as if the blows of life have done him in. And yet even as he nods his wife puts her hand on his leg, with the slow, distracted ease of someone moving under water. She's drunk. Her hand squeezes his flesh and his face lights up, with a hopeless, inarticulate love, a glow both crude and beautiful.

I sit and drink, while Popi entertains me with more of his pride. *"Él que no tiene dinga tiene mandinga,"* he says. "We Puerto Ricans all have a drop of black in our veins. That's why there has never been a race riot." In the 1700s the officials of Spain drew up a royal list of shades of *mandinga* on the island. "Pure Spanish and Indian made *mestizo*. *Mestizo* and Spanish made *castizo*. Spanish and Negro made *mulato*. *Mulato* and Spanish made *morisco*. *Morisco* and Spanish made *albino*. And on and on. *Cambujo, albarazado, barcino, coyote, chamiso,* and more, and more."

I hold out my cup of rum. Darkness has fallen and everyone is drinking; I'm actually sitting in the midst of a tremendous, human commotion. The celebration has begun. Bare lightbulbs swing on the front porch of the *casita,* so that it glows like a pink billboard in the night. Salsa pounds at my senses. Through the cyclone fence I can see the city, sense its violence, but here I feel safe. Someone hands me a plate heaped with food and a plastic spoon, and I taste the salty, luscious beans. More rum warms me.

I throw a chunk of pork to a cream-colored dog with sweet eyes.

"You're crying," Popi says.

I nod. I want Kim. I'm rudderless.

"Ah, that's good," he says. "It's good to cry."

"Why did you bring me here?" I ask a little later. Crying has inexplicably cheered me. There's a metabolism to grief—a cellular intoxication that finally exhausts itself. And then, for a while, you feel oddly buoyed, until the grief returns.

"To make the others jealous, of course."

"Come off it. I think you're actually sweet as sugar. Doesn't that sound like something *you'd* say?"

"Echas flores?"

"Hmmm?"

"Are you throwing flowers at me? You're a little flirtatious."

"Don't even think it."

"I'd say sweet as a field of sugar. I'd say *Tú eres mi dulce guajana,* you are my sugarcane flower." He smiles. "But you're beginning to learn."

"Can I stay here? I don't want to go back to my life at the moment."

"It gets cold on the floor of a *casita* in November."

"Right, and I can't speak Spanish."

"Anyway, I'm booked on a flight tomorrow morning."

"To San Juan? You already arranged everything?"

"It was easy. Will you come?"

"Popi, you're impossible. Besides, I can't get an assignment overnight."

"It's only a cover. Besides, I can get you one."

I look at him. "What do *you* know about journalism?"

"I have a friend who publishes a magazine for the tourist industry. It's in every luxury hotel in San Juan."

"A friend of your uncle's?"

He nods.

I set down my plate. "You're going to turn me into a domestic spy now?"

"You would make a terrible spy. You feel too much."

"I can be the bad cop if I want," I protest.

He laughs indulgently.

"For instance," I say, sitting up straight. "You pretend to be crushed by your situation. But you relish it."

His face clouds. "That's ignorant."

"You never got your hands dirty?"

"Like my uncle?"

"Right."

"I never did."

I close my eyes, lean back on the bench. "These people are your friends. Because you're proud of everything Puerto Rican. Except I've been watching them most of the night. They're afraid of you."

"I'm an islander. They are Neoricans," he explains. "There can be a barrier. For instance, a Neorican has to prove his manliness every day in the street, and so he walks as if he owns it. Islanders know the sidewalk can be shared. We are different."

"And what was that tête-à-tête you had with the albino when I went to the outhouse?"

"I thanked him."

"Yes, but do you employ him?"

"For what?"

"The albino—has he worked for your uncle?"

"Do you want to ask him? Shall I call him over?"

"Don't bother." I shove my hands into the pockets of my leather jacket and pull it tight around me. My mood is shifting again. "You answer questions like a guilty man. You should have just laughed them off."

"I'm sincere."

My voice drops. "Okay. Here's one more question. You said you followed Katie up here. Why are you interested in me?"

"You want me to talk?" he inquires flatly. "You'll simply be carrying secrets that could mean trouble for you. It doesn't endanger me if you know things. It endangers you. And who can keep a secret? I've never found such a person."

"I can."

He stares intently at his paper cup. *"Lágrima de mangle,"* he says. "Bootleg rum." For a moment he looks remarkably unhappy. "I never really worked for my uncle. Sometimes an errand that was a bit mysterious, but I was never part of the business."

Popi's mother says that when he turned five Nadal began to love him. It was a sudden love. He saw the boy coming up the steps, his fine hair slicked back, his smile impish. His mother had dressed him in a pale yellow shirt and shorts. Popi was small and perfect and he looked up at Nadal with a liquid, pure gaze.

He never showed his affection openly. He simply brought his sister and nephew to live with him, and felt his way along love's private corridors. He had the boy tutored. Sometimes he'd pause, head bowed, outside that classroom of one and listen while Popi recited phrases in French and Latin.

He only brought Popi on business once, late at night. They drove to a mountain house, where Nadal's bedroom was outfitted with scanners, receivers, transmitters and military unscramblers. He never touched the cocaine, but offered it freely to the men. He gave them a milky glass cutting block and a silver straw, but they poured it directly onto the flat back of their fists and snorted loudly into each nostril—the macho way of doing a line.

Popi sat with his uncle while Nadal monitored the cops on their walkie-talkies and his men opened gift boxes of Mac 10s with silencers. They went in back and sprayed bullets into styrofoam coolers packed with paper—a firing line of men under the mango trees, and a shopping-aisle display of blue-and-white speckled coolers. Someone handed Popi a Mac 10 and he murdered those coolers without a sound. Popi had never picked up a gun before.

Nadal came up and took the gun away, and it was the last time he took Popi along on business. He sent him to a private school in upstate New York a month later, and in the summers, to Spain and France. Popi was groomed to be a family prince, a kind of titular head of state, separate from the business. He was the heraldic coat of arms.

"But you didn't answer my question," I say.

"The albino was one of my uncle's men."

"Why is he here in New York? Why is he living like this? Did you pay him dirt wages?"

"He lives in this neighborhood but he's not poor. He supports seven families. He'd prefer to be the lion in a den like this than a middle-class islander in Hato Rey or some suburb. And I came here tonight to tell him he can still rely on a salary. Even if he never works again."

I'm silent for a while. "Okay. I guess I believe you."

He doesn't seem pleased. He stares at me, and then takes my hand. "I must be a little harsh, because it's getting late and we both need a full night's sleep."

"Go ahead."

Then he says something gentle and appalling. "When you came up here with me you forfeited your right to say no."

"No. There, I said no. No to what?"

"You'll be coming to Old San Juan with me."

I stare at him.

"I will be honest, since honesty seems to be something you desire. I'm not kidnapping you. I'm not even forcing you. I'm giving you an excuse."

"You're scaring me, actually."

"You want to go. You haven't admitted it to yourself. Don't you know that can get you into trouble, *mi dulce guajana*?"

"And if I don't go?"

"I'll escort you there, naturally."

I say quietly, "Am I going to get hurt?"

"Never," he says, and reaches out briefly to touch my hair. "How could I live if I thought this pale sun would be harmed. You'll be back in New York in a few days and you'll never see me again."

THIRTY-TWO

How can I understand your mouth and the world it displaced. What world can I live in now. Our first kiss was the kind that cauterizes as it cuts and leaves no clue, only miraculous feeling. And it went like water, like water, into my throat and soul.

In morning darkness I stand alone and catch the fleeting pornography of butt and thighs in my window, the cleft of self that invites endless violation, and I spread my legs for no one. My taste is me.

Then I dress and pack a few days' clothing in a black garment bag, and go to meet Popi at the airport.

A small irony: the postcard from Cob in my mailbox on the way out. My summer, he writes, was three weeks at Camp Winnebago with autistic children, then to South Dakota, Black Hills, Pine Ridge Reservation, Powwows, Sundances, Fry Bread, Corn Soup and the Spirits.

Strange, but I feel close to him now, as if I've followed his lead and wandered too far from myself. I just have to go further astray, it's the only direction left.

The limousine is waiting outside my door, as Popi promised. I sling the strap of my bag over my shoulder, and walk out into the street.

THIRTY-THREE

This is a city of openings. Everywhere archways trace a curve of inviting darkness in immaculate sun. Windows are cut out of hot, bright stone. I lift my hand and watch a melted blade of light move across my flesh.

Rains sweep through and vanish, leaving only a wet jungle light. It feels like juice pelting the terra-cotta walls and cobbled stone. I stand at the bottom of Calle de la Cruz, Street of the Cross, with Popi's chauffeur, Cesar, who's my bodyguard for the day. He's a moustached, beer-bellied man with a leathery face and generous smile, dressed in a short-sleeved shirt, tan slacks, and shiny loafers. When he speaks he makes big, expressive gestures with his hands, so that his elbow brushes against my breasts or thighs.

A few hours ago Popi dropped me off at El Convento Hotel, originally a Carmelite convent built by a noblewoman, and went to Arecibo to visit his mother. He promised to be back tonight to feed me dinner in his home.

While Cesar buys Cokes and cigars at a corner store, I stop at a phone booth and call my answering machine. There's another message from Kim. His tone is friendly, with the usual patina of quiet reserve. He tells me to call him at Cheeks' tonight or he'll try me again. I wonder how much Katie told him. There's also a message from Sherry. *Marvelous good news,* it says, so I call her back.

"Hey, Lynnie. How about stopping by my place tonight?"

"God, I don't know. I'm kind of in the middle of something."

"You calling from outside?"

"Yeah, from the street."

"Well, can you spare an hour? Kyros bought a bottle of Cristal and we want to share it with you."

"Sherry—does that mean you said yes?"

"Yeah, I'm getting married. Don't sound too thrilled, sweetheart."

"I am, it's only that—"

"Think of a good toast, one that will last at least a few years. When will we see you?"

"I can't. Sherry, I'm not even in New York."

Silence beats on the line. "You were in New York yesterday. What's happened?"

"I'm in San Juan."

"In San *Juan?*"

"Right."

"You're with Kim," she says.

"Actually, he doesn't even know I'm here. I came with Popi."

"You flew to San Juan with Popi?" I can hear the warmth draining from her voice. "The nephew? Are you sleeping with him?"

"Oh right. I'm playing Mata Hari of the Caribbean. Actually, Popi and I followed Katie here."

"So this is an obsession," she says sadly.

Cesar approaches me, and I hold up a hand, signalling a few more minutes.

"Listen," Sherry says. "I'm spooked now. I'll hold the champagne . . . I'm afraid if I open it when you're not around you won't get back. When *are* you coming back?"

"A few days. Sherry, I'm sorry. How come things are so weird and synchronous? Don't you ever wonder?"

"I always wonder," she says vaguely. "Today two of my old boyfriends called me. Today of all days."

"Drink the Cristal and I'll buy you another one." *I'm losing you.* "I'll call you tomorrow."

I walk with Cesar, who's still gesticulating and occasionally brushing my body with his hands, as if I haven't noticed that he's scoring surreptitious caresses.

I sit on an outcropping of the wall across from the Nadal residence. "Cesar, I know you're on the job, but why don't you cover me from Amanda's," I suggest, gesturing to a turquoise café around a bend in the road.

And I wait like a lover in thrall. Just sit and wait for Katie, while a strange exhilaration fills me. I'm certain this is the circumference of insanity—how could I feel euphoria now? This is what combat journalists experience when their senses are pierced and exalted by war, and they see a mesmerizing, seemingly slow, taffy-like choreography of bombs, guns, exploding skin and bones. They truly *see* —the good ones, anyway.

Katie's near, I sense her, cheeks burned and slightly peeling from a day at the beach, hair swept back with a bright plastic headband, wearing a t-shirt dress and black pumps and nothing else, no underwear, no jewelry. She's coming to this place where she was most herself.

After two hours of sitting alone, waving Cesar back to Amanda's a few times, I realize that tonight is not my moment to encounter Katie. But this almost preternatural sense that she's close—I can't shake it. And so I let Cesar escort me back to El Convento. He posts himself at a café table in the inner café, whose tiers of creamy archways and arcades once led to nuns' cells. There's a message from Popi, confirming his arrival at nine. *Dress up*, says the message. *I'll be inviting a few friends.* I go to my room.

Lucky that I brought a Betsey Johnson confection with me; black lycra top with silk spaghetti straps and a pleated chiffon skirt. The top is such a tight hug it makes me look flat-chested; the day I bought it, Sherry and I ducked down to an outré lingerie store in the Village that sells black leather underwear, edible handcuffs, and an assortment of push-up and strapless bras. "Naomi Campbell wears these on the runway," the dart-thin, sallow saleslady claimed, holding up two foam cups with erect foam nipples. They unnerved me, like seeing a storefront mannequin with pubic hair. I decided to go flat.

A scoop of black pearls on the neck, onyx earrings, and muddy shadow on my lids to bring out the highlights of my hair. The woman in the mirror is warm, slow and touched with a bit of Creole madness. She wants to walk into the sea, to stand on a little loveseat of cobbled street and count the admiring glances of men. Sugar kings and slaves are whispering to her.

Downstairs I join Cesar. Finally Popi arrives, clothed in black linen slacks and a dark gold jacket.

"Ever the young aristocrat," I greet him.

"And you are a flower, but I won't tell you which one."

"You've forgotten the name?"

"Oh, I know the name. But when I tell you, it means you don't fascinate me anymore."

"How many flowers do you refuse to name?"

He smiles. "Do you mind if we walk a few blocks to my home?"

This is the house Nadal built. Here is the sea-green stone. This is the courtyard made of ships' ballast. This is the house where Kim killed.

That is a wall of windows framed with red glass. This is the floor from Genoa, all marble, where guests are greeted. This is the place where Kim stood, wondering which archway to walk through.

These are the studded doors to the kitchen. Look up. Those are wood fanlights that resemble the rays of the sun, called *sol trunco*— cut sun. A mahogany counter, blue Spanish tiles. These are the urns filled with taro root. Here is the mortar and pestle for *sofrito*.

This is an archway, and another, yet another. Here is a gallery, and another, yet another. This is a suite of space and light. This is the house Nadal built. Here is the throne room, here is the war room, and a few guest rooms. Open this door. These are chairs with embossed backs. This is an earthenware urn, a leather screen from Cordoba, hand-tooled and painted. And here is another pierced fanlight, set with blue and gold stones, like a peacock's tail carved of wood. This is the tiled fire wall.

Here is a stairway, and another. Turning, turning, stairway to stairway. This is the hall with its white arches. Here are dark and bitterly sumptuous woods. These are shelves of pottery, those are shelves of saints. So many flowers and falling vines.

This is Nadal's bedroom, with folding doors of *capa prieto*, a native wood. Here a church tapestry, there a Spanish refectory table. Open the windows onto the sea. This is the room where Katie slept. That is the sewing spindle, and the four-poster framed with brocade. Royal lace is laid on the bed. Here is a carving of Saint Peter, and a gilded carving of a queen.

And now we descend. This is the garden at the heart of the house, like a pit at the heart of a fruit. What happened here? Come, don't be afraid. First walk through a stark and sun-drenched room, all white with white stone.

And we emerge into a violent Eden. Banana and grape trees weeping purple and yellow and green. An old wellhead that doesn't work. Stand here, in the cooling shadow. Don't be afraid. Stand under the old *nispero* tree. This is where Katie danced for men's hats. These are lilac bluestone tiles, in the form of a coil, a labyrinth of stone. Such circular mazes were built into the floors of churches for true believers. You can walk this maze to the center. See if you have a pilgrim soul! This is the flower at the hub of the maze, the one flower that will *never* be named. Really! It really has no name.

This is the house Nadal built.

"You've inherited a beautiful home, Popi."

"You flatter me. Now let me see to the dinner preparations. My chef has been working all day. Sit down. I'll bring you a drink."

"The old proverb of the conquistador was, *'Tiene su alma en su armario.'* He keeps his soul in his closet!" Popi sets his etched wine glass on the table and observes his guests' reactions.

Nine of us are dining by candlelight under the canopy of night in the garden, and we're in the grip of a philosophical fight. There's an elderly woman just back from Barcelona, with a wrinkled, patrician face, and her beautiful, Bacchus-like son, Javi, who has black hair and a pink mouth; a pair of men in their forties who claim to be wall-daters—archaeologists attempting to date the stones of the forbidding twin forts, El Morro and San Cristóbal; a middle-aged art critic who is spare, small and ugly—the seedy, ascetic ugliness of a man with a powerful mind—and his twenty-year-old lover, whose pear-shaped, luscious face is wrapped in a scarf like the young Anaïs Nin. Finally, I'm seated between a

Puerto Rican equestrian named Manuco and his graceful wife, Perri.

The centerpiece of the table is a coconut shell mounted in silver —the island's aristocrats once drank morning milk from such cups.

Popi has described each dish to me as they've been served: pork shoulder with tamarind sauce; a pie made of sweet plantains, ground beef and mozarella cheese; pink peas; pigeon peas; *mofongos* of fried plantains stuffed with lobster, pigs' feet and veal, served in a broth; steak fries cut from yucca root; a guinea hen paté; *pasteles,* a confection of root vegetables and pork that's shredded and mashed by hand, wrapped in a banana leaf, and slowly cooked. And, on several plates, steaming hills of rice and bowls of *sofrito,* a spicy condiment that Popi says is like music, improvised in every household.

"You parrot your uncle, Popito," admonishes Manuco. His voice has the staccato music of an island people, full of joking innuendo. "He always romanticized his Spanish heritage. He always talked about the sorrow of his defeated people. But it's injured vanity, that's all."

"Vanity? They're going to paint the stars and stripes on the entire Caribbean. It's relentless. Somebody's got to resist."

"Why? You should welcome another culture. When did Spain start to decline? When she pushed out the Jews and killed commerce. When she expelled the Moors and killed agriculture. When she purged her people with *autos-da-fé.*"

"I don't care a shit for influence. We need our dreams," Popi retorts. Once, he tells us, the *hacendado* rose out of a mahogany featherbed, bathed in a secluded stream, loafed in the starlight, sent his sons to study in Madrid. "Now we aspire to a second car and a color TV! Why do you think my uncle was so popular? Because he understood the old ways. Besides, it's embarrassing when you drive through our towns and see thousands of homes where they actually buy artificial grass when the tropical grasses are growing free. We are not just a tract of American real estate."

"Your uncle was a snob because it was useful," interjects Javi. "The twentieth-century Puerto Rican was never the sixteenth-century conquistador."

Popi says calmly, "Our family is different."

"How so?"

"After the Americans came, my family purposely destroyed itself," Popi says proudly.

"A fairy tale of your uncle's," Manuco retorts.

"But you know it's true! The other *hacendados*, they sold their land to American corporations, moved to the cities, and entered the middle class. We fought, with our own suicide. We let ourselves be broken. Better that way!"

"It was just bad judgment, and you romanticize that, too."

"Look, all we ever were to the Spanish was a military stronghold," says the wall-dater. "They were too interested in the gold in Peru to worry about making money here."

"Popi, you speak English, don't you?" inquires Javi.

"Doesn't it sound like it?"

"I mean that you don't speak Castilian," he continues. "You speak *English*. You already sold your soul."

"I speak French and Latin, too."

"Further proof there's no such thing as a real Spanish throwback on this island."

"You know what the *yanqui* policy was." He turns to me. "During the early years of the occupation they told us we had no devotion to our native tongue. Not like the French in Canada. They said our language was a patois that Spaniards found almost unintelligible, that it was necessary to 'educate' us into English."

"They alphabetized you," interjects the Colombian woman. "They taught you to spell and write. They didn't teach you to see yourselves differently."

"Then they gave us citizenship, but of course that was just before the war, good timing. Do they think citizenship is all we need to feel like Americans? The way a stick over the shoulder makes a boy feel like a soldier?"

"I do," says the Colombian woman. "I feel American."

"You're a piece of America, darling, that still prays to Jesus and still speaks Spanish."

"So?"

"So?" says Popi. "There's a dreamy sadness to our souls. *Regresar por las noches al vacío que producen las tardes de sol.*"

"In English, please," I ask him.

"We return at night to the emptiness left behind by afternoons of sun. A rough translation."

"Be careful when a young man quotes poetry," Manuco warns and turns to me. "What does the American lady say to all this?"

"I was afraid of that question."

"Why? This whole argument has been staged for your entertainment."

I glance at Popi; he smiles. "A bit, perhaps."

"I guess I think of America like a lion cub. One playful swipe of the paw and somebody's dead. We don't understand our own power."

"America is the biggest island in the world. Why should Joe American care about the fate of somebody thousands of miles away? I don't blame you."

"Enough," says Popi suddenly. "Time for dessert. Mango cheesecake, papaya flan, and a passion-fruit colada. These are sweets for the heart. As my uncle said, let your tongues taste what my wooden tongue can't say."

The waiter returns with plates of glistening sweets and frosty glasses.

"It's good?" Popi asks, turning to me.

"Way beyond."

"So," he says, twinkling, all his proud fire doused, "I still have a chance. *Salud, pesetas y amor, y el tiempo para gustarlos!*"

The guests are departed, and Popi and I have gone up to a terrace garlanded with hibiscus, to listen to the sea. Before us is a perfect view of La Perla, blue and red flags from the island's political parties waving on rooftops.

"The most picturesque slum under the American flag," comments Popi, as he pours two cups of *aguardiente,* firewater.

He hands me the glass. I think of kissing him. It's Kim's heat incubating in me. I feel as if I could set fire and lay waste to anybody, male or female.

"So what am I supposed to do? What's the plan?"

"Well, apparently you just missed her today. She ate alone at La Zaragozana, and went for a drink at El Batey. That's what I was told, anyway." He smiles. "She and I used to go to El Batey to talk. It's a shoddy place. The hand-grenade school of interior design. We would talk about everything under the sun. She told me I was her cotton-candy friend. She meant that I was sweet and didn't trouble her. My uncle, of course, troubled her deeply." He shrugs. "I think your approach is perfect. If you don't mind waiting outside my house, I believe you'll see her tomorrow."

"That's what I'll do, then. Where is she now?"

"Do you want me to find out?"

"She's being watched constantly?"

He nods.

"No, don't bother. It's just that she feels so close."

He sips his *aguardiente* and observes me.

"You're not setting me up, Popi?"

"For what? I need your help."

"Promise."

"I promise."

"What good is your promise?"

"As good as your trust."

I lean forward. "What did Kim do today?"

"He went to work. He went to visit his friend—"

"Cheeks?"

Popi nods. "Yesterday he took Katie in a taxi-cab to the airport. And he went back to Cheeks. That's all I know."

He puts his glass down. "You know," he says softly, suddenly, "I will never touch Katie."

"Never?"

"She had a love affair not only with my uncle but with this house, and she lost both. If she's innocent, she will come live in this house. But I won't touch her." Because, he tells me, everything must come from Katie. Months from now, maybe years from now. He'll be slow poetry taking hold of her soul. He wants nothing that she doesn't give freely. To be loved is the masterpiece. And when she loves, she'll have lost sight of everything except what he wants her to see.

THIRTY-FOUR

Stand here in the cooling shadow. Don't be afraid.
This is where he killed a man. How strange to stand
in the place where he stood. Now he's like a spider
web of silence laid over my face. Felt, but barely
felt. Like a wind that just died down. Won't I see
him again?

THIRTY-FIVE

Katie knows why I'm here—when she walked through the doors of La Bonbonería at nine-thirty in the morning, where I was drinking coffee and eating *mallorca tostada,* she simply stopped short. I watched masks slide in and out of place: amazement, fear, indignation, and finally, a canny awareness. She surveyed the coffee shop, which barely had an empty seat, stared at me, then turned and walked out. I waved a ten-dollar bill at a balding waiter in a white shirt, and ran after her.

We went wordlessly up the cobblestoned street, past jewelry and t-shirt shops. Just to piss me off, she stopped in a store that was rolling up the gates for morning business.

"I like these shoes," she said to nobody in particular, then marched into the store. *"Me gusta los zapatos cómodos de tacón plano."*

She bought them while I waited, embarrassed and rooted to the spot. It was like those dreams of humiliation you have as a kid where you unwittingly show up at school in your bra and cotton panties.

"Okay," she said when we stepped outside, back into the brilliance, "what the hell are you doing in San Juan?"

"I was eating breakfast. But then when I saw you—"

"*Why* did you follow me here? Am I supposed to be flattered?

Have you fallen in love with me? I've had a woman or two do that."

"I'm writing about Puerto Rican food."

"Gave up science? So go write your article."

She started to walk. Once again I followed and we went in silence past burnished streets, past gardens and courtyards and men fishing off a street called La Princesa, until we reached Calle Norzagaray at the top of the old city. In the distance I could see the tree-fringed peninsula that was once a leper colony. Katie and I just stood there.

We're standing there now.

"Can we talk?" I ask her again.

"Let's not and say we did." It's that cliché Kim uses, and she offers it in the same wry, mocking tone.

"I have the morning free. . . . Can't I talk to you?"

"Kim's gonna hate this. Actually, he hates anything complicated."

"I won't be around to care. It's over between me and him. I just want to understand some things."

"That's why you flew down here?" she mocks. "To *understand* things?"

"Listen, I came down, and it looks foolish and I feel stupid. But do you think I'd be here if I wasn't going crazy? This whole situation is killing me."

"You hardly even know Kim. What's your problem?"

I want to tell her. How I never knew what a virgin I was, untouched, half-heard; how Kim's patchwork of truths hid the truth; how I know too much, but not enough. But I want to keep my secret, too.

"I'll tell you," I say.

"Am I stopping you?"

We approach El Morro, a majestic, undulating skirt of green where tourists fly kites, kids play kickball, and lovers picnic. The fort protrudes in the distance.

Katie sits in the grass, kicks off her pumps and wiggles her toes. "So you're not planning on seeing him anymore?"

I shake my head.

"Mmm-hmm." She scans the sky, with its tendrils of cloud, and then says in a lazy tone, "I haven't sat here for ages. Seems like I got way too tight with four walls back in New York. How can you stand that city?"

"It's got everything, that's all. You have to be the kind of person who enjoys contrasts."

"You need to see homeless men curled up in gutters with scabs all over their legs to feel like you're really living?"

I laugh.

"So," she says, "you said you want to talk?"

"I do. Yeah."

"Good. Mind if I lie back and listen?"

She stretches in the grass, lifting her arms over her head and lolling there with an almost violent pleasure. There's something indolent and sublime about this woman. I can't take my eyes off her.

"I don't think you *know* how to talk," she says after a moment, her eyes heavy-lidded, voice sleepy. "You just ask questions and then do this disappearing act. So this is a test, kind of like how long can you hold your breath under water. Go ahead. Like you said, you came down here for something."

For Popi, I imagine myself answering. That would make her sit up.

For escape, I could say. From what? *From Kim.* It makes no sense. I'm still running headlong into his life.

For revenge. Kim thinks he can give me a medley of lies? I'll puncture each one, lay them at his door and leave.

For love. Love doesn't end, but what you make of it changes.

"For myself," I say finally. "I sit there writing about things you can't even see like quarks or neutrinos or viruses."

She seems as still as a statue in the grass.

"Kim got to me. Maybe I'm obsessed. But I can't stop or go back. It's like when a bird's born, did you ever watch that? The egg's smooth and warm and nobody would guess what's in there, and then it just starts to crack, from the inside."

Why won't she look at me? I don't know what else to say. I need to shake off this strange, carnal spell she's making.

She looks up.

"Oh come on. You're chickening out? I was listening."

"I'll continue. I just—"

"I don't mind spending the day with you," Katie continues. "At first I was furious. Invasion of privacy. But what the hell. Life is just a day-to-day thing for me now. I get through."

"What did you used to hope for?"

"Why should I tell *you*?"

"You've got to tell somebody, don't you?"

"Nobody, just nobody," she says vaguely. "Stop staring at me in that weird way."

"But you've been posing. You want me to stare."

We stare at each other.

"It's war, isn't it?" She sits up, slips her shoes on. "I guess I need company real bad. Come on."

"Where are we going?"

"To get my car. It's parked by the other fort. See that guy over there? He's been tailing me all morning and I feel like making him work for his money."

"The older man in the red shirt?"

She nods, then gives me a cool look. "You don't seem surprised."

"Well—" I seesaw between lie and truth, and for some reason I think of the percussive pulse when Kim unbuckles his belt in the dark. It's like a heartbeat, it moves in my neck and my fingers. I want more of him and can't get it. But she can give it. She's the next best thing.

"Go ahead," Katie urges, half-irritated. "You know something. Or you think something. I'd like one clean punch."

"All right."

She waits.

"Kim told me," I blurt.

"Told you? About me?"

"About Nadal—the drugs—the threats—"

"Who? The what? The threats?"

"The gunshots in the wall—the herb cure that didn't work—"

"Herb cure?"

"Being followed—the condo—hiding you—"

"Nobody hides me," she bursts out. "I make people notice me."

"I mean the condo in Isla Verde. It sounded like hell," I add, with a certain relish. "But Kim wanted to protect you. He'd do anything for you, I guess."

"Like sending his New York girlfriend down to spy on me?"

"Is that what you think?"

"I think Kim doesn't talk. So if he's talking like you say he is, the world's just fucked, everything's fucked."

She starts to walk, stiff and furious, a windup doll gone mad, and I follow, glancing once over my shoulder. The man in red isn't even looking at us. I wonder how a tail operates.

"Kim would never tell someone he'd just met about all this," she says. "He just never would."

"He didn't think our paths would cross."

"How much do you know about me?"

"I know mostly small things. Like one night you left him a message about wigs you saw in a shop window, these frosted wigs the native women wear, and it seemed sad and wonderful. And that was a reason he loved you, because you left those kind of messages."

"Wigs?" she echoes incredulously. "But what about Nadal? About me?"

"I know you went to live with Nadal, and became friends with his nephew, Popi, but mostly I know what happened after you came back."

"Who said I was friends with Popi?"

"Kim."

"Never," she says, in an extremely quiet voice. "I never told him."

"He must have guessed. Or maybe he asked around."

"Uh-huh." She rubs her eyes with her fists, then smoothes her white t-shirt dress, leaving an impression of damp palm-marks. Her arms hang at her side. "Some friendship. It was over practically before it began. Popi turned against me when his uncle did. Just like that. Pffft."

She seems dispirited suddenly. We keep walking.

"This is the house," she says a moment later.

We stare up at the sea-green façade.

"With the bullet holes intact," I reply.

"Bullet holes," she affirms. "Thirty-three of them. War wounds, you know." She goes up to the gate. "You don't know how beautiful it is. Sometimes I get a craving like an alcoholic just to walk through it again. Like things would be okay if I could sit in the courtyard and eat *carambola* and drink espresso like I used to do."

She turns, one hand on the gate.

"You do look like you belong," I concede.

Her hand tightens on the gate. "Maybe I wanna be alone," she says in a small voice.

"I'll go if you really want."

We just stand there.

"Is that what you call walking?"

"Katie," I say, stepping up to the gate, putting my own hand around the iron grillwork, my heart knocking, "I don't want to go. But I don't know what to do. I'm scared of you."

"I still can't figure why you followed me."

"I had to come see you. You started this whole thing."

Her hand slides slowly down the gate.

"I didn't start anything," she says, gesturing to the house. "He did."

She was standing in the lobby of La Concha after an ocean swim, in a gold bathing suit and black pumps, and she wanted that feeling of being the dead center of attention, so she flung her hair over her head and brushed her fingers through it again and again. When she looked up, unseeing, unfocussed, she sensed she was being eaten up by someone's eyes. Ah, the pleasure of being fucked for just an instant by a man in a doorway, across a crowded street, on a platform waiting for a train.

Somebody touched her arm. She would have kept going but the fingers tightened slightly, and when she turned the first thing she saw was a man's brilliant, brokenhearted, happy smile. A Humpty-Dumpty smile, shattered and full of hope.

She walked and he walked next to her.

"Where can I find you later?"

She felt careless and golden then, sensing other eyes on her, too, so she told him the name of her street.

"I want *your* name."

She told him.

"Just your first name?"

"That's right."

"May I see you?"

"No, but you can drive down my street."

He smiled. "Shall I park at the beginning or the end?"

She'd looked him up and down then and felt a little dizzy, as if she were at the site of a collision; his body seemed all massive thrust and his face so mild. His suit was perfect, shirt soft, voice clipped and beautiful, but he himself was a Cyclopean stranger. Even his hands were odd: small, delicate, but crudely thatched with black hair.

When his dinner companion walked up, Nadal invited Katie along, and they drove to a restaurant with an open stone bar and small tiled tables. Their table faced the sea. Even that first night he held court and talked like some kind of soldier-poet. He asked what had brought her to the Caribbean and she said peace.

"The Spanish people are so peaceful."

"But don't you know," he said, "that Puerto Rico's *serenidad* is not a Spanish trait? It's from Andalusia. Spaniards are bloody."

And it was some of the bloodiest who'd colonized this corner of the sea, he said, speculators and adventurers carrying a knapsack of flour and mining tools, and burning and roasting native Indians on their way, or sentencing them to slave labor in the gold mines. These Spaniards were so lavishly brutal that after a decade hundreds of thousands of Taino Indians were dead.

"It took time for the tropical climate to melt the Spanish will," said Nadal, "but catch us at the right moment, and we're still quick to fight. Read the newspapers and you'll find murders committed over a card game or a suspicion of infidelity."

"That's why I feel at home," Katie said, and she was sincere. "Anyway, there's another reason I came. I was practically dying of pain." And she told him about her arthritis.

His manner changed then, softened. "You left everything behind?"

"My home, my friends, yeah. But it wasn't like I emigrated to a different country. Puerto Rico is half-American, anyway."

He turned to his companion. "Another American who came here to be restored."

Each evening at dinner, talk gushed out of him, and it bore down on her: gloomy, cryptic, sentimental, savage. But then, at home, she suffered over Kim's reticence. She went from deluge to dryness. Kim sat in their backyard, reading one of his sailing books or listening to talk radio (a habit he'd picked up from Cheeks), his fingers massaging the ears of their labrador. His patience galled her.

"I'm not happy!" she burst out one night, standing in the lit doorway of the terrace.

"You were happy," he said, from the shadows where he sat outside. "But it scared you. Let yourself be happy again."

Rain, rain, everywhere, and not a drop to drink. Nadal was a nightly storm. He brought her armfuls of flowers with a proud correctness, as if obeying an old chivalric code. The waiters put the flowers in a vase, and wrapped them after the meal. Sometimes she'd bring them home—eliciting nothing but, "Those are pretty," from Kim—and sometimes she'd toss them into the sea, watching them disperse in the inky water.

It was Nadal's letters that she kept. Handwritten letters addressing her as a girl, a belle, he wrote, a jack-o'-lantern smile, *una sonrisa malévolo*, I can't forget you, how you looked last night, one Chinese slipper on, the other dangling, your sweaty stockinged foot, your ruffled dress, your strong face and husky voice, the things you say, *I'm gonna find myself, I keep changing, I thought I found myself once, I thought it was here in my solar plexus, 'cause I wanted to be a singer once, and I was trained by a guy who taught children with cleft palates how to speak.*

Everyone has a first and then a last love, he wrote, and it's the last love that stamps the soul. The first is simple, it's a flying leap into life. The last must be Gordian in its knot, it permeates every memory, seeps into every pore; counterpoint to fate. It becomes fate. And so the last love is always a shock and an exception. She might be his last love.

"But I'm not gonna fuck you," she'd retort.

"I don't need that now."

"But I'm never going to."

"Then we'll talk. Tell me what you like. For example, do you like the feel of silk on your skin?"

"If I say yes, will you buy me a silk dress?"

"A silk undershirt. How would you like the feel of my hand?"

"Where?"

His hand covered hers. She looked down, fascinated by the carved bits of nails, the reddened cuticles; his fingertips were mildly calloused, and they rubbed her skin tenderly.

"Why do you say I'm your last love anyway?"

"I'm forty-six," he said. "I can measure what is inside me."

Weeks of dinners passed and occasionally, when he was driving her home, she'd ask him to caress her leg.

"Stroke," was what she'd say.

He stroked her calf, one hand still on the wheel. His discipline was perfect. She couldn't imagine being fucked by this barrel-chested man. She'd stare at him, rapt and appalled, while his hand moved on her bare leg.

"How many times," she'd mutter, eyes half-closed.

"Was I in love? My mother, and one other person."

She wasn't looking at anything anymore, eyes closed, as his finger traced a circle on her leg. Her skin was a funnel-point, and he was the open funnel. Let this go on forever. Not him, not his strange, heaving body, but his soul-lust.

"I wasn't there when my mother died."

Like most Latin boys, Nadal said, he'd worshipped his mother. She didn't seem made of the sap and blood of Puerto Rico. The cream of her curved down from neck to shoulder to arm, a white *volupte,* thick and slow and heavy. She had a soft crown of black hair and startling blue eyes. But she suffered from some kind of craziness. He'd come upon her suddenly and she'd be standing rigid at the stove or before the radio, unseeing, and she seemed to be breaking apart inside, an inner shattering that had been frozen in time. It was as if he'd caught her at the moment before the thousand pieces of her flew asunder. She lived daily with this terror, barely bore up under it, and it was at complete odds with her beauty.

And the result, of course, was that men had her. She never resisted. She'd be standing in the doorway of their house, unseeing, like someone about to fly apart, and a man would stop, curious. Talk to her. Touch her arm. She needed it. She just yielded.

"*Y el criado?*" What about the boy?

"*Déjele en paz.*" Leave him in peace.

Nadal waited in the front room until it was over. The man left. His mother stood, quiet, the cream of her thick and slow again. She'd comb his hair and fix him a meal. Then Nadal went out in the street. His shame was everywhere.

Maybe she took money from the men. He never asked her. But when he was eight she sent him to a monastery in the mountains. She should have kept him; he preferred to be near her. She died a few years later. There was a strange, wild strength in him now. And it was masked with the mildness the monks taught.

He went to live with his father, who beat him almost as a matter of course.

When he was thirteen, he found the world of cocaine, a world where etiquette hid rage. It required his own madness, his own mildness. By the time he was sixteen he had so much money that his father stopped beating him. He also stopped working. The man became constantly drunk, and docile. "You're a good boy," he'd say when the cases of liquor were delivered.

His sister—half-sister—understood. She'd lean in the doorway, staring at her father, and say to Nadal, "You've stewed him while he's still alive. He's floating in booze."

It was revenge, and one approved by the victim.

"So who was your second love?" Katie asked.

"Well," he said, "when my sister was twenty, she had a child."

"Your nephew?" Katie laughed. "So I'm the real first love."

Silence.

"What do you need, Nadal?"

"To give you things."

"But why?"

"You're like a child on Christmas morning who comes to the bottom of the stairs and stands with her thumb in her mouth, terrified that she has missed all the presents. Don't you want all the presents, *querida?*" he asked, in the tone of a man inexplicably in love with a woman and therefore stirred and heartened by her every wish.

"I can still put my thumb in my mouth," she taunted, and sucked on her thumb. "But you know what you said before. You called me the apple of your eye, except in Spanish it's the children of your eyes."

"But that *is* love," he told her. "You almost give birth to the other."

"And what if we just stay friends?"

"We'll be friends, and you'll let me buy you dinner."

"What about sex?"

"Here's your street."

"But you want me," she said with her easy, cavalier cruelty. "And I let you cop a feel on my leg, that's all. What are you going to do about sex?"

She expected anger, but saw only the most incredible softness.

"I don't go without," he said.

I don't go without. Where? Who? But a woman knows when a man's belly-heavy with love and, for the moment at least, Nadal seemed to be. She forgot the conversation until a week later, when she stopped in an art gallery in El Condado Hotel. Nadal was standing on the second floor near the casino. She ducked around a corner and watched him.

He was wearing a starched pink shirt and black linen pants, and his silver ringlets were slicked into place with a coating of gel. Every time a woman stepped out of the elevator, his body seemed to tense a little and he leaned forward. When the woman turned or walked by, he'd relax.

He went on waiting and Katie went on watching, until a Puerto Rican schoolgirl appeared. He didn't seem to recognize her, but she smiled in a shy, almost worshipful way, pressing her schoolbooks to her chest, and walked up to him. Katie inched forward and heard him say in Spanish,

"Do you like me?"

She nodded, her head tilting up at him, the wide, shy smile on her delicate, brown face.

"You do?"

"Oh, yes," she said. Her accent was not Puerto Rican, but Dominican.

"How old are you?"

"Eighteen, sir."

"Why don't we go upstairs?"

When they'd disappeared, Katie went round to the casino and bought chips. Her hands were shaking and she couldn't fit the tokens in the slot, so she just stood there in front of the machine, staring at renderings of pineapples and papayas. At last she began to laugh; she forced herself to laugh. "I mean Christ," she thought, "it's one way to stretch out our courtship. Just go to hookers. I mean this means I can have my dinners forever." Finally she began to yank the one-armed bandit. "Hell, I'll tease him about this tonight."

The surprise came twenty minutes later, when he appeared again in the entrance to the casino. The girl was gone. So quick?

Katie stared at him and, sensing her stare, he turned slowly. When he saw her, he came forward, moving in a creamy, almost slurred way.

"What are you doing here?" she asked.

"A cultural exchange," he said.

His eyes were bright, he was soft with delight, unkinked, unwound, velvet. He gazed at her as if he didn't give a shit what she guessed or thought. He was not himself; he was pooled with pleasure.

A thousand hours of extravagant courtship couldn't have sparked her the way his mood did in the casino. He even took her hand, in a soft and absent manner, and said,

"We'll meet tonight?"

"Of course."

Had he noticed her "of course," its new modesty? He seemed almost bemused.

"I have something different planned."

"Should I dress up?"

"No, dress as you always do. It will be a special night," he said, and kissed her cheek before he left.

She stood in the casino, stunned, galled, pricked with shame, and—suddenly, against all she had ever expected of herself, against her natural taste, her pride, her need—hot for him.

That night he took her to a party in her honor at his house.

"I want you to know I'm never going to fuck you, Señor Nadal." *Not after what I saw today.* "Even in your house."

He smiled. "I didn't ask."

"Why not though?"

He took her to an unlit courtyard wrapped by four floors of balconies. The outline of hundreds of faces hovered on the stairs and terraces. Katie stood staring at the crowd, thinking, *I gotta illuminate myself,* while Nadal walked around the courtyard, lighting candles set in crystal cups.

The music and dancing began, hundreds of guests spilling down the stairs as if some dam had burst. That night Katie danced her heat, danced her rutting heat. One after another the men tossed their hats. Each hat was like a teasing slap in Nadal's face. At last they were hers, every hat but Nadal's and that of a young man at the top of the stairs. "I'll marry you all!" she cried out over the music, and that was when Nadal stepped away from the wall and said in a low voice,

"Katie, give me these hats."

"They're mine."

"You can take them home. I will have Popi wrap them for you."

"Who's Popi?"

"My nephew. You can meet him later. Come."

He motioned to an oak credenza under a tree. A rainfall of moss fell from the lower branches, cordoning off part of the courtyard, and they walked through it. Now they stood in perfect darkness; pots of small flowers could just barely be sensed.

He was staring at her but she couldn't see his eyes.

"When you were dancing out there, were you enjoying yourself?"

"Having the time of my life. What did you expect?"

"It was my present to you, *Catalina.*"

"*Catalina,* huh? Am I some Spanish hybrid?"

"You don't like the name?"

"Hey, my momma christened me Kathryn. Aka Katie."

"But it's *my* impression of you. Because I found you."

"You want to. Who said you did?"

He caught the inner bulb of her lip in his mouth and bit, delicate, hard. And he kissed her. She floated along the little driftwood-pain of his bite.

"You want to hurt me?" she asked.

"Even God has a shadow, why shouldn't we?"

"You think that's true?"

He told her that though he'd been orphaned at eleven, at twenty-six he'd found a teacher named Doña Nilda, a seer who'd taught him things. She taught him, for instance, that the body and mind were one. And so when Katie told him about her arthritis and how she left it behind, he thought that she might be able to understand him.

"I've done things in my life that were wrong. I'm so full of wrongness there should be no hope. But look how full of hope I am. Now that you've come. Doña tells a story of a man who believed he could only be happy if he made a necklace of the knuckles of a hundred men. So he killed a hundred men and collected a hundred knuckles and then as he was stringing his necklace he began to be sick. He knew what he'd done."

"What happened then?"

"He prayed for forgiveness."

"And?"

"I don't know the end of the story. I haven't been forgiven yet."

"Tell me you want me," she whispered. "Don't ever go with any hooker again. Promise."

"I won't go again."

"Did you do it a lot?"

"How high can you count? I think I'm glad you saw."

"Why are you glad?"

"I wanted to show you who I am."

They rejoined the party. Nadal introduced her to Popi. He was whimsical, a bending reed. Next to Nadal he looked like a sylph.

Sometime in the night Katie wandered upstairs, and Nadal followed, mounting the stairs silently. She noticed him shaking when he swung the carved doors to his room, and shut them behind her. All the shutters had been opened, and she could almost breathe the sea, but he went to close each one. The four-poster bed was topped with brocade, the cutwork sheets inlaid with lace. Candles had been set along the floor of his room and he blew them out.

He was shy, he told her. Even with prostitutes he didn't undress. His body was caked with hair, and his shape was strange.

"You hate your body."

"I do."

"Well, I can't see a thing."

"If you don't want to touch me I understand. I'll do every-thing."

"That's not my style, señor," she teased.

She unbuttoned his shirt. Her hands moved in amazement—repelled, intrigued—over the swirls of hair on his enormous back, like fossiled etchings in stone.

"In the morning," he whispered, "I'll be downstairs in my robe, eating breakfast. And you'll join me."

"You never wake up in bed with a woman?"

"I never will."

"The way you talk about him, I can't imagine he was a drug dealer. Who is this man?"

"Who *was* this man."

"I'm sorry. He still seems alive. Not just for you, for Kim, too." I open my window. We're driving into the rain forest. The jungle plants are mutant in their giant scale. "Was it hard leaving Kim?"

"It tore me up but I didn't care. I knew where I belonged."

"With Nadal."

"Nadal," she echoes.

"How could you give up the sex, though? I mean with Kim."

"For you it's the first time, so you think it'll never happen to you again. Oh, don't give me that look. I know about you. A born-again sex freak. But after a few years you'll be with somebody else and it *will* happen. Then Kim will be your first but not your only."

"But he's so good. Even his touch is different. And how many guys can stay hard even after they come?"

"Not that many. But some. Enough."

"Was Nadal one?"

"I told you he was quick, didn't I?" She grows quiet. "But I kind of liked that. I did. When he got inside me he couldn't stop himself. This enormous man, this terrible excitement. I was the only woman in the world who mattered."

"So, after you made love, that's when you knew you would leave Kim?"

"When I walked into Nadal's house. That house," she throws her head back, "that house was him. Like walking into the man himself."

"I can imagine."

The night Katie left Kim she pulled out drawers, up-ending them and stuffing their contents into black garbage bags. Shoving those drawers back into dressers, she kicked them into place. Kim stood like a deaf and dumb sentry, never once asking her to stay. Was he catatonic or just following his old rule of steadfast kindness?

"Say something," she snapped, finally.

"Nadal is a drug dealer," he offered.

"So's the United States government and just what do you think my doctor's doing when he hands out tranquilizers and charges double? I'm not judging *any*body."

"Try and stay out of it anyway, will you?"

"You think I'm gonna start selling?" She laughed. "Or snorting?" Then she shook her head. "I'm in love. Is that enough?"

Not a muscle moved in his face. "That's enough."

"Hey, you weren't supposed to say that. This gentlemanly shit is gonna kill me."

They smiled at each other suddenly, and Katie turned another drawer over on the bed, spilling balled-up tights, lace leggings, camisoles, and t-shirts that still bore price tags (she always bought two shirts, in case the first wore out). She threw a pair of tights at Kim. "Basket!" He tossed them back to her. There was a complicity between them even now, a kind of ironic tolerance of their differences.

"Any other advice for me?"

"Packing like a whirling dervish doesn't help."

"Well, I can't pack slow. And look, I know I shouldn't leave, I know if I weighed the damn thing I'd stay." She paused, and added, "You saved us for years."

Her sudden softness must have hurt. He whistled at the dog, who leapt toward him. "You'll be back," he said, and left the house.

She opened another drawer, slowly now, and lifted a heap of underwire brassieres in her arms. The plush and flimsy silk, molded by wire loops, seemed a symbol of her contradicatory self, and she stood there, unable to pile the bras into a bag. Finally she stuffed them in her purse, as if that were a halfway measure, and she might still return them to this house, this man.

But Nadal made her forget. Nadal covered her life like a warm shadow. That night she stood at his front gate while he carried her bags inside. He moved like a heavyweight boxer in a trance—his soft face a smudge in the evening light. For an instant she balked. Kim, with his clean lines, had been so comfortingly American.

He gave her a room of her own down the hall from his, and introduced her to the two sisters he kept as servants. The younger one, broad-hipped and brown-skinned, Rosa, would be hers. He went to get the last load of bags, and Katie began to open one of the garbage bags and dump her clothes on the bed. Rosa sidled up to her, saying in Spanish,

"Please, let me fold these for you."

"That's okay."

"Please," said the servant, gently pushing her back.

"I can fold my own things. But thank you."

Rosa grew quiet, then began to pick up a t-shirt and smooth it.

"Really, I don't need help. I have to figure out where I want to put these things."

She went on smoothing the shirt and began to fold it.

"You like that?" Katie said. "You want it?"

Nadal came to the door. "My servants are not beggars."

"I just thought she might want it."

"Their wants are not your concern."

"Well, I can't really use her help right now. I need to do this myself."

"Don't you understand you must let her do it? I brought her out of the ghetto, a family of twelve. All her pride is in her work."

"In folding my clothes?" Katie scoffed.

"It may seem strange to you, but this is her fate and she has embraced it."

"Okay," said Katie, shrugging.

And Rosa smiled. *"Gracias,"* she said. *"Gracias, señorita."* She just kept thanking Katie for being allowed to fold the clothes.

"I never saw anything like that," Katie said in a low voice. She turned to Nadal. "With her around all the time, I'm gonna get fat and lazy."

"You have a choice. You can watch her work, or you can come with me."

On his four-poster bed, he pulled her to him and held her in his lap like a daughter.

"Y poco a poco me olvidé de vivir," he said. *And little by little I forgot how to live.* She understood he meant his life before she'd come.

"Look at those angel's trumpets," she says now. "See 'em? I love driving in El Yunque. You know how I learned to drive? At two in the morning I snuck out my window and climbed down a tree and drove my parents' car around town. Then I'd sneak back in between the two branches of the tree, which I'd named eleven and twelve. So my mother would say what time did you come in last night and I'd say, 'Sometime between eleven and twelve.' "

"I pulled the same kind of trick when I was a kid. I loved horses but my parents wanted me to take piano lessons. So I asked them to put the piano in my room. I'd tape myself playing, and put the tape in my recorder."

"Then you'd sneak out?"

"Exactly."

She laughs. "Look at that," she exclaims. "The Rainforest Restaurant. You wanna stop?"

"Sure."

"You know, I'm happy right now, talking to you. I don't care *who* you are anymore."

"For today we'll be friends," I suggest.

"So, okay, friend." She laughs. "*Friend,* I gotta know the whole deal with Kim." She swings onto the side of the road near the restaurant and parks. "Uh oh. It's about to rain. See those trees? They've got these huge leaves with five fingers. See? Whenever it's gonna rain the leaves turn up and you can see their silver undersides."

I look at the steep hill of silver-white.

"And after the rain they all go green again. So how did you meet Kim? I didn't believe your line for a second."

I start to tell her.

THIRTY-SIX

The day after someone is murdered in La Perla, a burial celebration is held. At high noon you can hear the belch and smack of gunfire, and you can't take tour groups to El Morro or San Cristóbal without scaring the tourists.

There are rare times when rage or calculation or a mix of both teases the funeral calvacade up into the city itself. That's why Nadal's house still stands with bullet holes, a living badge of vulnerability and hatred in honor of the master chef whom he killed for cutting the kilos.

La Perla. Katie says in the morning you find hypodermics scattered along the benches at the top of Old San Juan. A cripple called the garbage man retrieves them to sell to addicts later in the day, down in El Caballo—the horse—a tail of the slum near San Cristóbal.

The police pull an occasional raid, and the junkies oblige and let themselves get arrested because otherwise the cops will just plant their own drugs and raid those. Everybody knows a fed because his nails are manicured, and dealers' hands are always grimy from handling the coke. Years ago the government bought the shacks nearest the water, tore them down, and paved a road between the rocks and waves. When you stand on that road and look straight up you see the backs of houses on high stilts, in reds and yellows, and above them, shaggy grass and horses grazing. A few of the homes have pools on the roof and marble inside.

La Calle de los Cuernos (the Street for Cheating Spouses) glints with bleach and water swept from homes with big, thatched brooms by women who daily hose down their floors. Painted into the dirt outside buildings are the words, *"Dios es amor."* Chickens and pigs wander freely. You can smell horse manure and hay, meat sizzling in oil, and ocean spray.

Standing in La Perla, Katie says, is like coming home. Nobody judges you there. You can just sink into that proverbial hole in the wall and be nothing but yourself. In the piercing light of a tropical afternoon in La Perla, nothing in the world seems dangerous anymore.

THIRTY-SEVEN

In a tin hut by the sea three men stood, while Nadal rubbed cocaine into the skin between his thumb and forefinger. Methodically, dreamily, his fingers rubbed, while Katie leaned against the door jamb watching. He seemed to be stretching out the transaction, as if he wanted her to remember every detail.

Like all men in love, he claimed that he was a changed man. He took her everywhere, as if he were preparing a foreign bride, educating her in all the customs of a new country.

They'd celebrated her move with a drive on the old Ruta Panoramica, the kinked and threadbare road that careens across the volcanic spine of the island. It took two days. Travelling at night in the mountains Katie felt certain she'd entered the womb of darkness itself. Nadal drove about five miles an hour, through sheets of rain, sounding the horn at each hairpin turn to warn oncoming cars.

Everything he said seemed absorbed by the colossal scale of nature. *The mountains here are sublime, and what does that tell you about the sublime? It has no morality,* he said. *These mountains are my home.*

And she herself felt a detached mood of acceptance; she was willing to witness anything, even when they stopped in a house in Utuado and watched four men disembowel the body of a dead priest. The priest was being shipped from Colombia to Canada, with a stopover in Puerto Rico. He had been on their list of senators, police officials and journalists who received payoffs, and had agreed to let his body be packed with bags of cocaine after he died.

The Ruta wound from town to town, and whenever they emerged from the dank and gorgeous forest they saw a *Marlboro* sign tacked to a tree trunk and a blond mutt lying on the street like a mascot, near a house at the top of the hill. It was exactly the same each time. The *casitas* were wonderfully garish, painted in Day-Glo hues. There was humor in the colors, as if the houses were mocking nature and knew the joke was on them.

Each day was different, but their nights never changed. In bed, under cover of complete darkness, there was only Nadal's talk, loamy, rich and dark. *There is no place on this island that's more than fifteen miles from the ocean. We have an old proverb. If you try to walk away from your life, you come to the sea so soon you have to turn around and then you meet yourself while walking back.*

He let her unbutton his linen shirt, remove his cufflinks, slide her hands over his body. It never ceased to repel and intrigue her, the feel of matted hair on his torso, his craggy, fleshy arms and chest.

"I get to know you like a blind person," she'd say. "You're really so embarrassed?"

"If you sat at the River Ganges in Calcutta with a leper who talked like me, would you let him kiss you?"

"Of course not!"

Maybe a woman, Nadal went on, who has lived for years with stumps for arms and a pink, scarred lid grown over one eye, a leper woman who indifferently brushes away the flies that feed on her rotting foot—that woman might see him as a beautiful man. "It's no trick of sight. She wouldn't see my deformities because she's accustomed to worse in herself. Of course, I've exaggerated to make a point."

"No, Señor Nadal, you're just the vainest man I ever met." She laughed, half-irritated, half-awed. "The way you talk. Deformities. You're demented. You're nothing but a madman." She kissed him. "Keep the dark if you want."

*　*　*

But he was changing. On the day he'd promised to take her to La Perla—a kind of final initiation rite—he left the door to his dressing room ajar and she surprised him dancing naked before the mirror, shutters closed, waving his shirt around his head and singing softly to himself in Spanish.

She stepped back instantly, ready to close the door. But—his gaze still riveted on the mirror—he now began to sing in English. He was grotesque and magnificent, and knew it, and no longer cared. "My love is new," he sang. "And my servants and my nephew are sleeping, and I dance in my room alone." He turned to her, smiling. "Look at me, *carita*. Look at me."

Now Nadal sat in a folding chair, rubbing cocaine into the flesh between his thumb and forefinger. Katie hovered just outside, watching the gloomy faces of the three men who stood opposite Nadal.

"Darling," he said finally, without looking up.

She shoved her hands into her jeans and waited.

"Darling," he repeated, and stood, framed in the pink aluminum doorway. He smiled at her and told her that, as always, she looked like a girl on Christmas morning. "Come, sit. Join us."

She sat on the chair, and waited for the show to begin.

"Who is the cook?" Nadal asked in Spanish, although he knew. It was the fat man with the bald head, whose skin was wrinkled like a breakfast crepe. His eyes were expressionless.

Nadal held out his hand and the man came forward, inspecting the skin, peering at the white dusting of impurities. His broad, bald head nodded lower and lower, revealing three cracked and lugubrious furrows, and it seemed almost as if one could read those lines as one reads a face—its private, inarticulate grief and pride. He made a clucking sound and his head bobbed slowly, balefully, until finally he sighed and turned to the others. Then they conferred in Spanish.

When the men looked up, Nadal was holding a sleek pistol. Katie crossed her legs and folded her hands, to let everyone see she was just the audience and knew nothing.

"Well," Nadal was saying with gentle irony, "my reputation. My reputation cannot endure this. Who would try to cheat me? Better still, why?" Nadal began to talk of the Spanish heart—how like any Latin male he had a yearning for the codes of truth and honor, and an even deeper yearning to prove that honor through bloodshed. Virgins, bulls, men and gods; the world must be made to bleed.

The men watched him, huddled together in the terrific heat of that tin room, baffled by his flight of rhetoric—and in their puzzlement they already seemed to have lost.

"If I walk out now," he concluded, "it will be all over Latin America that Nadal almost let himself be cheated and I will be cheated again, and my friends in Colombia will lose respect for me." He paused. "I really don't understand," he said softly. "Was it because I told you the girl was coming?"

The cook's head bobbed almost imperceptibly.

"So. You've all heard that Nadal lost his head over a girl? An American girl. You thought to yourselves he would never kill a man in front of this white lily. It's not the money that tempted you." He was silent, then asked the cook, "Would you die for honor?"

"Honor," the cook echoed in a faint voice.

"My honor," Nadal corrected him. "You two can live," he added to the men on either side of the cook, and then he shot him.

She remembered the two men kneeling beside the chef and heaving him onto the foam mattress. She remembered how Nadal turned to her, slow, careful, full of hope.

And what did he see? Katie's hands at her face. She didn't say anything. She held her face as if her head might come off.

A tin hut. A dead man. That was Calcutta. That was the leper. She turned and ran.

She ran up narrow cement stairs, kicking off her shoes and scooping them into one hand, stumbling against the enormous white piping someone had laid as a banister, ran past hay and manure from some horse's stable, past rusted walls, abandoned lots, little candy stores, pigs, chickens, old women, hammocks. She ran up into the city, along the curving sidewalk with its keyboard of white posts, down to the great white sheath of Casa Blanca and

through a secret stairway like a jewelry box of stone, down Paseo
de la Princesa and La Puntilla, to the old gold of docks and cruise
ships, where finally she walked by the water, carrying her shoes as if
they were flowers she would lay at some grave, if she ever found
the grave.

THIRTY-EIGHT

This is how it was when Kim took Katie back:

She arrived at his door about nine P.M. The house was dark. She found him in a chair in the living room, contemplating nothing. There was peace in this small home.

For a long time she stood in the middle of the room, trembling. His silence, his patience—they had complete power over her now.

"I can't go back there," she said finally.

"You can stay here for a while."

"I'm scared."

"Of him or of me?" came the wry answer.

"Have you . . . been okay?"

He was quiet.

She sat at his feet and put her head against his leg. "Have you missed me?"

"I've done a lot of thinking, as they say." He breathed out slowly. "I knew you'd be back."

Touch me, she thought. If you touch me, I'll know it's okay. Tell me a thousand times you're not going to forgive me, but touch me.

She sat there, her cheek against his leg, and waited to find out her fate. Touch me, touch me not. Touch me not. Touch me.

At last his hand moved slowly through her hair.

THIRTY-NINE

e've lingered for hours at The Rainforest Restaurant, and at
last we get back in Katie's car and drive to the city. Once we
hit the highway she puts down the hood and speeds, her
chestnut hair slapping her face as if she were the reckless heroine of
a movie.

"We're back where we started," Katie says as we reach Old
San Juan. "Want to stop and watch the sunset down in the cemetery?"

"It's right next to La Perla."

"You can't climb over the wall. Besides, you think I'm so
fucked-up I'd show my face in La Perla again? I'd get killed. The
cemetery's safe. C'mon." Katie parks the car and we walk. "What
hotel are you staying at?"

"El Convento."

"Spare no expense, huh?"

"I can write it off my taxes."

It's like walking into a castle, down this deep, curved hook of
road. The gouged mortar of the wall rises behind us.

"So, you never did tell me. Did Kim take you back that night?"
She gazes at me, cool. "You mean did we nooky?"

"That's not the word I'd use."

"Yeah? What would you prefer?"

"You know how it is with him."

"Did we fuck," she says flatly.

"Katie," I protest.

"Hey, earlier today you made me sit and listen to the same stuff. How our stud puppy couldn't get enough up in New York."

"It wasn't just sex."

"Well, this was," she says stubbornly. "You bump against Kim in the hallway and he's ready. It's not such a sacred thing." She shades her eyes for a moment. "Hey, we're in luck. The gate's open. Somebody just got buried."

Here white graves are garnished with angels, rising and falling down to the brink of the sea. Look back and the massive wall, ancient poem of earth and ice, stands solid against the sky. Through another gateway is a chapel laced with arches. Walk up the ring of steps and you see four arched openings, one fitted inside the other in an illusion of symmetry and eternal return, and beyond it a scarf of blue.

"Yeah, I started sleeping with Kim again. And it drove Nadal mad."

"Makes sense," I say tightly.

"The man still loved me. He was too proud to take me back, but he was crazy with jealousy. He thought I was going to betray him. He thought I'd go to the cops."

"But *Kim* tried to go to the cops. So Nadal wasn't wrong."

She's silent.

"And you went straight to Kim that night. I can almost follow Nadal's line of reasoning. If you'd gone to a hotel and come back the next morning—but to go to Kim—"

"I'd just seen a murder and one of those guys could have been trailing me. I thought I could die. It was fucking terrifying. What could you know? You didn't watch him kill a man."

"Yeah, but I know the feeling when someone you love does something unthinkable."

"You are one arrogant sister. You'd better save your breath. You *don't* know."

"Okay. And there are things you don't know."

"Brilliant. Home run. Stick to science."

She walks out of the chapel and weaves her way among the white slabs. Then she actually walks on a grave, climbing onto a sarcophagus, and from there onto the top of a mausoleum.

"I'm sorry," I call to her.

"Forget it. I already forgot it." She begins to tiptoe along the edge. "I can tough almost anything out," her voice floats back. "Like, I used to be afraid of heights. When I was a kid I never could have done this. But I trained myself by walking around the edges of rooftops in San Juan. Now I can take on any roof anywhere. Bring them on—Taj Mahal, the Empire State. But I can't be alone, not since he was killed."

"You're not alone."

"I got you, babe," she says sarcastically. "Hey, look." She jumps down. "There! Now wait for a second, okay."

She walks a few steps and suddenly kneels before a simple grave. I come up behind her. Nadal. The name floats on stone, one word bears the inflections of a whole life. A white chalice is the only decorative touch. I wonder what he meant by it—an offering, a mockery?

"So," she says, "you want to have dinner with me tonight?"

"Because you can't be alone?"

"Just say yes or no."

"Yes."

"Come this way. The sun's starting to set and we'll have a great view."

"Katie, there's something I don't understand."

"Shit, we're back in reporter mode again."

"Why didn't Kim bring you up to New York?"

" 'Cause I hate New York."

"Then why did he choose New York?"

"He went ahead of me to set up a life."

"But you can't go north because of your arthritis—right?"

"Who knows." Three years ago, she tells me, she stopped at a gumball machine and said, 'If it's green, my arthritis is gone forever.' It was green, and she brought the gumball home, placing it in an abalone ashtray. It stayed there for months, and then one morning she popped it in her mouth. "Now it's inside me," she explains. "Luck is green, right in here."

"But New York?"

"*What* are you getting at? Ask Kim, not me." She twists a lock of hair around her index finger. "He missed Cheeks. He left me here for a while because Nadal was dead, so he figured I was safe."

A light rain mists the air. I join Katie on a slab of marble, and we look east to the crooked tin and cement roofs of La Perla. They seem like steps one might mount straight into the carnelian sun above.

I say, "Don't you ever wonder who killed Nadal?"

"The same fuckers who watched him kill that cook. The ones who put bullet holes in his house." Her voice drops. "Kim holed me up in that condo but I left every couple of days and sat outside Nadal's house. Don't you think he was watching from one of his windows? Sometimes in the condo I'd get this funny feeling, all those hours alone, and I could tell that he was calling me. I'd pick up the phone and hear silence on the other end, and then a hang-up. Nobody except Kim was supposed to have the number but," she concludes with a touch of pride, "Nadal had friends in the police department who could have traced it."

She even went to Nadal's seer, Doña Nilda, a fat black grand-mother who wore homemade caftans and rhinestone reading glasses. Even her rotary phone had rhinestones glued onto it, and she used a laminated gold knitting needle to dial numbers. "She's the one who gave me the herb cure. But she told me I'd be moving back into his house. I really wanted to believe her."

"Where was Kim in all this?"

"You've got to understand," she says very softly, "I was hunted. Everything went dark in one split second. I just couldn't get it straight. I hardly knew what I was doing. I still don't. Anyway, Kim never knew I left the condo."

"You're wrong. He had you watched. Katie, you have no idea how far he's gone for you."

Just the first breath of the secret between us now, and I feel my body trembling. I trace Kim's name, unseen, on the wet marble.

"He told you he had me watched?"

"Right."

"So both of them had spies on my tail."

"He was trying to protect you."

Soft and slow, like the rain itself, the truth drifts toward her. But she just shrugs.

"Then why didn't he come visit me ever? He had me imprisoned in Isla Verde."

"Do you ever stop thinking about yourself?"

"Do you ever stop asking questions?"

"He could have left you, but he tried to save you."

Finally she says, "He did leave me."

"I don't mean it literally. You know what I mean."

"One day he just didn't call. And the next day he didn't call. I wasn't reading newspapers or watching TV anymore. I thought he'd been killed. It took me weeks to find out it was Nadal who was dead. So then I thought, maybe Kim's alive. And I started checking, like some war widow. New York was the third place I checked. I followed him up there." She stands. "I can't think about how I hurt him. It's getting dark. We'd better go before they lock us in."

At the cemetery gate she hesitates. "Look, neither of us is going to be with him. He's just got to be on his own now."

She's had both men and lost them both, and she seems certain that somehow she's taken them with her. The three of them lost and perfect. That's what she wants me to see. I have no part in this lofty tragedy.

We walk up to the street. I say: "Do you want to know what he did for you?"

"Okay. Tell me something I don't know."

I tell her Kim was the one who killed Nadal.

Time slows when I say it, *Kim*, each moment clicks, *killed*, in place like, *Nadal*, a transparency, and I feel
a deep glacial thrill
as if a tourniquet just tore
triumph gushing through me at long last
I feel power, feel reckless, thoughtless, cruel, tender, true—
Click, and Katie's face goes still
Pieces of her life fall into place
Click, click. A rattle, a kind of caterwaul.

"And you came down here like this—"

She turns from me, turns to El Morro, turns to Nadal's house.

Click. She puts her hands on either side of her head, as if blocking a piercing noise. And starts to walk, unbelievably, toward La Perla.

FORTY

I'll play reporter. I'll ask the questions.
Why did I tell Katie about Kim?

FORTY-ONE

Kneeling in the briny grass, my arms around her, telling her she can go to Kim. Touching her wet face with my fingers. Smoothing her shirt soaked in rain. Pulling her to her feet, lifting her like a child, carrying her like a sleeping girl. A thousand tender images pass through me as I watch her go.

Holding her. I want to.

Rain running gutters down my neck and back. Katie's walking as if there were no rain at all. Like a tribal woman balancing baskets on her head. Like a person just blinded. Down the road to La Perla.

I follow. Warm shadows and a mulch of papaya rinds, tires, papers, chicken bones, shoes, condoms. At a distance I track her. Ditches and drainpipes flooded with fluid, tar paper, bottlecaps. The watery clap of a woman defecating in a trench.

We descend and descend, down a necklace of broken steps, past windows cut from tin, children crouched beneath a cardboard tent, clucking chickens. Past houses on stilts, bulked and clumped like barnacles. To a long road by the sea.

She turns left, and left again, hypnotized and slow, mounting steps until she reaches a green house set on high stilts. I stop under the house, inhaling the must of urine, salt and mud, and watch her raise both fists and bang at the door. No answer. Still she bangs.

At last she lowers her fists and rests her head against the door.

And then a light bursts in the window, glides through the dark, scattering like sequins on the skirts of rain. She looks up.

The mouth ajar, the eyes wide and still. I steal close, under cover of the house. Her dazed face is tilted with hope into the pool of light. That face, it's my doing. My doing. It's my doing.

The light blinks off, and La Perla is silent. So I step into the womb of rain. I go to her.

There will never be a record of this night. All she can say is I told her something. She won't always look like this. Unrecognizable. Every pulse of her retarded, as if she can't metabolize the truth and so has slowed down until she's become almost aboriginal, without thought or guile, like an exposed heart beating strange, ancestral beats.

"Me," she says finally.

"What?"

Her voice is deep, the vowels drawn and stretched as if altered by a synthesizer. "It was because of me."

"Yeah, but you couldn't have stopped him."

She lowers her head.

"Katie, it's dangerous, this place. Come on."

"I can't go back up there. Here I can stand it." She turns away. "This is Nadal's house. Where he first took me."

"This isn't his house. His house is in Old San Juan."

"This is his second house," she repeats in her stubborn, slow voice.

"This is his house, too?"

She says, "He took me here. He sat me by the pool. He said now you belong."

"Let's get out of here. The only thing that's saving us is the rain. This whole slum is deserted."

"And he said I was the little girl on Christmas morning. That was my favorite part. 'You are my Christmas present.' I am the Christmas girl."

"Come on."

She looks up at the shell of green tin. "Nobody judges you here."

When I lace my fingers through hers and tug, she walks, unresisting but without volition. I guide her through the streets of La Perla as if she were drugged, harmless for now and uncommonly beautiful. At the top of the old city, safe again, I don't look back. We go to the gate of Nadal's house and I ring.

"She's innocent," I say, when Popi comes, dressed in white shorts and a black cotton shirt. "But I think I've—I think I've—"

He unlatches the gate. Suddenly Katie is still, observing him closely—an animal scenting its hunter, yet unaware that it has already been sighted. She goes on staring as if he doesn't yet see her.

He comes near, breathing shallowly. His hand moves to her face. He touches her hair. Lightly he strokes, in silence, then slowly lets his hand drop, like a boy who's had his first kiss.

"What's happened to you?" he asks.

"I'm going to melt," she says.

"Then we'll take you out of this rain and dry you off," he says.

"I told her that Kim killed your uncle."

He's silent. Finally he asks, "She didn't know?"

"She had no idea."

"So why did you do that, Lynn?"

"I don't know. It's terrible. I don't know."

"He did it for me," Katie says slowly.

"If you take her hand, she'll go with you."

"*Carita*, there's hibiscus on the bureau in your old room, and bottles of Medalla in the ice chest. You can stay here tonight." Popi turns to me. "See the man in the red turtleneck outside?"

"That man was following us today."

"He'll take you to my car and drive you to your hotel. He'll also arrange for your flight out tomorrow morning."

"You want me to go?"

"Of course."

"So this is the end?"

He doesn't answer.

"Can I call to find out how she is?"

"You already went too far."

"But you were the one who brought me here."

He breathes out slowly. "All right. I will let you know."

"Thank you."

As they walk to the house Katie half-turns and looks back. That dumb, soft face seems not to recognize me.

"He said those who have had some misfortune . . ." She pauses, searching, the way a foreigner searches for a word in a new language. I have the feeling that she wants to offer help. "Those who have some misfortune . . ."

"Don't talk now," Popi orders.

Then she sighs. As I walk away I hear her voice, "You know my favorite thing he said? He said you are my Christmas present. I am the Christmas girl."

FORTY-TWO

When I was twelve and Cob was fifteen we had a
white dove. I called her Maia, after the mother of
Hermes, and he called her Maya, the Sanskrit word
for illusion. We'd let her fly around the house while
we yelled out her name, evoking entirely different
universes, one thronged with petulant and passion-
ate gods, the other a heart of emptiness coated with
form.

She was the only completely happy creature I'd
encountered. She'd kiss our toes and fingers, cleaning our imaginary quills with her beak as if we were
bald birds. At night she'd settle on her perch, ruf-
fling her feathers until she looked enormous, and
her lids would slowly shut in sleep.

When spring came, I let her outside. Our neighbors warned me not to let her loose, because their
terrier might attack her. But I wanted to see her
dart into the oak tree, lift her tail and sing. At evening she'd wait on the roof of the woodshed. I'd
lift my hand and she'd fly to me, tiny pink talons
curving around my index finger.

In July, I was sunbathing in our backyard when I
heard an explosive, muffled sound, like someone

violently shaking out a rug. I kept sunbathing, but the sound went on—so I went round to the deck to investigate. Maia was half-buried in a fantastic swirl of snowy feathers, and the dog was leaping joyfully at her.

I scooped her up in one hand. She was a palpating, stunned thing, beak parted to show a parched tongue. Her head bobbed and snapped forward and then she was dead. I found out later his bite had pierced her lungs.

Of course I wept, and nobody said I'd tempted fate. But I remember a flicker of malice and curiosity, the first time my neighbors warned me. In my own fashion, I killed Maia.

Cob understood. I found him later that week, crouched in the driveway, torturing a beetle with a twig, flipping it on its back so it lay kicking at the air. We knelt together on the warm asphalt, watching the beetle's dance. Finally Cob let it clasp the twig and turned it right side up, and we both observed the long moment of almost reverential stillness before it scuttled off.

Those are small crimes of childhood.

FORTY-THREE

Like Nadal's mountains, New York stands outside any moral compass, and so I return to it. I take the airport bus to Grand Central Station, where I buy magazines and chocolate and call Sherry. I know why Kim came to New York after the murder, even though he no longer liked the city. Here, where inferno and paradiso lie in waiting on every corner, you can always belong.

Sherry says to call him.

"If you don't he'll think you blew him off because of the murder."

"So?"

"So that's like a condemnation. It's not fair."

"So?"

"Just call him."

But I don't.

When the phone rings I let the machine pick up. I turn down the volume. I don't play my messages. The red light blinks, and whenever I come into my room I look at it. He might not have called. He might have. The blinking light is like an unopened letter. It's like looking for him in a place where I can't find him. I need to look. But I don't want to find him.

I won't touch myself. I lie in bed, hot ash waiting to cool.

* * *

Three days later I'm walking down Broadway past the Times Square Tickets Booth, where a Wednesday matinée crowd of a few hundred has converged, hoping to buy half-price seats. And I stop and dial Cheeks. He seems pleased and surprised, and I arrange to stop by.

His living room is a kind of warm, dishevelled retreat, a friendly disorder of books and knickknacks, like the home of a professor.

"So," he says, "I left you several messages."

"I haven't been playing my messages."

"Oh. Well, I wanted to invite you over, but you beat me to it."

"I thought maybe I could talk to you."

"Ditto." He settles into the couch, hitching up his corduroy trousers. His baby-bear face crinkles into a smile. "Ladies first. What have you been doing with yourself?"

I tell him I've spent the last few days alone, walking and thinking. I walked through Chinatown and bought vegetables I don't know the name of, and across the Brooklyn Bridge and back, and under the FDR where homeless men were making fires in garbage cans. And into Alphabet City and Loisaida, and Gramercy Park where all the dogwalkers were out, and St. Bartholomew's Cathedral.

"We're up to Fiftieth Street," he says gently. "By the way, is this about Kim?"

"Yeah."

"He hasn't heard from you in a week."

"Are you going to try and get me to call him? Because I won't."

Cheeks shakes his head slowly. "No. No. What would you like to tell me or ask me?"

"You're his oldest friend."

"Family, almost."

"Well, here's a dumb question. But I just have to ask it. Why did he want me when he was in love with somebody else?"

"You mean Katie?"

I nod.

Cheeks hesitates. "Does it matter? He seems to be through with Katie."

"They were staying together in his motel room."

"Au contraire. Kim was staying with me."

"I've *been* in that motel room."

"Honestly. As soon as Katie came up, he moved in with me."

"And let *her* stay there?"

He nods. "He doesn't want me to see her. He doesn't want me to know why they've split."

"But he never told me he'd moved in with you."

"I'm not sure you gave him much of a chance. He dropped off his suitcase and clothes, went straight to work and then to your place. He said you two talked all night. And that you haven't spoken to him since. Now, look, I'm the kind of guy, if somebody I love sprays a crowd with bullets, I'll ask the police, 'What did those crazy people do to upset him?' Whatever Kim has done, I still love him the same. Is there a reason you don't want to see him anymore?"

"I just can't."

"My dear, you say that guiltily."

"I don't want to see him."

"Well, then, will you answer me something about yourself?"

"Yes."

"Are you glad you met him?"

"I wish I'd met him under other circumstances."

But, I know, circumstances reflect who we are. I could only have met him this year, in this place, in this way.

"But if it had to be like this," I add, "well, I'd take it all again."

FORTY-FOUR

You ask nothing of me. You stand in my doorway—
you came, you say, because you have something to
tell me—and I can't say what I feel.

It's no trick of sight, what I see in your face. You
surrender and are unchanged, you lose hope, and
the sea-carved clarity of your face is unaltered, you
ask nothing, and your mouth is still tender. You ask
nothing of me.

I followed your face from that first night.

I wandered, came home to your face.

FORTY-FIVE

"I didn't come here to change your mind," he begins. "I know you don't want to see me anymore. Cheeks told me when I got home tonight."

"I'm glad you came."

He brushes his matted hair; his fingers come away wet. "He said you would be," he answers, bewildered. "I told him he was crazy."

I turn from him, because if I keep looking I'll touch that sweat-licked face.

"What else did he say?"

"That he'd been waiting fifteen years to play father. And now he had his chance. He practically ordered me to come here."

At the kitchen we pause. "Go ahead," I say, and he opens the freezer door, so that the familiar white fog flows out. He opens a beer and then says,

"Cheeks said that you ran into Katie."

"You're volunteering information? Without a question first?"

He smiles. "You didn't call me for a week. I kind of missed your questions."

"How about a trade?" I suggest.

He leans in the doorway. "What are the terms?"

"Our old terms. Except me first this time."

"Fair enough."

"I guess I should start in the Royalton."

"Why the Royalton?"

"That's where I went to visit Popi and tell him about you."

"Lynn, I already know most of the facts, and the rest I can piece together."

"But you—you know I betrayed you?"

"Katie called me this afternoon."

"You know what I did?"

He looks at me and says calmly, "Most of it. What I don't know is why."

That's the hard part. I'll try to answer. It's not that I did something unforgivable. It's not that I hurt you and Katie. It's this. Ever since Cob left I've been asking questions. That's kind of obvious. I suppose I don't have to say it, but I can't ask him questions. I don't know where he lives.

So I hunt down people's secrets. But I knew this about myself already, this is not my discovery, this isn't even what I really want to say. But I found out secrets. Sometimes I suffered for it. I never stopped myself. I could sense people with a kind of canny and yet uncanny sight, and I'd go with my calibrated questions into their hearts. I'd see the one thing I wasn't supposed to see. Like Stephen on the street with his girlfriend.

Down into the part of the heart that doesn't want to be questioned. That used to be the only magic in my life. Really. I used to feel like a magician standing on an empty stage, and suddenly I'd pull at a little corner of cloth peeking out from somebody's sleeve, and all these colored scarves all knotted together into one long flag would come out. Keep pulling and pulling. One secret is always knotted to the next.

And in your case, it was murder, and I couldn't get all the scarves. So I pulled from Popi, and Katie, and I got them, right? And now I can't be with you but that's not what matters.

Oh, these are baby steps. I'm standing before you now and trying to show who I am. And I wanted to do this for you. You don't have to forgive me.

*   *   *

But I cannot describe this. His face has the barren richness of rock in high desert. His eyes all dark pupil. Then his lids shut, and one tear, like the bee's sting, slips.

Give it to me, I'll drink.

Later: "Is Katie still with Popi?"

"His mother has come, and she's been giving Katie baths and taking her for walks on the beach. She's living in Nadal's house, after all."

I walk over to the window. The lit awnings of the doorman buildings look like a display of parasols.

"Popi's going to tell his family about you."

He comes up behind me. "I know."

"I'm scared."

"Katie said—"

"Go on."

"Katie said she'd made an arrangement with Popi, and I was free."

"I know the arrangement. He'll marry her."

Kim's jaw tightens.

"You don't like that, do you?"

"She doesn't want to owe me her life. She'd rather I be in debt."

"It's more than that. She cares about you."

He lowers his head.

"Kim, I know when Katie came back to you in San Juan you were lovers."

"How do you know that?"

"She told me."

"And you trust your source?"

"Well, that's the point. Because she also said you were lovers up here. And I just want to know when you slept with her."

"I didn't."

"She said it's not such a big deal with you. And I just want to know."

"I didn't."

"All right."

"It is a big deal with me."

"It's a horribly big deal with me."

"Well, this is something I came here to explain."

That first night in the motel he stayed with her, holding her face while she slept. About five A.M. he brought his suitcases to Cheeks, took a shower, and went to work. That morning I'd called him, saying only, "I met somebody who told me about you." He came to me that night. The next day he stopped by to see Katie for an hour, bringing ten sunflowers in his arms. Their stubbly yellow and black blossoms hung on curved stems. He filled the metal waste-basket with water and put the flowers in as Katie talked.

"I was walking up Madison Avenue today and I had that feeling again like I used to have in Galveston and San Juan," she said. She'd closed the door of the motel room, and was standing straight and still, her chin lifted and held there, eyes unfocussed.

"Like even though I'm only five foot three," she said in a strange monotone, so unlike the rough music of her voice, "and dressed in a t-shirt and jeans and I have straight brown hair, that I'm scaring strangers and I'd better be careful not to crush any buildings and not to step on anyone. Like somebody's going to stop any moment and say, 'What happened? Did somebody run over your dog with a truck? What happened to you?' I figure I should try to hide this look on my face, whatever it is, but then I decide not to. You know why?"

"You always looked like this," he said.

"You know why?" she repeated.

He shook his head.

"Because it's something. I've got something left. Right?" She looked straight at him. "I mean I don't have you anymore. Am I right?"

"I'm here, aren't I?"

"You had no trouble at all staying away last night." Her eyes moved down his body, but without that familiar, prickly heat. It was as if she were missing, and suddenly he wanted to do some-thing to make her appear, like a boy who switches on the light in a dark bedroom, just to see the reassuring topography of bureau, bed and lamp.

"Hmm," she said. "I'm wrong, you did have trouble. Okay. I'm glad. And I can see you're dying to get out of this room. You want to go with me into the lounge?"

"I like the privacy here."

"Sure it's private, but the lounge has a different wall," she quipped. "Sometimes people feel like looking at a different wall."

"No thanks." He sat on the end of the bed and said awkwardly, almost crudely, "Katie, I'd like you to go home."

"Home?"

"To San Juan."

"Are you coming with me?"

"I don't think you want me."

"Don't shove that excuse off on me."

"All right, then. I'm not coming with you."

"And I'm not going. I need you."

"Like this?"

"Like what? Of course like this."

"Against my will?"

She shrugged and went to the window. "I'm your will. Isn't that why you chose me in the first place?"

He laughed, irritated. "Even you don't believe it."

"You chose me," she insisted, a little deflated, but indignant nonetheless. "You stood there waiting for something to happen. You stood there like somebody who could explode if he was touched in the right way. So of course a woman had to come on to you."

"I won't argue about it."

"Kim, I don't know how to calm down." She felt like a soldier who'd become accustomed to gunfire and sleepless nights. It was war, but it was a place, a home.

"You're incredibly tired, aren't you."

They were both silent for a moment, startled by the softer tone in his voice. She walked to him. He took her hands, with their familiar strong fingers, creased knuckles, blunt nails.

"I just want somebody to wipe that look off my face that scares people." Then she leaned against him. "You haven't decided yet. I know you're uncertain."

"Maybe I am," he said quietly.

"I only care that you are," she replied. "I don't give a shit why."

"If I go with you, Katie, you'll wait to get strong, and leave me, and I'll stay on in that house. I'll be like one of those guys whose name nobody can remember, like the clerk at the hardware store who knows where all the nails are."

She stared at him.

"I didn't want to live in that house forever," he added.

"Then don't," she said flatly.

She went to the sink, turned on the water, and let it run over her hands. He could see her shaking. "This damn water is cold. I can pretend it's hot, so hot it would burn. Did you ever notice they feel almost the same, being scalded and frozen?"

She came to him. "Try it." Both hands on his face. "Which one is it?"

"Cold."

She shrugged.

"All right. If you won't have me, Kim, I'm going to travel. I'm in the mood, you know. I'm in the mood for disappearing."

"Where would you go?"

"I'd *disappear*. I dunno. Bali. Jakarta. I'd go check out some tribe that practices magic. Y'know, they dance and anoint you with oil and whirl a red-hot axe around your head."

Closing her eyes, she started turning in a circle, arms raised and bent at the elbows. "The only therapy for passion is confession. That's what the *curandera* told me."

"Doña Nilda?"

"Of course." Katie spun slowly in her circle, and let her head drop back. "I confess," she said, her voice soft gravel. "I left my man for another. I want him back. I confess."

It seemed that she was more alive than other women.

She was dancing in his hotel room. She talked about a red-hot axe, and he saw it.

Her eyes were still shut but her body sensed him approaching her, and her dance slowed. The slowed tempo drew him. Her arms dropped, her dance stopped.

"You'll do it now, won't you," she said. "You wouldn't touch me all this time but now you will."

"I can't."

He was in her circle of fire then. Why not touch?

"With your mouth," she said. "Please. First."

Unzipping her black denim miniskirt, shimmying it down her legs. Wearing orange tights, hitched up awkwardly over her muscled belly, and no underwear. He saw the moss of pubic hair underneath. She stretched the elastic waist with crooked fingers and let it snap and laughed. Then she pulled the tights off with a quick, brusque motion.

Hands closed into fists. Saying nothing; lying back on the bed, hand between her legs, watching him with half-lidded eyes. He came forward, shaking a little, exactly like a man who had for months resisted a dangerous medicine that, only if taken in careful doses, won't kill him. She kept her hand between her legs, mocking a fig leaf.

He knelt then at the narrow bed. Put his hand over hers, felt the earth of her. Then rocked a little, wary.

She leaned up on one arm and said, rough and lyrical, *"Vénte Conmigo. No Puedo. Abre Paso. Éstate Quieto."*

"What are you saying?"

She smiled. "They're the names of my favorite cures from the botanica. I'm using them on you now, darling. You know what my personal, absolute favorite is? The Double-Fast Luck Spray. Double-Fast. Can I try that on you?"

"It'll probably slow me down."

"Vénte Conmigo. Why are you waiting?" She shook her head. "You're able to resist me because you've got some other female. The one you said is taking the edge off. Who is she? You met her here—or back in San Juan?"

"Here."

"How?"

"None of your business."

"You're embarrassed? You met her on the corner in spike heels? What does she do?"

"She's a writer."

"Would I like her?"

"I doubt it. I like her."

"Are you trying to make me jealous?"

"Are you jealous?"

"I'm considering becoming jealous."

He smiled. "What are you going to do about it?"

"I don't care if you see another woman. I just don't want her taking the edge off. That edge is for me."

"You own it?" He stood, body tensed against a flood of feeling. He had his own quiet strength, and it was enough.

Presently she swung her legs over the edge of the bed and grabbed for her tights and skirt.

"Forget it. Might as well get dressed for the last act," she said. "Where are you going now?"

"I told you on the phone. To Cheeks."

"He'd probably want to see me, but I won't push it. I'm done testing you."

"Was that all it was?"

"No."

"Do you want to stay here? Or do you need a return ticket?"

She looked up at him. "I guess it's my turn to be good."

"Just how are you going to be good?"

Presently she said, "Shit. I'll do what you ask. I'll go home."

But when he left, it was he who lingered at the door, and she who touched his cheek. Just a brief caress, unlike her. The touch of a mother sending her child off to his first day at school. As if these four years she had been his strength, and had let him believe he was her protector so he would love her.

He crossed the street. When he got to Cheeks', he called me. I wasn't home, and he left a message, giving Cheeks' number, and lay down to sleep.

He touches the small of my back.

"There's no cherry left," I tell him.

"There's always cherry left."

"You'll find it?"

"In the dark with a blindfold."

FORTY-SIX

There are nights when the gift seems indistinguishable from the curse. When Katie, whom I imagine standing at the window of Nadal's house—looking out at an emerald sea, turning with a sigh toward Popi—seems still one with Kim, and therefore me. She follows Popi quietly down the stairs to dinner, where he entertains her with amusing anecdotes. He is air and flight—luminous, childlike. Is she lonely? Is she grateful?

After dinner, perhaps, Popi's mother—Nadal's half-sister from his father's second marriage—massages Katie in a marble bath, and her head sinks with pleasure. Her chestnut hair pinned up, pearls in her ears, she taps her fingers on the rim of the round tub, and then the fingers hesitate, then tap again, as if seeking some lost inner rhythm. Popi's mother pours essence of orange and neroli onto Katie's skin and massages, humming Spanish love songs. *"Lloro y añoro mi jardín azul,"* the woman sings.

There are nights when Kim seems free, and other nights when he doesn't talk. Then he sits in the dark, as if he were back in his living room the night

Katie returned. His life is now, and will forever be, a life lived for Nadal. Murder is an act which must be balanced, again and again. But, as Nadal said, even the man who killed a hundred men and collected their knuckles, believing that would bring him luck—even a necklace of knuckles can't be judged. Each of those knuckles belonged to a man. Each of those men had a story. Who can hear them all? Sherry, who cheats on Kyros. Kyros, who knows. Katie, who came to New York uninvited. Kim.

FORTY-SEVEN

A few weeks have passed and one night Kim and I are on Cheeks' roof, listening to his radio show on a battery-run ghetto blaster, looking out over the roofs of brownstones—which rise and fall like the keyboard of a player piano. José has just left us to crash on a couch downstairs.

"It's hard to believe both Popi and José are Puerto Rican," I say.

"Blood changes in a new country. Islanders think Neoricans have turned white and spit up English." Kim's lightly calloused fingers touch the back of my neck. "Nadal said in Puerto Rico every step told a story about your ancestors."

"You quote him like an old sage."

"Sometimes the things he said come back to me."

"What else comes back to you?"

He smiles. "You're subtle. What would you like to know?"

"What he said that last hour."

"If I tell you, don't go running down to Puerto Rico again."

"Are you joking?"

"And if I tell you," he continues, "don't say it changes things."

But he seems curiously at ease. He's been waiting to tell me. He seats me on the fire escape at the back of the roof, leans back against the rusted iron railing, and speaks.

* * *

That final hour was Kim's secret, his silent happiness, the alibi he would never use.

In that last hour, Nadal sat at his oak-carved table, his garden moist with light, and talked. Kim let him talk. Let him dictate the terms of his death—like a kind of improvised last rites.

But his voice was soporific.

"Como boca de lobo," Nadal said softly to Kim. "After Katie ran from me, I was in the mouth of the wolf and I could see nothing. I know what she thinks. That I've ruffled up all my feathers and am too proud to forgive her for what she did. She held her face in her hands as if her head was about to fly off. She ran from me."

"Why didn't you just send her back up to your house?" Kim said suddenly, as if he'd just been yanked out of a light sleep, his head nodding languidly and then snapping up. "Why did you make her a witness?"

"I told you, if I had sent her away that evening, the men would have seen my weakness, and it would be the beginning of a long decline. This business is a war."

"So why did you choose it?"

"You see, I built the life I wanted."

"You had to build it with drugs?"

"I built it, that's all. People have said, 'Nadal, he's a good man.' It was never that simple. An employee of mine was dying. I told him I would take care of his family and pay their bills for the rest of my life. I told him, 'Your only job is to live. I want to boast that I know a man who was shot six times in the heart and still lived. It's good for business.' And he lived. I kept my promise, but it wasn't only out of goodness."

"You never loved anyone?" Kim asked suddenly.

Nadal was silent. "Is that what you want to ask me? Or do you want to know how a man like me can love? I've loved. Three times."

"That's not what Katie said."

"I loved her so much I broke my rules. I went against my instinct. I made her part of the family."

"And you were willing to destroy her."

Nadal grew still. Minutes passed. His eyes focussed on nothing.

"I haven't destroyed her," he said.

"How will you ever know?"

"Listen to me. You'll see."

"It's your hour," Kim shrugged, leaning against the wall, relaxing a little.

Nadal told how in a tin hut by the sea, in the silence and heat, he'd gazed at the three men before him. They'd seemed unbearably sharp in their outline, like paper cutouts pasted against the aluminum wall, or ducks in a row at a carnival. Their faces were smug and sullen. He could almost hear their thoughts: You should never have brought the girl down. An American girl! Love stays in the bedroom. How can we negotiate now? She might go to the police. Our employer knows you will never make this mistake again, and he will try to forget it, but you must pay for the favor. Take the cocaine quietly. Pay. And get rid of the girl.

"They were right," Kim interrupted. "You could have allowed yourself one mistake. You could have sent her out of La Perla. There was room for that."

"There may have been."

"But you didn't."

"No, I did not."

"And then you tortured us."

"You went to the police, remember?"

"The police were all on your payroll, there was nothing we could do. And why did you have your crazy witch doctor poison her? Her skin was burning up." Kim put his head in his hands. "I couldn't touch her."

"Doña's a good woman," he said. "If the herbs were strong, it was to burn out love."

"That's bullshit. It was a bag of fucking poisonous herbs."

"You don't know what Katie needed. *Con permiso*," Nadal said. "May I tell you what you did wrong?"

"Don't bother. I won't believe it."

"I'll tell you anyway. You decided she should be happy. You even decided the shape of her happiness. You were certain it was perfect, you were righteous in your certainty. Something like a Christian missionary. But you cannot take another person's night away."

"No," Kim said uncertainly.

"You can't protect her. She doesn't want it. One day you'll be able to pardon this bitter truth."

"I wanted to protect her," Kim shouted. "You wanted to kill in front of her."

Nadal smiled. It was an odd, relieved smile—a shy smile—the wrong smile for the moment. "Why do you think I wanted such a thing?"

Kim watched the man. Well, I've got the gun, he thought. I can say anything. "You were lonely, fucking lonely. You had nothing. That's why you talk so much, even to me now. You're lost and you're a bastard and you're lonely."

"I can explain myself."

"You don't have forever. I'm not your biographer."

When Katie ran from him he went numb, a merciful numbness in which he wrapped up the deal, buying the cut cocaine for a quarter of its price, walked to his Lamborghini and drove home. It was only when she returned, shaking the locked gate and crying, and Popi refused to let her in, that he suffered. The way she held her shoes in one hand, and rubbed her eyes with the other, her look of incomprehension, how her head dropped in exhaustion as she turned away—all were like symptoms of a sudden illness, one that he had carried for years without feeling. Now, when he looked at her, he saw his illness.

Every few days she came to sit outside his house. He stood at his window. He could live for that. *Y de noche mi corazón despacio. Mi vida despacio.* His heart slowed. His life slowed. He was entranced and it was unbearable.

Even so, when too many hours had passed and she finally slung her leather bag over her shoulder, folded up the newspaper she'd taken along to read but never looked at, and uncrossed her legs, preparing to walk away, he felt the agony of the betrayed. When she was gone, he raged. He devised torments. He imagined her dead.

Love would let her go. Hate would lay siege. Let him choose love, but in life he could not do it. Because she was gone from him. Because she sat outside his house. Because when he saw her he became crazed. He stood at his shaded window, feeling nothing but love, and when she left, he paced his room, feeling only apocalyptic fury.

Maybe Katie had been his soul's last gasp. Maybe he'd brought her down to La Perla to destroy his soul. Wanted her to watch him kill.

"I am Spanish, a Catholic," Nadal said. "I do believe in a soul."

"Go on," Kim said. He was overcome by a strange, narcotic terror. He had to hear what this man was about to say. The gun was too fucking heavy. The sun was too fucking hot. "Finish!"

And Nadal said those who have endured some misfortune will always be set apart by it. They can follow the call of that misfortune, they can seed affliction in others, until they are so alone that no one can reach them.

But it is that same misfortune that is their gift, and their bridge back to humanity. They must make their way back. He'd tried to make his way back through love. In a tin hut in La Perla on a sunny afternoon he knew he could not.

Now death was honorable. And suicide was not.

The next moment was as brief as a single breath, impalpable, insensible, a lonely flutter of hesitation. But that flutter cast so distinct a shade.

Kim put the gun down.

"In these last days I am suddenly drawn to the 'sí' word. *Sí, sí, sí.*"

"Yes to what?"

Nadal gestured to the gun.

How still the man stood in his green garden. Against the brick and flagstones of his green garden.

And so Kim said it. "You want to die?"

"That's why I waited for you."

Waited for you.

After Kim shot him, Nadal put his arms round Kim's shoulders and let himself be carried. His body was heavy, warm; Kim could feel in it all the honey of relief and release. The man collapsed against him, softly sweating, and as Kim helped him over to the wall, he could smell the soapy odor of his fine cotton shirt. He asked Kim to stay with him.

"What can I do for you now?"

"Just look at me."

And so he looked. The man was so still it seemed he'd long ago ceased to exist, like a chalked saint on the crumbling fresco of a centuries-old church.

And he remembered Nadal lifting one hand, as if to silence Kim, even though he wasn't speaking.

"Guava shells," Nadal said. "Soursop. Tamarind juice. Fields of sugar. The nuns in the courtyard. Their ivories clicking."

He paused, weakening.

"Go on," Kim said hoarsely.

A man fingering the fine parchment of old illustrations.

He said, "Espresso with rum. My house. My nephew who is mine. The morning she left. I danced. Who in the end shall say that I was not the happy *caballero* of my home?"

FORTY-EIGHT

Dear Cob,

This is number 117. For years now I've been writing you, and the plastic box that contains your postcards also contains my letters back. Tonight I'm on my bed in my blue silk robe, knees bent, notebook balanced on my knees, writing you by hand.

Remember once you said man is a little better than his reputation, and a little worse? I wonder if you'd say the same thing now.

I always thought you took your love away. Now I think differently. You were afraid if you lived near me you'd claim my life, and my only purpose would be loving you. I'd never marry or have children or even meet somebody like Kim. I don't have to tell you who Kim is. You can imagine such a person. If I'd never met him, you'd still own the virgin in me.

I can see you at nineteen, in your attic room at Cornell, sitting at a parson's table. Papery light fills the room, like the scratched and luminous glow in an old black-and-white movie reel. You're bent over your empty table, working out the math of two lives, yours and your sister's. On your side, you calculate an inborn weakness. You need her too much. To balance the equation you must go. But even then you sense another, more shadowy reason. I don't know that reason. I still can't guess.

It's an act of betrayal, but there's love in it.

I have my own life now. I no longer blame you. I'll even quote you the words of a dead man. He said those who have endured some misfortune will always be set apart by it. But it is that misfortune that renders them human and will someday set them free.

ABOUT THE AUTHOR

JILL NEIMARK is a journalist whose assignments have taken her to Romania, Cyprus, Honduras, the French Caribbean, and all over the United States. She lives in New York City.

FICTION   Neimark, Jill.
Nei
         Bloodsong.

3/303

DATE		
JAN 6 1994		
JAN 19 1994		
FEB 11 1994		
MAY - 2 1994		
JUL 1 1994		
AUG 1 8 1994		

BAKER & TAYLOR BOOKS